WHAT PEOPLE ARE SAYING ABOUT

BLACK AND DEEP DESIRES

What mad excitement! Gunpowder plotters, Jacob⸱⸱ intrigue, Transylvanian shape-shifters — all written ⸱⸱ ⸱ked in rich and smoky pungent prose.

It's as if Hilary Mantel, A⸱⸱⸱ ⸱got together at a diabolical W⸱ few bottles too many in the w⸱ ⸱p with this rollicking manuscript. Gra⸱ ⸱ess, our leading Shakespearean scholar, has had ⸱ ⸱un bringing his historical knowledge to bear upon an unmissable romp.

Roger Lewis, author of *Seasonal Suicide Notes* (Short Books 2009) and *The Life and Death of Peter Sellers* (Century 1994).

In this exciting fiction, Graham Holderness shares and enters some of the passions that swirled round Shakespeare in his lifetime. Religion, politics, and sex are all turned up to a deadly degree. We move from Stratford to Transylvania and into the Inferno, but the intensity is leavened by demonic wit. There's even a posthumous cameo by Christopher Marlowe! This is literary criticism off the leash, and there are many incidental insights. The novel ends with the physician play-goer Simon Forman coyly propositioning the Bard: 'How do you feel about collaboration?' And of course Holderness himself is winking as he does so....

Ewan Fernie, Chair, Professor and Fellow of the Shakespeare Institute (University of Birmingham) and author of *The Demonic* (Palgrave 2013).

A very clever and well organised novel, a successful balance of historical fact and apt quotations with a well-timed ingenious and rather fun plot ... wonderful.

Alexa von Hirschberg, Bloomsbury Fiction.

Black and
Deep Desires:
William Shakespeare,
Vampire Hunter

Black and Deep Desires:
William Shakespeare, Vampire Hunter

Graham Holderness

**TOP HAT
BOOKS**

Winchester, UK
Washington, USA

First published by Top Hat Books, 2015
Top Hat Books is an imprint of John Hunt Publishing Ltd., Laurel House, Station Approach,
Alresford, Hants, SO24 9JH, UK
office1@jhpbooks.net
www.johnhuntpublishing.com

For distributor details and how to order please visit the 'Ordering' section on our website.

Text copyright: Graham Holderness 2014

ISBN: 978 1 78535 063 4
Library of Congress Control Number: 2015932357

A CIP catalogue record for this book is available from the British Library.

Design: Stuart Davies

Printed and bound by CPI Group (UK) Ltd, Croydon, CR0 4YY, UK

⦿

We operate a distinctive and ethical publishing philosophy in all
areas of our business, from our global network of authors to
production and worldwide distribution.

For Marilyn

Stars, hide your fires;
Let not light see my black and deep desires.

William Shakespeare, *Macbeth*

Play

1 July 1606. Hampton Court Palace

Roughly Abraham manhandled the boy's head, gnarled old fingers clutched in the tight yellow curls, forcing him down onto the altar stone. In his right hand, sharp against his son's vulnerable, offered throat, the keen sacrificial knife. Isaac lay athwart the stone, legs helplessly askew, extended wrists tightly bound in subjection. Cold the old man's grey-bearded face, ruthless, undeterred. A springtime bloom of fair young beard flushed Isaac's cheek with gold, gold never to grow to autumnal ripeness, never to know the natural rhythm of reaping. Cut off in the blossom of his youth. He is brought as a lamb to the slaughter, and as a sheep before the shearers is dumb.

William Shakespeare stood before the great series of tapestries by Pieter Coecke van Aelst, commissioned by Henry VIII, that decorated the walls of the Great Hall at Hampton Court, depicting scenes from the life of Abraham. Here was the Departure of Abraham; the Return of Sarah; the Meeting of Abraham and Melchizedek. There God appeared to Abraham; there was the Circumcision of Isaac and the Expulsion of Hagar; there Eliezer and Rebekah at the Well.

But it was the panel depicting the Sacrifice of Isaac that most of all compelled his imagination, and to which he returned, again and again. To slaughter one's own son, as if he were no more than a sacrificial beast! To violate the highest commandment of your religion, and your race! To shed your own blood, the blood of the covenant; the blood that is the life, and is required by the Lord of every man. Once William had talked with a wise Mohammedan, who told him that in the holy book of Islam, the Quran, the same story is told, but with a difference. There the boy, whose name is Ishmael, is asked what he thinks Abraham should do, and gives his own judgement on the proposed massacre of innocence. "Oh my father," he says, "do that which you are commanded. God willing, you shall find me obedient."

William thought of all the sacrifices he had seen performed to appease the hunger of such a savage God, from the excommunication of Elizabeth I to the Gunpowder Plot. He thought of *Regnans in Excelsis*, of the Papacy releasing English Catholics from their allegiance to the English crown, provoking them to assassinate their queen, committing them inexorably to the altar stone. He thought of the Catholic aristocracy, encouraging the Gunpowder Plotters, while they remained aloof in their gated mansions, isolated like his own Mariana in her moated grange. He thought of Thomas Percy, calling on the Earl of Northumberland at Syon House on the eve of the Plot: of Northumberland's disavowal and survival, and Percy's violent death. Even his own father John, encouraging him to stand up for a faith that he knew had become indistinguishable from treason. All through the colossal wreckage of history, in the future as well as the past, grey-bearded old men obediently offering their sons for slaughter on the altar of some corrupt ideal, some perverse and wilful thwarting of God's revealed, manifest will.

For there it was, in the tapestry, as in the scripture. The countermand. An angel appeared to stay Abraham's hand. A wraith-like figure, slipped easily between the warp and weft of the embroidery, as through the lacuna between two worlds. An angel of history, the winds of futurity blowing back the locks of his hair. With an extended finger, touching the father's head, bidding him cease.

Why thus? William asked himself. The artist might have done it in countless different ways. The angel could have seized the boy, and pulled him to safety. Or grabbed the wrist that held the knife. No: for the appetite for undesired sacrifice, the willingness to murder at a whim, lay not in the sacrificer's hand, nor in the victim's obedient subjection; but in the patriarchal mind, that labyrinth of murderous thoughts, curling and sprouting like the grizzled elder's beard, tangled as the branches of the thicket where Abraham found the ram. Confusing love with blood, loyalty with murder, deference to the divine command with a reign of terror unleashed by men, under the banner of an unjust law. Behold, I give you a new covenant: that ye love one another, as I have loved you. *This* is the word of the Lord.

William heard laughter and noise in an adjacent corridor. The players began to file back into the hall, instinctively hushing their rowdiness as they entered and took their places on long benches behind the dais. It was the kind of room that compelled silence. The company was at Hampton Court to rehearse William's newly-written "Powder Play," the play commissioned by Robert Cecil after the collapse of the Gunpowder Plot, now become *The Tragedy of Macbeth*. Today was the dress rehearsal, and Robert Cecil himself was to be present to approve the production.

And there alongside him was William's comrade-in-arms Dr Simon Forman, his notebook at the ready. William had not seen Forman since the burning of the Globe theatre had finally extinguished the last remnants of the Gunpowder Plot. But knowing that Forman was an avid playgoer, who wrote up detailed descriptions of the performances he witnessed, William had invited him along to observe and take notes.

Cecil was seated, surrounded by his entourage. The audience was gathered. Let the play commence.

From Dr Simon Forman, his *Bocke of Plaies*

To Hampton Court on 1 July 1606 to see *The Tragedy of Macbeth*, by William Shakespeare. There was to be observed first the 3 Vampyr sisters, terrifying but comely with their sharp teeth and bright red lips, seeming to hover invisibly through the air.

"When shall we three meet again," said one, "In thunder, lightning, or in rain?" "When the hurlyburly's done," rejoined the second, "when the battle's lost and won." "That will be," said the third, "at set of sun." For the Vampyr may come abroad only in darkness. "Where the place?" "Upon the heath." "There to meet with Macbeth."

Next to be observed, Macbeth and Banquo, 2 noble men of Scotland, riding through a wood, there stood before them the 3 Vampyrs. And they saluted Macbeth, saying 3 times unto him "Hail Macbeth, king of Scotland shalt thou be hereafter." Banquo cared nothing for them, and so rode on. Macbeth alone asked the sisters how he might chance to become king. They said that they could give him eternal life, and all the strength and power he would need to seize the crown, if he would submit to dwell in darkness, and feed on living blood. Macbeth said he would do so gladly, and so the Vampyrs fell upon him, bit his neck and drained his blood. And so they made Macbeth a Vampyr.

Macbeth returned at night to his own castle, and told his wife what the Vampyr sisters had said, that he should be king. Then Macbeth told her of the Vampyr's power, and that they had granted it to him. She begged her husband to do the same for her. And so Macbeth fell upon his wife, and bit her throat, and tore at her breasts so the blood ran freely down, and stained her pure white dress. And so she too became a Vampyr.

That night Duncan the king came to visit them and stayed in their castle of Inverness. Macbeth and his lady saw this as their opportunity to murder the old king in his bed, and to seize the crown for themselves. And so they went to his bed at midnight, and stood on either side of the bed where the good old king lay sleeping, then fell upon him in the utmost savagery to bite at him, and drain his heart's blood. "Ah," said Lady Macbeth, her mouth all bloody, "I have given suck!" "Yet who would have thought," said Macbeth, "the old man to have had so much blood in him?"

Nonetheless they drank it all, and left the old king drained as dry as hay. Also they cut off his head, and stabbed him through the heart, so that he would not in turn become a Vampyr. And when Macbeth had murdered the king, the blood on his face and hands could not be washed off by any means. Nor from his wife's hands, which had held the old man's throat as she sucked his blood. Wash them as they may, the stain and spot of blood could never be removed. By which means they became both much amazed & affronted.

Macduff and the king's son raised an army and came into Scotland and besieged Macbeth's castle of Dunsinane. Next we saw Lady Macbeth walking, as it was thought, in her sleep, but her nocturnal wanderings were indeed the night-walking of the Vampyr. The Lady held a bundle before her, which seemed at first like some stuff, but then the bundle began to cry, so we knew it to be a baby. The Lady held the infant tight against her breast, as if to give it suck. But then to our amazement, she seized upon the child, and sank her sharp teeth into its throat to drink the blood. Thereafter in great anguish of spirit she cast herself from the castle walls into the river below, where she died. For the Vampyr cannot endure water any more than sunlight.

Hearing the news of his lady's death, Macbeth resolved to sally from his castle and face his enemy. Then Macbeth fought with Macduff, and Macduff vanquished him, and unseamed him from the nave to the chaps, and tore out his heart, and cut off his head. And they took branches from the trees of Birnam Wood, and pierced his heart with the green wood, for this was the true way to kill a Vampyr. And Duncan's son Malcolm was restored to the throne.

1 July 1606. Hampton Court Palace

Silence. William thought the play brilliant, masterful, awe-inspiring in its tragedy and terror. It had brought back to him all the horror and sublimity of his own recent encounters with the arch-assassin Guy Fawkes, with the Gunpowder Plot, and with the plague of the Undead; so much so that when Lady Macbeth leapt to her death, he shed a secret tear in memory of Ilona, his own late, lost, lamented Dark Lady. Forman sat in silence, staring at the page he had written, as if he too were seized with the overmastering power of the drama, or of the memories it released.

But only one opinion mattered, of course. Cecil's. Was he pleased? Delighted? Indifferent? As usual nothing could be deciphered in the opaque liquidity of his eyes. He sat for a while in silence, looking at William.

Plot

20 May 1604. The George and Dragon Inn, Southwark

William's first glimpse of the Gunpowder Plot conspirators, some two years previous, had been to see them huddled close in the yard of The George. Though the early spring sun was warming the old grey cobbles of the inn yard, the five men lurked beneath the gallery, in the shadow of the building, shunning the light, clinging to the dark side. So obvious a pack of desperadoes William could scarcely imagine. Muffled in heavy cloaks, though the day promised warmth; eyes glittering from under their tall, broad-brimmed hats; beards jutting pugilistically forth to challenge the innocent air. They were whispering loudly amongst themselves. *If I were Captain of the Watch*, he thought, *I'd arrest them now, just for looking like that.* He knew only two of the men – Thomas Percy and Robin Catesby – the latter tall, handsome and charismatic, who now welcomed him with an affectionate embrace.

"This is Shakespeare," he informed his companions. "He is to become one of us." The others nodded briefly to William, then ignored him and returned to their discussion. The smallest of the three unknowns, a young man with sad eyes and a reticent chin, was remonstrating with Catesby.

"Did you not say we were to meet at The Duck and Drake in the Strand?"

The others sniggered, as at some private joke.

"How many times have you been in The Duck and Drake, Tom?" asked Catesby.

"None, that I can recall. But there's many a London inn I've never been inside."

"The reason why you've never been inside that particular one," Catesby continued with assumed gravity, "is that it does not exist."

"What?"

"There is no such inn," said Percy. "You would be searching for it still, if I hadn't called you from across the road."

"It was a decoy, Tom," explained Catesby. "A false trail for any government spy trying to track us."

"It's just a pity," put in Percy, "we forgot to tell you."

More laughter, as Tom's drooping nether lip jutted in a truculent pout.

"Think of it," said Percy. "In the future, when we are known to history as the men who brought England back to the true faith, they will search in vain for the place where our plot was hatched. Historians will pore over maps; pilgrims will comb the streets; men will waste their lives in a fruitless quest for the whereabouts of the old Duck and Drake in the Strand."

"And the real ale of The George and Dragon," added Catesby, "is better far than the phantom brew of The Duck and Drake. Let's in."

They filed upstairs to a garret room, simply plastered and timbered, with a small lattice window overlooking the busy, traffic-impeded high street. Side-boards were furnished with food and drink, capons and pasties, ale and wine. There were no serving staff. With the door firmly closed, the five seated themselves around a table. Their hats and cloaks off, William was able to observe them. All five men produced from their clothes short clay pipes, and pouches of tobacco. The pipes, liberally stuffed with the weed, were lit from a match they passed around the table. Each man drew in the pungent cloud in long inhalations, drinking it down to the lungs, and from the nostrils puffed out wreaths of smoke.

"Now, William," said Catesby, sounding refreshed, "these men are your brothers in this great enterprise. Tom Wintour, who hankers after The Duck and Drake; Jack Wright; and Guido Fawkes."

Tom, recovered from his discomfiture, nodded pleasantly. A more reserved greeting came from Fawkes, a very tall man and powerfully built, with thick black hair and pointed beard, a prominent nose and red apple cheeks, a large downward-sloping moustache, and eyebrows that slanted strangely upwards to give him a perpetually quizzical expression. Wright was also a large Falstaffian man, stout but sprightly. He was burly with pleasant features, now distorted in a scowl of suspicion as he stared at William.

"Jack?" said Catesby. "Are you all right?"

"I don't like 'im," he said in a harsh northern accent. "I don't like 'im one bit."

"Why ever not?" laughed Percy.

"I don't like the look of 'im. Once he knows our business, may we not be discovered?"

William cupped a hand to his ear, as if finding Wright's speech hard to understand.

"Jack, Jack," said Percy soothingly. "You can't talk to William like that. He's a genius. He's the greatest writer of our time. His plays are known as the best in Europe."

"And," added Catesby, "he is one of us. His mother is an Arden. His father signed the Testament at my father's house when Campion was with us. You need not fear him."

"Well," said Wright, mollified. "I'm sorry. Let me shake hands with thee."

"I have no idea what you just said to me," returned William, "but I will take it as an apology. The insult to me I forgive, right readily. But your offence to my mother tongue is unpardonable. For speaking English in that barbaric way, God may forgive you, but I never will."

"Nay, nay, Will," said Catesby. "Don't provoke him. He's a good fellow, and the best swordsman in England. Best beware his blade."

"I wasn't thinking of challenging him to a duel," said William.

"But I might put him in a play. As a choleric Yorkshire jackass."

"Ay, the pen is mightier. But we are all here of one company. Percy is my cousin. Jack went to school with Guido in York."

"I am surprised he went to school at all. And I did not know there were any schools in York. They clearly do not teach boys to speak English."

"Come, enough of this folly," Fawkes interjected. His saturnine composure was nettled by the continual jesting. "This is not a playhouse. We have a serious matter in hand."

"Well then," said Catesby. "To business. William, we admit you of our council. We have all sworn an oath, as you must do. Here is the *Little Office of the Blessed Virgin,* on which we have all sworn." He placed on the table a small book, bound in brown calfskin, with decorated spine, and gold lettered title on a red morocco backstrip. "Kiss it, and swear. By the Blessed Trinity. By the Holy Sacrifice of the Eucharist. By the Body and Blood of Christ. By the dolours of the Blessed Virgin Mary, Queen of Heaven, Star of the Sea. Together, all of us, in life and death. One heart, one mind, one mission. To kill a king."

All crossed themselves, on breasts and lips. Reverently William kissed the book, and assented to the oath.

"Amen. Now, we have debated endlessly of the 'why' in this business. This king, who has broken every promise he made to our Catholic brethren; who has fined and repressed us to the point of penury; and who now moves to persecute us with grievous penalties – this king must die. Today, we are here to speak of the 'how.' We have talked endlessly, gentlemen, and done nothing. But how do we get close enough to this king to take him off? None of us are trusted, even you, Percy, though you be a Gentleman Pensioner."

"Gentleman or pensioner," said Percy shortly, "James would as soon have me near him as a cockatrice."

"And none could bear a weapon anywhere near him, save his Scottish lords, whom he trusts with his life. But now we have, among our number, one who has privilege to come close enough to the royal person to almost touch him. One who has the prerogative to carry a sword, albeit a toy one, close enough to reach the tyrant's heart."

Eyes levelled at William, in search of a reaction. His face remained illegible.

"William here has killed many a king in his plays," said Percy. "He is the royal playwright, and an actor in his own plays. He could write himself a part, the character of some revenger perhaps, and bear a real sword in place of his buttoned foil. His weapon would be ready in his hand. He could approach the king at some necessary moment of the action. And so, the deed is done."

A ruffle of approval swept the board.

"Did you not have a play," said Catesby, "*Homelaicte* I think it was, a fine comedy, in which a prince stabbed the king who murdered his father? And did he not do this at a play?"

"Approximately," said William. "But …"

"Can you not play it again?" Catesby continued. "Have at the Player King, and stab the real one? Not in jest, but in earnest?"

"A tragedy," said William.

Fawkes glared at him. "Only for those who love the king."

"No," said William with some asperity. "My *Hamlet* was a tragedy, not a comedy."

"Really?" said Catesby, bemused. "I distinctly remember laughing."

"I foresee one disadvantage to this plan," said William. "And that is that the assassin cannot hope to survive the assassination. It is a suicide mission."

"Why man," said Fawkes belligerently, "we all risk our lives in the very act of being here, and speaking of such high treason."

"True," replied William. "But in this scheme only one would die for sure. The rest of you may risk your lives from a safe distance. You will kill your king, and live to tell the tale of the poor player who perished in your cause."

"We have no fear of venturing our bodies," said Percy earnestly. "You know that. It is a matter of who can get close enough. For that, William, we need someone like you. As the prophet Isaiah says, 'whom shall we send? And who will go for us?'"

"I wrote another play, a few years ago, *Julius Caesar*, the tragedy of Caesar's death in the Capitol. Those who swore to kill him agreed that all should strike a blow. All should share the common guilt. All should bathe their hands in Caesar's blood. Now I will gladly place myself in such peril for the Cause, even at risk of certain death. But only if you will all risk with me. One for all; all for one. Or if one alone, then none."

"He has something there," said Percy. "We are like generals who order their troops forward into ambush while we stay safe behind."

"Could we not disguise ourselves as Players," put in Percy, "and so join the action?"

"We could all of us wear masks, and appear in the play," said Wright, catching on. "At the signal we could deal with the Scottish lords, while William here dispatches James."

"Such a play," said William gravely, "would have to be a Dumb Show, in every sense. For not even a Scottish king could understand your speech."

"But do you think it could be done?" asked Catesby earnestly.

"No," said William. "The actors are too well-known at court. We are all normal size. No disguise could conceal the identity of this Magog, or his companion giant Gog over there."

"Then what?" said Percy. "Catesby brought you in with this service in mind. You say it cannot succeed. What else?"

William brooded for a moment in silence. "Your plan," he went on, "is the assassination. How many attempts have been made on the king's life?"

"Since he came here, only the Main Plot that I know of. In

Scotland he was endangered many times. The lords Gowrie and Angus seized and held him when he was but a boy. Young Bothwell laid fire at his door. One Ruthven assaulted him and was run through."

"Yet he lives still. What of the old queen, her late majesty Elizabeth? How many attempts?"

"Many."

"Yes, many. And all failed. I saw my cousin Arden's hacked-off head grinning back at me on London Bridge. His death did not improve his appearance. I saw Babbington hang, choking and blue. Saw his privy members sliced off like the tail of a radish. Saw his belly slit across, and his entrails tumble out before his very eyes. Have you smelt a man's entrails? Saw him dragged to the block and quartered like an animal. He could not kill Elizabeth. Neither could the others."

"But these are not the only kings in the world," said Fawkes. "Think of France. Henri III, the last of the Valois kings, was murdered by Jacques Clement, a mere Dominican friar. Or the present king, Henri. More than one assassin has reached his very side. One came close enough to cut his lip. Those who failed in England show us the way. With more courage and resolution, it can be done. It falls to us who follow to complete their mission."

"You are men of action, men of the sword. You think naturally of killing: the quick lunge, the subtle thrust. I am a poet. You think with your sword-arm; I with my imagination. You think small. I think big. If you had seen my *Caesar*, you would know the fate of those who think to crush a tyranny by ending the tyrant's life. They were men of belief, like you; soldiers on a crusade; honourable men. Caesar was their sole enemy; Caesar they killed. And those they left alive, Marc Antony and Octavius, lived to destroy them. Brutus and Cassius died in ignominy by their own hands."

"Are you saying we should kill all the great lords who support the king?" said Catesby. "Such a thing is not possible.

We have not the strength to destroy so many at one blow. And if we had, such wholesale slaughter would shake the people's loyalty to its roots. They would find it barbaric, intolerable. Is it not impiety to send so many, all at once, to perdition? Such a sight becomes the battlefield, but here would show much amiss. We cannot wage total war in the streets and houses of England."

"Again, you think with your muscles, not your brain. You think only of killing by hand. Of stabbing a man to death in full public view, leaving you standing there for all to see, blade smoking with hot gore, the blood-boltered murderer. There are other ways. On what occasions would you find king, princes, bishops, lords, all assembled together in one place?"

"Some royal birthday, perhaps?"

"In church, where we cannot touch them?"

"On a state occasion?"

"My Caesar," said William, "was killed in the Capitol."

"The Parliament House?" Percy grabbed at the idea. "But to slaughter them all, that would take an army. We are but few."

"Shut the doors and set a fire," suggested Wintour. "Burn the house down, and all of them in it."

"Impossible," said Catesby. "A fire can be doused. Some would escape, most likely James himself."

"No," explained William. "You must advance on them in silence. In secret. So they do not see the danger until it is too late. You must come at them from nowhere."

"You riddle with us, Player," said Fawkes. "Speak plain."

"We Catholics cannot live in the light of day, but inhabit a perpetual night where none can see the truth of what we do. We are like ghosts who cannot endure the daylight."

"Was there not a ghost in your play, Will?" asked Percy.

"Think," William went on. "Where is our faith housed in these evil times?"

"In the Holy Church."

"In the Blessed Sacrament of the altar."

"In the breasts of the faithful."

"Good Catechetical answers, all. But where is it, in reality, physically present, here in the world? Where do we harbour our priests? Where are our Masses celebrated? Where do we hide when the king's men hammer at the door?"

"Priest holes."

"Secret chambers."

"Hidden passages."

"Exactly. That is our domain. We inhabit the darkness, and shun the light."

"But God, in the beginning, divided the light from the darkness," said Wintour, "and saw that it was good."

"So He did," replied William. "And yet, ever since the coming of Our Saviour, His faithful children have been found worshipping in the dark, hiding from the light of day. Think of St Paul, lying in the shades of his prison cell. Of the Christians in Rome, hiding in crypts and catacombs beneath the city. Of our own priests and martyrs, walled up in the shadows of a priest-hole, buried in blackness, with nothing but their own filth for company. So it has been for 1600 years. The children of God are always those who dwell in darkness, and the shadow of death."

Percy and Catesby glanced at one another, as if beginning to understand. Wright continued to scowl in suspicion. Wintour looked intrigued, Fawkes fascinated.

"You know the work of Little John the carpenter?"

"Of course. Nicholas Owen. He has fashioned priest-holes and secret compartments in all our houses. A master of cunning contrivance and curious craft. But these are places to hide, not sally-ports for ambuscade."

"There is another place where Little John exercises his skills. In the theatre we also have hidden compartments in which actors can conceal themselves, and from which they can emerge. Most especially under the stage. There, in the darkness, men and boys may hide from the light of day. But then they issue forth into the light, from the trap, at the designated time."

"Yes!" cried Catesby. "Your Ghost came from beneath the stage! Through the trap-door! He was in his night-gown. I remember. That's what made me laugh. I told you it was funny."

"The trap-door is a portal, a permeable barrier between two worlds. The space beneath the stage is a place of darkness, that we may identify as another world. In our plays, fiends from Hell emerge, and drag the damned soul down to fiery torment. A ghost from Purgatory rises and freely walks the earth. The dead may rise from their graves at the necromancer's command, and prey upon the living. Do they not call us devils, children of Satan, instruments of darkness? But who is it that has cast us into this Hell? Let us rise, then, from the darkness of the tomb, like ghosts to haunt the living. Let us issue forth, like demons from the pit, to tear the flesh from our oppressors' bones, and drain our enemy's blood."

"So we attack them from *below*," said Percy, at last seeing the practical application. "I see. Is there a cellar beneath the Parliament House?"

"Certainly," said Fawkes. "There is an undercroft. Right beneath the floor of the House. Used for storing firewood, old broken furniture, empty barrels."

"Could we not take possession of such a place?" asked Percy. "Clear the space and secure it. Fill it with a troop of armed men, sufficient to the task."

"But there are many adjoining apartments," Fawkes continued. "Numerous chambers on that lower level. Some of them are leased, I believe. They are not private places. You will find men working there, night and day. There is no access to the cellar without being detected. We could not infiltrate and hide a company of men there in secret. Someone would see us."

"Even if we could gain access, the odds are still too great," observed Catesby. "Surprise lasts only a few moments. Guards are everywhere, and reinforcements at call. We could not hope to meet them all. Meanwhile, the king escapes."

"Who said anything about an armed assault?" said William. "That could be done at any time, if you had the force. But you do not. And that is why you need to think beyond the tried and trusted, think beneath the obvious. Say you have taken possession of that cellar beneath the House. Say you secure it. Lock it up. Keep others from entering. What then? What other means of assault are open to you?"

The blue smoke of their pipes had by now woven an opaque smog, through which the conspirators peered in silence at William, who vented a sigh of frustration.

"I really do have to spell it out for you, don't I? How was James's father killed?"

Light fell upon them in a blinding rush.

"Gunpowder!" said Percy. "He was blown sky high at Kirk O'Fields."

"Two barrels of powder," said Fawkes, "lodged beneath his chamber."

"He was in his night-gown too," put in Catesby. "Now that really *was* funny."

"But that was but a small explosion," said Wintour, "merely enough to kill one or two men."

"But all you would you need to kill more men," said Fawkes, "is more powder!"

"Blow up the Parliament House!" said Catesby in wonder. "How much powder would be required?"

"Thirty or forty barrels," said Fawkes. "Placed right beneath the Chair of State."

"Would it work?"

"Of course it would work. The whole building would be devastated."

"Think of it," said William. "What is a building? A haven; a harbour; a shelter from nature and the hand of war. We can live inside it, love inside it, conceive and bear our children, and it will protect us. The young can grow up in it, the sick recover their illness. But turn that building into a weapon, and we can be destroyed by the same roof and walls that have protected us from weather, and climate, from wild beasts and wilder men.

"I saw a town in Italy, after an earthquake. It was a heap of rubble. Those who died were beneath it, killed by their own homes. The shepherds, abiding in the fields, were pulling the dead from the ruins.

"You have all seen buildings engulfed by fire. The house becomes a shroud of flame that murders with a blaze. Only the houseless go free. Think of the Parliament House as a weapon. A cannon, say. Charge it with powder. Ram it full of human shot. Light the fuse, and discharge it at the moon. The house becomes the lethal instrument that slaughters all within. Kill them all, with one blow. The be-all and the end-all."

A pregnant silence, heavy with tobacco and thought. The conspirators all stared at Shakespeare with something like awe. The ingenuity! The scope and scale! The depth and breadth of imagination! Not one of them, with all their military experience, crusading zeal and organisational ability, could have thought up such a scheme. It had to emerge from the fertile mind of an artist, a poet, a dreamer. For it is only the imagination that can body forth the shapes of things unknown.

"It is a stroke at the root," said Catesby, breaking the silence.

"It would bring about new alterations," said Percy, "in religion, in government, in the whole realm."

"The effect would be terrible," said Wintour. "So many casualties. The innocent slaughtered along with the guilty. This is how it would be seen: as murder, not tyrannicide. The king, yes. But the queen and princes? The royal babes? All the pretty chickens and their dam, at one fell swoop?"

"The cubs must be put down, if they are with their sire," said Fawkes. "And the queen is mother to his heirs. It has always been so. If they live, we die. Unless we can seize one of them and make him serve us."

"What of the Catholic lords," Wintour went on, "our friends, relations, patrons? What of Monteagle, Stourton, Northumberland?"

"Casualties of war."

"But I fear that to destroy the Parliament House, which so many hold sacred as the temple of law and the seat of government, may turn many against us."

"Why man," said Percy, "it is in that place they have done us all the mischief! It is there they have devised their fines, their taxes, their arrests and executions. All the injuries and oppressions from which our people suffer, stem from there. What better house to serve as the place of their punishment? There they would give the death blow to the Catholic cause. There we would hope to bring upon their heads the same end they have designed for others."

"There is divine justice in it," said Fawkes. "Samson brought the Temple of Dagon crashing down on the heads of the Philistines. It will be seen as the will of God."

"It is true," murmured Catesby. "The nature of the disease requires so sharp a remedy. In necessity as great as ours, the harshness of the deed should have no effect on us, in view of the cruelty and unbridled barbarity our enemies use towards us. We only work against life. They rob us of what is dearer than life: our goods, freedom, honour, and every shred of hope for our posterity. What man is there so lacking in religion, so shallow in his knowledge of God, that he would not despise, for the sake of these, everything else in the world, including life itself?"

"And yet," Wintour went on, refusing to be cowed by their opposition, "it seems to me that such an act may strike the heart with fear, but not inspire it with love. Think what a quantity of blood we must spill! From such a holocaust there may spring an enormous hatred, and for us, a reputation for infamy among those we have bereaved. So great a blast may blow the horrid deed in every eye."

"That tears may drown the wind," said William thoughtfully. "Tell me, all of you, when a man is put to death on the scaffold, why is the act of execution rendered so dreadful, so obscene, so shameful that even the most hard-hearted man will close his eyes to shut out the horror? If a man must be put to death, could it not be encompassed with dignity and respect? He may be hanged, quietly, in private, his priest by him, his relatives near, the officers of the law looking on to ensure justice. Let him wear his own clothes, a sober suit of black, and be allowed his own private prayers. Let all be decent, and modest; let him be taken off with gentleness and mercy. He has done wrong; he deserves his punishment; now he is gone, to trouble the state no more.

"Instead of this, what do we see? Cruel exposure of obscene nakedness. Coarse laughter at a man's weakness and fear, as he shits and pisses and whimpers his way to ignominious death. Vicious torment visited on a wretched body already enfeebled by torture. Emasculated, ripped inside out, gutted like a fish, quartered like a carcass on a butcher's stall.

"Now why is this dreadful pageant thought necessary? Is it to prove the power of the state, that can apply such wanton cruelty at will? Why no, for that power is already manifested in the execution itself. Is it to show that the punishment must fit the crime? No, for the punishment exceeds the crime. I will tell you: it is to compel belief that the horror of the penalty must imply an equally horrid offence. The terror of the execution creates the enormity of the crime.

"When you see a man thrust a sharp blade into another man's body, say one hot afternoon in a tavern yard, seemingly random and unprovoked, your very being cries out, *why?* What prompts that man to exercise such violence on another? There must be a motive we cannot see; a reason, albeit one we cannot know. And when you see a man torn to pieces on Tower Hill, or in St Paul's yard, this is also what you feel: there must be a reason. What is being done to him, could not be done, if it were not for the absolute enormity of his wrongdoing. The crime fits the punishment: the punishment defines the crime. There is an equivalence of dread. Terror breeds terror: blood will have blood."

"Repel force with force," added Catesby.

"And so it is with this Gunpowder Plot, as we may call it," William continued. "The scale of the violence will map the scope of our injuries. The dismembered corpses strewing Westminster will put all in mind of those innocents for true religion quartered on the scaffold. The ruin of their Parliament House will equal the destruction of our church. And from its ashes we will rise the phoenix of the one true faith."

"Let it be so," said Fawkes. "We have our Plot. And so, gentlemen, it is time for us to stop talking, and to do somewhat, here and in England."

"We'll need a house in Westminster."

"We'll need powder."

"We'll need weapons."

"You Percy," Fawkes went on, assuming command, "will secure lodgings. In your capacity as Gentleman Pensioner."

"Aye."

"And I'll gather the powder. Catesby: you undertake to secure a lease on one of the apartments adjoining the cellar under the Parliament House."

"I will."

"Jack, a store of weapons?"

"We may start with these," said Wright, fetching from a side-table a roll of cloth which he unwrapped on the table. Inside it lay five of the most beautiful swords William had ever seen. He took one up, and examined it. It featured a forged iron guard, consisting of round bars and an up-turned shell, the obverse chiselled with graphic illustrations. The quillons were long, straight and tapered, with turned finials, and the integrated knucklebow connected with double bars to the shell. The blade was over a yard long, and deeply engraved with scenes from the Bible, depicted with exquisite precision and skill.

During one of his Spanish voyages, Fawkes had travelled to the little walled town of Toledo, south of Madrid, sought out Juan Martinez, the most celebrated swordsmith of the day, and commissioned him to forge a number of weapons to a specific design and scheme of decoration.

First the master craftsman had heated his furnace to its full intensity, and shaped the sword, firm and strong, folding over three layers of steel, and hammering them together into a gleaming blade. Then he made the grip, formed from twisted wire, alternating silver and iron. Lastly he added the curved guard, forged for strength, and shaped for beauty.

With many a wonder did his cunning hand enrich the blade. On the shell he wrought the creation of the heavens and the earth: the land and the sea, the sun and the moon, and the stars that glorify the face of heaven. On one face of the blade he wrought also the image of Paradise, Adam and Eve with the serpent, and their banishment from the garden for their original fault. Then he wrought Cain slaying his brother Abel, and Noah delivered from the flood, and Samson groping the temple-posts to overwhelm the world.

On the other side he wrought the Annunciation, and the Nativity of Our Lord, and the Temptation in the Wilderness. And there, towards the point of the slender blade, etched in miniature, were scenes from the Passion of Christ. It was a speaking story in steel. Here Jesus stands before Pilate, and is condemned to death. Here he shoulders the cross, and begins his long journey down the Via Dolorosa. There he falls, and meets his mother. Simon of Cyrene helps him, and Veronica wipes his face. He is stripped, and nailed to the cross, and dies. He is deposed, and laid in the tomb for his last human rest. One short sleep past, he wakes eternally. Death once dead, says the sword's sharp point, there's no more dying then.

William replaced the weapon on the table with a kind of reverence. He was moved almost to tears by such artistry, such craft, such precision revealed in the chasing of the fine lines into obdurate steel. And he was struck to the heart by the fanatical piety of men who had troubled to acquire such ornate and decorative weapons to prosecute their bloody cause, when in fact any old iron would have served. They truly were modern-day crusaders, or warrior-monks, like the knights of old, the Templars and the Hospitallers, who took that long hot road to Jerusalem to deliver the Holy Sepulchre from its infidel occupiers. They burned with a devouring flame of religious zeal, an absolute devotion to a mission that demanded, and cost, not less than everything. Though he could never wield such a weapon himself, it was an honour simply to be of their company. And so it was with a feeling somewhere between devotion and love that he left them, and made his way north through the dark narrow lanes, back to his lodgings in Silver Street.

Tunnel

24 December 1604. Westminster

Percy was leading William through a Cretan labyrinth of dark narrow streets, in the direction, as far as he could tell, of the Palace of Westminster. It was a raw, cold afternoon. Percy's hat was pulled down over his face, and a long cloak concealed his clothing. Every so often he stopped, crouching into an embrasure or doorway, and surveyed the street behind them. To William these precautions seemed both absurd and exciting, like a childhood adventure glimpsed through an adult's recollection. Satisfied that they were not being followed, Percy turned a corner and yanked William into a porch beneath a protruding clapboard penthouse. He rapped on the door with a soft, coded knock of short and long taps. The door opened quickly to admit them, and as quickly closed again behind.

William could not see who had let them in. A dark passageway led into the house. Through the window he could glimpse a small garden, with an outhouse, roughly-constructed from old yellow bricks. The garden seemed surprisingly well-tended, with a covering of bright green turf. There were no flower-beds. Behind the outhouse he could see a pile of timber, straight lengths of trimmed and chiselled lumber, neatly stacked, and partially covered from the weather.

Fawkes and Catesby sat at a table in a low-ceilinged room. Wright lay sleeping on a rough truckle bed in a corner. Wintour was not there. The air was foul with Nicotan. Fawkes and Catesby seemed physically exhausted, grimed from head to foot with reddish mud, black soil and yellow clay. White tracks showed on their faces where the sweat had run down and cleared the dirt.

A table was piled with food and drink, pies and cooked meats and bottles of wine. Another table bore a heap of pistols and powder flasks.

"How goes it?" asked Percy, taking off his hat and cloak.

"Well enough," grunted Fawkes. "But slow."

"We have until 7th February next year," observed Catesby, as if the date were fixed in his mind. "Slow, but sure."

"Would someone like to tell me what's going on?" asked William.

"Here," said Percy, "we may talk freely. Everywhere else the city is full of ears. The houses listen. Even the air cannot be trusted. Sit down and take a drink, Will. Is there wine?"

The others gestured towards the side-table. They seemed too tired to stand up. Percy poured for all of them.

"We rented this house from one Whynniard, a Keeper of the King's Wardrobe," Percy explained to William. "He lodges elsewhere. On the other side of that wall is a chamber. Next to that chamber, the Palace of Westminster. We are within a short distance here of the Prince's Lodgings, the Painted Chamber, the House of Lords itself."

"Good God," breathed William.

"Holy is his name," said Catesby automatically. He was almost asleep.

"From here, the Parliament House is within our reach. But proximity is not power, and reach is not strength. We follow your Plot, you see, William. To come at them unseen, out of the darkness, to strike from below, like demons from Hell. We are digging a mine from under the floor of this next room, into the vault beneath the House of Lords."

"Old mole," said Catesby sleepily. "Like your ghost, William. But not so fast."

"The mine will take us to below the cellar, and we will break through the floor to enter it. We will have the powder stored safely elsewhere. You will know where, when the time arrives. For now the work is to dig, to excavate, to undermine. We labour at night, when there is no-one abroad to hear our noise. It is cruel work."

"Your turn," said Fawkes.

"Ay," said Percy. "Come, Will, let me show you the mine."

Percy took up a lantern and led William into an adjoining room. The floorboards and stone foundations had been removed, and in the centre of the chamber gaped a large hole, a good three yards square, buttressed on all four sides with planks of timber, and with a turned round crosspiece laid over the gap. William peered over the edge, and gazed down into darkness.

"How deep is it?"

"This is the shaft," said Percy. "Twenty feet or so. We surveyed the ground between here and the Palace, and dug deep enough to allow for variation in levels. The tunnel leads off from the foot of the shaft, and will run beneath our chamber, below the foundations of the Palace, and then directly through the floor into the vault beneath the House of Lords. Once it is in place, we will introduce the barrels of powder."

Percy picked up a couple of short-handled shovels, and held the lantern over the shaft. A wooden ladder was nailed to one side.

"Coming down? Here. Hold the lantern."

William disliked confined spaces, but did not wish to show any fear. He had been down a coal-mine in Warwickshire, but could not honestly say he had enjoyed the experience. He raised the lantern over the shaft, and Percy clambered down into the darkness. When he reached the bottom, William followed. At the foot of the shaft a low tunnel disappeared southwards. It was no more than four feet high, and a little wider. Stout baulks of timber braced the reddish brick-earth at the sides and above, shoring the tunnel and preventing collapse. These pit-props were placed at intervals of a yard or so. Plank stretchers squared off the joists, and the roof was roughly sealed with floorboards from the house.

"Little John showed us how to make these," Percy explained,

pointing to the props. "You cut them a little too long, and bray them in with a lump hammer. We had a few falls before we brought him in." He dropped to his knees and scrambled like a rat into the tunnel. William was obliged to follow with the lamp. The floor of the mine was wet: the river was not far off. As they shuffled through, William noticed that in places the walls were formed from the deep, residual sandstone on which London sits. Laboriously the conspirators had chipped and cracked their way through solid boulders.

"That one took us a week," said Percy proudly. "Almost killed me."

Some yards further on, they reached what in a coal-mine would have been the face. A blank wall of yellow clay, scattered with small stones, and flints, and bits of quartz that winked in the lamplight. Piles of excavated earth lay waiting to be cleared, and two empty buckets stood ready to hold it. William set the lantern down. Each man took a shovel and began to fill the buckets.

The work went slowly in the confined space, every movement condensed and miniaturised. But at last the buckets were full. They crawled back along the tunnel, each dragging a heavy pail of red and yellow brick-earth and clay. When they reached the shaft, Percy climbed up the ladder and threw a rope over the crosspiece. William attached a bucket to the rope, and inch by inch it was hauled up and over the edge. The second bucket was raised in turn, and William followed, still holding the lantern, up the ladder. As he reached the top, a familiar face greeted him over the lip of the shaft.

"If it ain't Master William," said the face, in a hempseed Oxfordshire burr. "Rising from the grave, like the ghost of your own father. Remember me?"

Nicholas Owen, or to use his soubriquet, Little John, was a dwarf, a carpenter, and a Jesuit lay brother. He was also one of the most remarkable men of his time, if only for combining these incommensurable qualities. This was the same Owen who had provided the recusant population of England with the opportunity of practising their faith in the darkness of secrecy and concealment, since it was he who had constructed that baffling maze of tunnels, secret passages, priest-holes and oubliettes that enabled Catholics to harbour priests, conduct masses and conceal the elaborate properties of their faith. Owen had also worked in the theatre, which was how Shakespeare knew him.

"'Ow did that trap-door work, then?" he asked, as he helped William to haul himself clear of the shaft.

"Like a dream," said William. "We pushed it open from below, and it swung up, paused, and slammed backwards onto the stage so the audience gasped with fear. Before they'd even caught sight of the Ghost!"

"Ay, I thought it would."

"But what brings you here?"

"Why, I've been helping these gentlemen with their little tunnel. What do you think of it?"

"It's perfect," replied William. "And now I know why you're here. You're the only man I know who could stand upright in it."

Owen laughed, took one of the buckets and dragged it outside. Percy and William took the other between them. Owen pulled his pail to the outhouse in the garden, opened a low door and disappeared inside. Following him in, William was surprised to observe that the outhouse contained nothing but piles of earth.

"Here we store the earth from the tunnel," said Percy from behind him. "So it cannot be seen. Then at night we lift the turf and spread it over the garden."

"I see," said William. "Eventually the garden will be so high you'll be able to jump down into the Palace."

They returned to the house and rejoined the others. Fawkes and Catesby were engaged in an argument. Wright still lay on his bed, but awake and listening to his fellows.

"It's hard work, Guido, I know. But it can be done."

"How long have we been working on this tunnel?" asked Fawkes.

"Two weeks exactly."

"And what proportion of its necessary length have we excavated?"

"About a quarter."

"Six more weeks then. We will never do it. Not before Parliament opens on 7th February."

"Then we will increase our efforts. Speed up the work. Double our shifts."

Wright groaned, and his head fell back onto the mattress.

"We are exhausted already," said Fawkes. "We must finish by the New Year. We will need time to install the powder. And while we slave down here, there is other business that remains undone. Our plan to seize one of the young princes, or the Princess Elizabeth. The securing of more horses and armour, musket, pikes, shot. Keeping the Catholic nobles on our side. All this goes by the board, while we play at being miners."

"Then there is only one other solution," said Catesby simply. "We bring more men into the plot."

"My brother will come in," said Wright. "And Tom's brother, Christopher."

"If you can trust them, then let us have them in," said Fawkes impatiently. "But no more. How often have we agreed that the circle must be kept tight and strong? There can be no room for a weak link."

"Speaking of weakness," put in Percy, "where is little Tom?"

"Wintour has gone to the Palace of Westminster to hear the news," Fawkes replied. "He should have returned by now."

"I'll go seek him there," said William, fearing another summons to the underworld, another hour inhaling the dark dust.

Fawkes shrugged. "Aye. Tell him to get back here."

William left the house, and crossed over to the Palace. Cold was falling with the darkness. His breath smoked in the raw foggy air. It was Christmas Eve. The taverns were full of drunken revellers, soaking themselves in ale and wine, with no thought for the morrow. A holy day. As William picked his way carefully through the dark streets, light streamed from the windows of ale-houses, lighting up a heap of rubbish, a pool of vomit, a dead cat, a drunk helplessly sprawling on the ground. Ragged voices bawled out a Christmas hymn.

Lullay, lullay, thou tiny child …

A pretty young whore fluttered her tongue at him from a doorway.

"Wha' ya want for Christmas, 'andsome?"

"Not a dose of the clap from you," replied William, "that's for sure."

"Too late for you, you bald-headed bastard."

The great mediaeval hall towered above him. Crowds of people milled round the doorway, jostling, pushing, shouting to one another. A pair of noblemen came out of the hall, richly dressed in immense furs, and were immediately assailed by a throng of the desperate, the needy, the merely curious. Their attendants beat back the importuners, and the lords were escorted to their waiting carriage. For a moment William caught a glimpse of the brilliantly-illuminated hall as it must be seen from the outer darkness of deprivation. Like the lonely dragon in an old poem he had once read, looking across the dark fens of alienation towards the bright lights of the mead-hall, hearing the sounds of music and laughter, and nursing an inconsolable hatred, deep in his wounded heart.

William slipped through the crowd and entered. From the shadowy loft-space above, the great timber angels that buttressed the roof looked down inscrutably. The session of Parliament seemed, from the empty benches, to be over for the day. A group of courtiers in sober black, conversing together on the dais, were putting their papers away, as if some announcement had just been made. He caught sight of Wintour standing at the edge of the platform, and pushed through the dispersing crowd to join him.

"What's the news?" William asked him in a whisper. "Good or bad?"

"Hard to say," was Wintour's reply. "Parliament is prorogued. But not to 7th February. Till 3rd October."

"October?"

"Ay. It gives us more time. But it puts off our venture."

"More time for the tunnel?"

"Ay. But the iron is hot now. Who knows if it may not have cooled by the autumn?"

Together they left the building, and returned to their house of conspiracy.

"Well?" asked Fawkes.

"Prorogued," said Wintour. "To 3rd October."

"3rd October!" exclaimed Fawkes. "A reprieve! We can finish the tunnel, as planned, by the New Year. Then we have a whole nine moons to do the rest: get the powder, raise the horses and arms, plan the coup. Talk to our friends abroad. I see in this the hand of Providence. It gives us a greater earnest of success. We have more time."

"More time for digging," said Catesby dejectedly. "What fun."

"I can't feel my hands," said Wright.

"Let me counsel you," interjected Owen, who had quietly come in from the outhouse. "You gentlemen be delicate. Not used to such labours as these. And 'tis the evening of Our Lord's birthday. Why don't ye all take a rest? Go home for the night. Take a bath, a drink, some food, get some sleep. William and I will take your shift tonight. He was a poor country boy, like me. He's used to hard graft."

William tried to remonstrate, but was seized by a fit of coughing. Dirt blocked his throat. "I think I already have a case of the black lung," he said, spitting dust.

"You were only down there an hour!" exclaimed Percy.

"I'm used to the fresh air of Paris Garden," said William. "To breathing stale beer, rank sweat and steaming horse-shit. Not subterranean London brick-earth."

"I'll look after him," said the little man, slapping William hard on the back. "Don't fret."

The others were too desperate for rest to resist, and so wasted no further time in quitting the house, silently and cautiously, one by one. William was left alone with Owen, who gathered some lengths of timber from behind the outhouse, and threw them down into the shaft, together with a hammer and some other tools.

"You fit then, boy?" he asked William, and shinned quickly down the ladder. William followed, again holding the lantern. Owen was already up at the face, proceeding to prop the work the others had completed. The labour of setting the props, banging in the cross-beam, and adding the stretcher seemed effortless in his practised hands. Meanwhile he talked away to William, who crouched over the lantern and listened.

"It ain't right that gentlemen should have to do work like this. Not that they ain't up to bearing hardship, as they do in the wars. They're tough lads. But God gave us different gifts: some to work with their hands, some with their minds. To each his own. Those chaps could do more in an hour with their thinking and talk, than ever they can do down here with a pick and shovel. Mr Percy, now, and Mr Fawkes, they can dig with the best. But young Wintour, and Wright: good men, capable and clever, but useless bastards down the pit."

"You do swear a lot for a priest, Nicholas," said William, admiring the little man's versatility.

"Oh, I don't swear as a priest, Master Will," said Owen earnestly, his accent losing some of its bumpkin vernacular. "No, I swear as a carpenter. Even St Joseph must have cursed now and again. When the hammer hit his thumb."

"So you keep your identities quite separate, then?"

"I do. I'm three things, as you know. A Jesuit, a midget and a craftsman. It sounds like the beginning of a joke, don't it? 'A priest, a dwarf and a carpenter walked into a tavern….' Here, Will, with your wit, you could finish it for me."

"So the priest said to the carpenter," improvised William, "'Make me a crucifix.' 'You'll never,' said the dwarf, 'get me up on one of those things.'"

Owen laughed in delight as he hammered in a joist. "No, I keep my trades distinct. This job, now, I do as a carpenter. They know I can do the work, and keep my mouth shut. As a priest, I don't know why they're digging a hole in the ground under Westminster. They don't tell me. If I overhear any talk of treachery, why I just forget it. Do you think I remember everything I hear in confession? If they asked me for spiritual counsel, I'd tell them what the church tells me: that all good Catholics should be patient and obedient, and do nothing to stir up the powers of the state against them."

"And have they asked you?"

"No," he replied, wrestling a length of floorboard into position above the cross-beam. "Not once."

"But you must have your opinions, as a priest, on what you know, as a carpenter, is being undertaken here? Do you think, for instance, just for the sake of argument, that a believer should take action against a king who persecutes the church?"

"Our Holy Mother Church has often preached tyrannicide as a just cause. In the case of our own poor country, she trusts in the Lord, and hopes for a better day. God has caused the death of many an evil ruler. Pass me that piece of planking, will you?"

"In such cases, their deaths must be God's will," William replied, giving him the piece of wood. "But take another case: what if a man set out to kill an evildoer, but cannot reach him without harming innocents, caught in the way? What of an army, whose bombardments slaughter civilians alongside military? What of the man who plants a bomb, hoping to destroy his enemy, knowing that many who have done no harm will also die in the blast?"

"I've known many soldiers torment themselves with such questions. 'Tis a hard decision, and great cruelty, to kill innocent men and women. But many enterprises would have to be given up, and many opportunities lost, if we invariably forwent such sacrifice. Our faith holds to the doctrine of the just war. You know, St Augustine. It is essential, for anyone prosecuting a just war, to observe the principles of justice. If the death of innocent people is something accidental, and by no means desired by the man who wages the just war, and if he hates this consequence, he may, without violation of justice, allow their death. He is not obliged to cease waging war, notwithstanding the damage done to innocent parties."

"And is this true theology?"

"Ay, it is. We call it 'double effect.' A single action has two consequences: one good, one bad. A man undertakes an action. If the good effect countervails over the bad; if the bad effect is involuntary; and if the one cannot be brought about without the other – then his conscience is clear."

"Is this not equivocation?"

"Of course. There are for a Christian many instances where two incompatible things are equally true. Christ was both God and man. Our Blessed Lady was both virgin and mother. God made the world, yet permitted men to nail Him on a cross. *Communicatio idiomatum.* We cannot reconcile such truths to one another. Yet we give them equal weight, we speak of them as one."

"I see. Very persuasive. They don't call you Jesuits for nothing."

"I would hope not. But understand one thing: none of these men has confided their intention to me, or to any other priest. It is an article of faith with them. They do not want to involve the Catholic clergy in whatever enterprise it is they pursue. If it is a capital matter, and it fails, they will all die. Some of them will be tortured first. They do not want their priests to suffer the same agony of torment, the same shameful death. Not one could bear to see a priest, who has brought them, in his own hands, the body and blood of Christ, hung up in iron manacles, stretched, racked, maimed."

"Would they do such a thing? Would they do that, even to one such as you?"

Owen stopped work, and fell to examining a knot in a piece of timber. "Because I am small, you mean? Because my body has already been twisted, and broken? Because even a wild beast would hesitate to inflict cruelty on such a poor, bent, crippled creature as this?" He held out his hands for Shakespeare to examine, palms upwards. Each of his wrists was scarred with a dark red cicatrice. "I was brave enough, or if you like enough of a fool, to preach the innocence of the blessed Edmund Campion. This is what they did to me. They locked the manacles on my wrists, threaded them with a chain, passed a rope through the chain and hauled me up till my feet left the ground."

"I'm guessing that didn't take long."

Owen laughed. "But I told them nothing. Now Campion's a saint in heaven. I long for nothing so much as to meet him again, when I too am called to Christ's supper. And now I must drive this face a foot deeper before morning. You clear the earth behind me with the shovel, and fill the bucket for me, William, there's a good boy. But understand and remember this: no Jesuit priest is involved in any conspiracy against the king."

"And anyway, you're just a carpenter."

"And a dwarf."

Without delay Owen set to work with his pick, attacking the clay deposits with short, concentrated blows, hacking vigorously at the wall of earth. William had swung an axe in the open air, but had never done such work in a confined space, where there is scarcely room to pull back the pick before striking with it, so all the power of the blow has to come from the workman's shoulders and hands. It is backbreaking labour. The earth crumbled and flaked off, here fragmenting into sandy powder, there coming away in thick kneaded clods.

The tiny man stood in the low tunnel, and William took the shovel and began to clear the earth behind him. Soft lamplight illuminated their labours. The poet and the priest, thought William, digging a mine. How grotesque. What are they seeking? The empty tomb? The Nibelung's gold? The lost plays of Sophocles? What lies at the end of this tunnel: bliss, treasure, glory? Or pain, disappointment, death? Is it the path to a brave new world? Or just an empty hole in the ground?

24 April 1605. Silver Street

"Master Shake-a-spear?"

The boy leaned nonchalantly against the door-post of William's room, hands in pockets, hat slouched on his head, exuding the supreme self-assurance of the London street-urchin.

"Approximately. What is it?"

"Master Percy, 'ee wants you. Dahn the 'ahse."

William's Warwickshire ear had never become attuned to the harsh carillon of Bow bells. He could just make out "Percy."

"Darn the arse?"

"'Ass right. Dahn the 'ahse."

"Oh, down the house?"

"That's what I said, innit? Speaks English, don't I? What you keep repeating me for?"

"Is that your message?"

"Nothing wrong with my words, mate. You ain't got no reason to mock my vocabulary, you toffee-nosed bastard."

"I hope you don't expect me to pay you for this."

"No need, mate. Don't need none o' your piss-poor pennies, you pen-pushing ponce. Already been paid, by a real gentleman. He give me a whole groat. See?"

"Spend it quickly," advised William. "With your capacity for insult, you can't have long to live, you abusive young villain."

The boy was already on his way down the stairs. "Yeah, lah-di-dah, use long words at me, why don't yah? I'm as good a man as you are, any day. I'm a Prentiss, mate."

"Fuck off," shouted William after him. By now Mountjoy had stuck his head out of the workshop door to see what the commotion was.

"Wat is all zis badinage? Go away, you naughty garcon, you."

"Up yours, Froggy," the youth called back over his shoulder.

"And retournez not to zis quartier. Zis is a quartier respectable. We don't want none-ayour sort 'ere, you Cockeney whoremonger."

"There'll be no glass left in your winders by next week," was the response. "I'll vouch for that."

"Oh God." William put his head in his hands. Perhaps it was time to move lodgings. In any case, by October he would either be living in a royal palace, or dangling on the end of a rope. Briefly, that is, pending total evisceration. He pulled on his boots and went down into Silver Street.

He reached the house, gave the secret knock and was admitted as before. Percy stood guard outside the chamber of the mineshaft, gloomily peeling the shell off a hard-boiled egg. Fawkes entered shortly afterwards. He had been sent for too.

"How goes it?" asked William.

"You need to see," said Percy shortly.

The three of them descended the ladder, and joined Catesby, Wright and Wintour at the end of the tunnel. They were not working, but sitting despondently side by side. Their faces, grimed and grained with dirt, showed little expression in the flickering lamplight.

"Tell them," said Percy shortly to Catesby.

"Tell us what?" asked Fawkes suspiciously.

"Look for yourself," Catesby said simply, and held the lantern towards the wall of earth at the end of the tunnel.

"What am I looking at?" asked Fawkes. Easily the tallest of the men, Fawkes had spent little time cramped in the tunnel, and was less familiar with its topography. William knew immediately what they were talking about, and cursed softly under his breath.

Where there had been a flat face of clay and earth, with the occasional extruding boulder, there was now a massive stone wall. Constructed from blocks of sandstone tightly packed, still held firmly together by mortar that must have been laid centuries before, the foundation wall of the Palace of Westminster decisively closed off their excavation. Immeasurably thick, obdurate and resistant, built to withstand all accidents of water and earth, of fire and air, it looked like a wall built by the giants who had once inhabited the earth.

"You said we would undermine the foundations," Fawkes said accusingly to Catesby. "That we would dig below them, and so reach the cellar floor."

"Yes," said Catesby angrily, spitting black dust between his feet. "But who knew how deep these walls would go? No building has ever been grounded like this. They must have raised their foundations on top of an older wall. There's no way we could have known. Anyway, there it is. If our measurements are correct, it must be all of twenty feet thick. To pierce it will be a protracted and cruel labour. And every blow we strike will echo and re-echo round the neighbourhood. We will rouse the devil himself with such a din, let alone the night watch. And then more tunnelling on the other side. It's impossible." His head dropped on his folded arms.

"We have to revert to the first plan," said Wintour. "To gain access to the cellar. Perhaps we can lease all the apartments up there, and have the whole space to ourselves."

"Not in six months, you won't," said Catesby, who had spent much time exploring that avenue. "Or even a year. They just won't sell. The sites are too valuable."

All fell silent. The earth began to close in on them. In the silence a slight dripping of water from the roof seemed to splash loudly onto the timbers. From somewhere in the soil around them came the muffled squeaking of rats.

"Right," said Fawkes, with the air of a man who is taking charge. "We will abandon this for the time. Get Owen to replace the floorboards over the shaft. Lock up the chamber. I will go abroad to fetch help. I will find men who will do anything, and say nothing."

"What men, Guido?" asked Catesby.

"Men who owe no allegiance to the king, and have no fear of death," Fawkes replied. "The rest of you, get back to your daylight duties. If any of the leases fall vacant, seize them. But we can't rely on that happening. Start to gather the powder at the house in Lambeth. Store arms, ammunition, horses. Spread the word among the Catholics we can trust that a change is coming. Don't despair, comrades. God is with us. Our time is coming: a great day in history. 3rd October 1605. The day of the Gunpowder Plot."

Help

1 August 1605. New Place, Stratford

Silent and dark was the old house. By the light of a flickering hand-held candle, William paced through its many rooms, slippered feet scuffing the cool polish of the oak floorboards. Shadows scurried before him and clotted in corners. Everyone else was in bed: Anne, Judith, Susanna, the three white-shifted women of his household. The night was his time.

He had returned home to Stratford for the summer with some reluctance, since normally there was little there to welcome him, save wifely indifference and filial importunity. On arrival, though, he found himself strangely happy in the big house, with its pleasant gardens: the flower-beds, the knot-garden, the flourishing mulberry tree.

London had become a nightmare from which he was glad to awake. He had entered the plot motivated by the same crusading zeal that moved his fellow conspirators. It was not difficult to believe, as he still believed, in the justice of the cause, since it was a conviction shared by many more than would ever dream of taking up arms in its defence. His acquaintance, however, through family and recusant connections, with the conspirators, provided the means. It had been easy to fall in willingly with men who shared his faith, and would dare anything to defend it, come rack, come rope. He himself had provided the opportunity, by applying the full power of his imagination to the practical exigencies of terror. He alone among them had the capacity to think the unthinkable, to envisage the obscene, to bring to realization strange images of death.

Had the event taken place, as planned, on 7th February, then all would have been over, the insurrection victorious or crushed, done or undone. That was how he had pictured the denouement of their hopes: a hasty preparation, a heightened readiness, a sudden blow. Victory, or death.

The protraction of the plot to the autumn changed everything for William. His motive remained unshaken, a commitment to the old religion something akin to a Roman resolution. But it was his imagination, that very power that enabled the cunning ingenuity of the plot in the first place, that began to balk at the reality of its execution.

In London the plot had crescended to an incubus that lay over him in sleep, and pressed his breath. Every moment was an expectation of discovery, a terror of arrest. As he walked the streets, he would see a strange man observing him closely, then looking away. Did he know? In the theatre, as from the green-room he peered across the flat wooden stage to survey the audience, he would catch sight of men who seemed to be looking around the theatre more than at the play, seeking someone, searching perhaps for him.

No-one was more accustomed to leading a double, or several, life, or lives, than he. As a writer, he existed in multiplicity, the continual discordant crying of many tongues, the incommensurable chattering of a thousand voices. As an actor he played many people, assuming a hundred foreign faces, donning a hundred inscrutable masks. Often he lost all sense of a personal identity, his being fluid and interpellated: losing his own voice in the hubbub of others, finding in his own face a mirror reflecting back only what others saw, the observed of all observers. Often he felt he had never really been anyone. As if he wrote about so many people, because he wanted to know what it was to be a character. Acted so many roles, because he wanted to know what it felt like to inhabit a personality. No one man was as many men as he. But he never felt there was anyone inside him. As if he were a dream someone else had failed to dream.

But once he had entered the plot, it was as if his identity had been fixed and formulated, his character defined and pinned down. He had become someone, albeit only another character he played: a Catholic, a recusant, a conspirator, a terrorist. By multiplicity of being, he had evaded capture, eschewed possession, flown by the nets of identification: none could pluck out the heart of his mystery. Now, fixed in a terrible singleness of self, he was offering his mind to be deciphered by interrogators, his body to be impounded by authorities, his heart to be plucked out by an executioner. He had been everyone, and no-one. Now he was William Shakespeare, Gunpowder Plotter. Born, Stratford-on-Avon, 1564. Died, Tower Hill, 1605.

He set the candle down on his desk, and turned back to his play, *Measure for Measure*, hoping to hide from his thoughts in someone else's dream. The Duke of Vienna, Vincentio, is commissioning Angelo to assume his authority. Angelo, to the external observer, is a man of solid character, legible identity. No-one can doubt who and what he is.

> There is a kind of character in thy life
> That to the observer doth thy history
> Fully unfold.

The Duke, on the other hand, wishes to be no-one, to disappear into obscurity, to pass beyond knowledge. He confers on Angelo not only his power, but his very being:

> In our remove be thou at full ourself …

Now more than ever, to restore that negative capability! To remove, to exit into offstage invisibility; to let some other be at full oneself. To go where no observer can my history fully unfold.

He started. What sound was that? Nothing but the chink of a bridle, the clatter of a horse's hoof in the lane outside. How every noise appals me. He listened. Silence, and the sounds of night. A fox barked clear and cold from the nearby woods. He heard the owl scream, and the crickets cry.

Then a sudden terrible hammering sounded at his front door. Whence is that knocking? His hand trembled so much he put down the pen. Who was it? He heard the old manservant, grumbling and cursing, haul himself out of bed and unchain the front door. A man's voice. Was this the moment? Could he escape? How does one prepare oneself for arrest, torture, execution? Should he wake Anne, and say good bye to her?

The old servant tramped up the stairs to William's study and tapped on the door.

"Gentleman to see thee, sir. In the kitchen."

William went downstairs, and was mightily relieved to see Jack Wright standing in his scullery, cloaked, booted and spurred for travel.

"Now then, lad," he greeted William familiarly. "A nice big house thou hast here."

"Big?" replied William scornfully. "I'm the only one of you who doesn't live in a castle."

"Maybe so," laughed Wright. "A nice little place then. We've had a letter from Guido."

"Where is he?"

"Constantinople."

"Constantinople? I thought he was going to Flanders."

"So did we all. Seems he went a bit further."

"What does he say?"

"Well as yet we've no idea. Being as how we can't read it."

"So I was right about your schooling, then?"

"Nay. We can all read English. This is written right bang through in French. Dost read French, William?"

"Why, yes. So Guido concealed his message so well that his own companions cannot decipher it."

"Ay, well. He did it for the best. At least you can be of some use now. Get me a drink, will you, and some bread and cheese. I'll rest while you read the letter. Then let me know what it contains."

William called back his manservant and gave the order. When Jack had refreshed himself, he led him upstairs and showed him a couch in the corner of the study. Then he spread the letter on the desk and began to read.

From Guido Fawkes to Robin Catesby, *et alii*
15 July 1605. Constantinople

My dear brethren in Christ -

I send this letter to give you an advance earnest of success, at least as to my part of our mission. I am on my way home, bearing with me the means of our deliverance, in the shape of a body of men we may put to work to accomplish the final stages of our sacred task. My search has entailed some labour, no little hardship, and many, many miles of travel. Even now I know not how long my journey home may take, since though my coming hither was by land, my return must needs be by sea. Why this is so requires some longer explanation, which I set out below. Let me assure you at the outset that I will soon be with you again, by the grace of God, and furnished with the wherewithal to bring our great task to a successful conclusion.

As you well know, I undertook to travel overseas in quest of men both capable of completing the labour we could not effect ourselves, and irreproachable in point of trust. This has been no easy task. There is no shortage of fellows, among the mines of northern France, skilled in such work, and poor enough to set themselves to anything. But they have not the education or understanding to be trusted with a secret mission, and would betray us by a careless word. At the same time I was able easily to find, among our co-religionists in Europe, many a man who would die for our cause; but they are like us, gentleman, scholars, priests and soldiers, unfitted to the exigencies of subterranean labour. Equally there is everywhere, in every country, a class of men desperate enough to venture anything for hire, but useless for our purpose: such reckless villains and cutthroats as would shame our cause, and ruin our reputation.

Still I persisted with my inquiries, taking advice from some of our brethren in the Spanish territories, and received from them a promising suggestion: that I should travel further eastwards, into the lands of the Turk, where slavery is universally practised. Among the Ottomans, they informed me, it is possible to find men who can be bought, body and soul, from their owner. Such men could be put to any kind of labour, at no cost to the proprietor, and would bestow in return an absolute loyalty based on fear. They are so cruelly used by the Turk, that the least act of kindness offered to them by a new owner would bind them in a passion of slavish adoration. Among these poor wretches are many, so I was told, who had been forced by the Ottomans to convert to the Mohammedan religion, and would delight in nothing so much as the restoration to them of their true and native faith.

And so I travelled through the German lands to Prague, where I rested for a few days among friends who recalled the company of the blessed martyr Edmund Campion, of sainted memory. They gave me a new idea, which was to make my way into the Christian domains over which the Sultans hold suzerainty. There, they said, I might find, among the ancient aristocracy of the old kingdoms, noblemen who hold their own subjects under an absolute feudal power, and in addition take advantage of Ottoman customs to exercise this power in a form of virtual slavery. Such landowners would be easier to treat with, they advised, than the Turk, and would be able to provide men of no less obedience and docility. And so I travelled from Prague into Hungary, making inquiries as I rode, and finding my way to the city of Buda, on the Danube, which the Turks call Budin Eyalet. There I learned of a nobleman, resident in the neighbouring country of Transylvania, who would surely be able, so my advisers assured me, to satisfy my requirements. None could recall his name, which seemed to me unusual, though they knew precisely where he was to be found, in what part of the country, and where his castle is located. Locally, they told me, he is known simply as "the Count," and letters sent to him at his ancestral seat would safely reach him.

And so from that beautiful city on the banks of the Danube, I sent letters to the Count, setting out my requirements, informing him of the recommendations I had received, naming him as a suitable supplier, and emphasising my need for both speed and confidentiality in our business transactions. I received, by return of post, a most courteous reply, inviting me to travel into Transylvania, and to the Count's castle, where he would be happy to discuss my needs, and negotiate with me a mutually acceptable price for his services.

Leaving Buda and crossing the Danube, I had the distinct sensation of quitting the West, and entering the domains of Turkish rule. The Count's castle lies in the eastern region of the country, in the midst of the Carpathian Mountains, one of the wildest and least explored regions of Europe.

The guides appointed to take me through the Borgo Pass to the Count's castle are Slovaks, men who know the mountains. The closer I came to the Count's domains, the more strangely these people behaved towards me. They would perform any service required for money, but seemed most reluctant to assist me in my journey. They dealt with this dilemma by taking my gold, but ritualising every transaction with a strange liturgy of superstitions, crossing themselves repeatedly, and holding out two fingers to ward off the evil eye. It was not me they feared, I soon came to realise, though I was to them both a stranger and a foreigner. Their terror was inspired by the place to which I was directed, and the man I was travelling to meet. Did the Count hold some kind of sway over them? I knew very little of their language, communicating with them only in German; but soon acquired definition of a few of the words that were continually in their mouths – such as *ordog, pokol, stregoica* – which seem to signify such terms as Satan, hell, witch. One word in particular they kept repeating, but always in a secretive and muttered undertone: something like *"Draco"* or *"Dracul."* Being a devoted soldier of Christ, I feared nothing of their mumbo-jumbo. But when I slept at night, I took care to keep my crucifix round my neck, as well as my sword at my side. These precautions they seemed to approve, and my caution bolstered their confidence.

Not without some difficulty, then, I finally arrived at Bistritza, from which the Borgo Pass leads to Bukovina. The Slovaks were to guide me to the castle and leave me there. The evening was closing in by the time we reached the vicinity of the castle. The closer we came to our destination, the more agitated my companions became. Notwithstanding the steep climb, and the sweat-lathered exhaustion of our horses, they rode up the pass as if the devil himself were pursing them. I gathered, from their continual glances at the sky, that they were determined to reach the castle before night fell. But the sun was dropping in the sky as fast as our horses' hooves could carry us up the pass. Soon the road we traversed, at times a mere stone ledge skirting a tremendous precipice, was wreathed in twilight, while the rays of the setting sun still flamed gold against the distant mountain peaks.

The Slovaks lashed their horses into a frenzy to cover the last few miles, and at last reined them to a halt. There was the castle, a tall and ruinous black pile, squatting on a flat platform of rock split off from the side of the mountain. On all four sides of the fortress, the sheer precipice plunging a thousand feet to the valley below. The only means of access was a natural stone bridge that spanned the gorge, and joined the castle to the cliff-ledge on which we stood.

I say we, though in truth I had found myself suddenly alone. Turning about in my saddle, I was astonished to realise that my companions had all vanished, melting into the gathering darkness even more swiftly than they had hurtled hither. What terror could induce them to prefer the hazards of the road we had traversed, and plunge themselves headlong into that dangerous darkness, rather than endure the briefest sojourn in the region of the castle?

The light was failing. Ahead of me the stark outlines of the castle showed not a chink of light from any of its windows, and its broken battlements stood black against the fading remnants of the sun. Resigned perforce to my solitary situation, I wasted no time in dismounting, and leading my horse gingerly across the stone bridge, risking a brief glance into the depths of the gorge below. I might have been overcome by the horror of such height, but I could glimpse moving shapes far below me in the undulating shadows of the valley, and hear from below the howling of wolves. The sound began to frighten my horse, so I had enough to do to soothe him, and persuade him to cross the chasm. In any case, better to brave the dangers here, whatever they may be, than perish in the jaws of such creatures as those!

I reached the front entrance of the castle, a great wooden door studded with iron nails. Still no light was visible from within. Ascending the steps, I lifted a huge iron knocker and let it fall against the scarred, ancient wood. The sound echoed through the hollow spaces of the house. Perhaps the Count was from home. Just as I was about to give up hope, and just as the very last patch of sunlight vanished from the highest of the eastern peaks, a light sprang up from within the castle, and advanced towards the door. I heard the sound of heavy chains, and the grating of an old key in a rusty lock. Creaking and groaning, the door opened.

Standing within was a very tall elderly man, with long dark hair, streaked with grey, falling over his shoulders; clean-shaven but with a heavy moustache, also grizzled; and dressed from head to toe in black, who greeted me with all courtesy. I was after all expected. Holding the lamp aloft, he bid me leave my horse by the door, and enter, freely and of my own will, his house. I did so, and followed him up a great stone staircase, into the rooms of the first floor, which were as ruinous as the outside of the castle, though richly and comfortably equipped with well-made furniture, all in an antique style, and all dusty from apparent disuse. The walls were covered with old tapestries, such as I had seen before in the homes of our nobility: faded with antiquity, but still of immense value. He led me through into a dining room which was illuminated by a log fire burning in the hearth. The table was set with food and drink, a welcome sight to a weary traveller. The Count encouraged me to sit and refresh myself, excusing himself from joining me, since he had already dined. I fell to, and within a few minutes found myself sufficiently refreshed to take some measure of my host and my surroundings.

For all his strange reputation, and the fear he evidently inspired among the Slovaks, the Count seemed to me a typical nobleman of these parts, elderly and cultivated, well-mannered and courteous. He reminded me, in his reclusiveness and antique ways, of some elderly Catholic lord from our own Midlands counties. I learned immediately that his name was Dracula, and that he was descended of that ancient and heroic lineage, the Szekelys, traceable back to Attila. So that word the Slovaks had repeated, in such an undertone of fear, was nothing more than the Count's family name! He was certainly odd-looking, but in ways that agreed with his status as *boyar*, a title similar to our *baron*. His features were aquiline, with a long straight nose, a strong chin and large eyes that varied between a luminous brown and an opaque black. His hair, as I already described it, fell in waves around his shoulders, a fashion one would expect to see in a much younger man. The large dark moustache was grown horizontally across the face. His skin was extraordinarily pale, as if he shunned the sunlight. I chanced, as hospitably he poured into my glass some excellent Tokay, to touch one of his hands, and found it to be icy cold, more like the touch of the dead than the living. The heavy moustache partly concealed his mouth, but beneath it one could see very bright red lips, and when he smiled, a pair of large protruding canine teeth.

He welcomed me to his country, and assured me that in principle he would be able to meet my needs, if his services were found suitable, and at an agreeable price. I explained my requirements in detail, of course veiling the true nature of the project. I needed a body of men I could take back to London, men capable of excavating a tunnel, work which involved breaking through an enormously thick wall. With a mixture of courtesy and business acumen the Count carefully avoided prying in to the details of my project, while showing an extensive and practical knowledge of underground exploration. How many men would I wish to obtain? he asked. I said about twenty, or twenty-five. Such a number would be easily supplied, he said, of men who would astonish me with the strength of their arms, and their ability to stick to a task. They would readily hack their way through my wall, or with astonishing speed tunnel round it, whichever was my preference.

There was just one caveat he insisted on placing on our negotiations, for avoidance of any doubt: and that was that his men could only work at night. Why, I replied, that is exactly what I need, since this work can only be carried on under cover of darkness. Nothing could be more suitable to my needs. And what will your men do during the day, I asked, wondering how we would be able to accommodate them within the confines of our little house. Why, they will sleep, he said. They work, and they sleep. Nothing else. But again, he said, I must explain all peculiarities of this transaction, since I would not have you in any way disappointed in what I provide. My country has some unusual customs that will seem strange in another place. Your ways are not our ways; Transylvania is not England. Not only do these men sleep during the day. They can sleep in only one place.

And where is that? I asked. In their coffins, he replied. Resting on a bed of earth from the soil of their homeland. Now in truth this struck me as very peculiar indeed, though it could hardly be more convenient for our purposes; yet I had heard of such a practice among certain monks of an extreme devotedness, who would sleep in their coffins to keep a perpetual remembrance of their end, and to be ready at their Saviour's summons to return whence they came. Are your men then very religious? I asked. Why yes, he replied, they are. Their existence is a continual devotion. Their very life is a prayer. He seemed to like this last phrase, since he delivered it with a kind of inscrutable smile that might have been mistaken for irony.

You have said, I put to him, that these men will not require any form of payment. That is the case, he replied. They are bound in a very ancient order of servitude, and would not dream of taking wages for their work. Then they are paid only in kind, I suggested, working in exchange for their food and lodging? No, he said, there is no need to feed them. They will find their own sustenance, in their own way. He did not seem willing to expatiate further on the topic of food and drink. This I could not understand, and I found it necessary to press the matter, to a point which seemed to provoke the Count to a certain well-concealed but deep-rooted anger. Do you mean they will rove forth and steal food from the neighbourhood, as do the gypsies? My work is of a very confidential nature, and I cannot afford to attract attention by having my men creating a public nuisance. Master Fawkes, said Count Dracula, in a voice of some subdued annoyance. Let me explain something to you. My family is of a very ancient lineage, and my name in these parts both respected and feared. We Draculs have a right to be proud: the blood of Attila flows in these veins. Now I would not have you suspect me of any underhandedness in this business. I have been open and honest in telling you of the strangeness and oddity you will find in the men I can supply you with. To me it would be a matter of personal dishonour to hold anything back, or to mislead you in any way. I can furnish you with the men you need. But I would not do anything so shameful as to sell you a bunch of thieves.

I was ashamed to have nettled the Count's pride by my careless question. I am deeply sorry, I said, to have offended you. My ignorance, not my malice, is the cause. You have said yourself that your ways are strange, and in this case I do not understand them. If I do not feed these men, how will they provide for themselves when they venture abroad in the daylight? At this point Dracula's face could not conceal an expression of dark amusement. Why, he replied smoothly, who said anything about them venturing abroad? They will live where they work, and under no circumstances would any one of them seek to go abroad in the daylight. They have lived underground all their lives, and have become resourceful in finding the means of existence in that subterranean gloom. I do not seek to know what creatures of the darkness they catch and eat – the bat, the mole, the rat, the mouse? Who cares? They fend for themselves. Believe me, Master Fawkes, you too should not be troubled by any such concerns.

I had to be satisfied by this explanation, though in truth I was still mystified at the strangeness of it all. What kind of men work all night, sleep all day in their coffins, and feed on the creatures of darkness, never seeing the light of day? What of discipline, I asked, among the men? How should I keep them at their work? That is simple, Dracula replied. As you have yourself indicated, these men are very religious. They have a great fear of – God (he seemed to hesitate over the word, as if inhibited by some devotional piety), and that fear is transmitted to those they believe to be God's representative. Such am I to them, their *boyar*, their Master, their Lord. And such you too, Master Fawkes, will become. I observe that you wear the insignia of your faith proudly on your breast. Keep that sign about you at all times. Ensure that anyone else you depute to supervise these men is similarly equipped. They fear nothing so much as the images of your religion, especially the cross. They fear also the bread and wine and oil of your sacraments. Occasionally you may see one of them become restless at his work of the night, prowling around as if seeking escape. He may even snarl or growl at you, baring his teeth like a wild beast. Confronted by such disobedience, you must simply show the man the cross, or a piece of your sacred wafer, or a drop of your Holy Water that has been blessed by a priest. He will be dominated by the power of these images. He will shrink from you, and return obediently to his work.

And what if one of these men should commit a crime, I asked, and be condemned by lawful process to the ultimate punishment? What kind of justice should I impose? What kind of justice? Dracula repeated. In one word: summary. Cut off his head, pierce him through the heart, and bury him in his own coffin. Neither he nor his companions would expect anything less. But how gloomy our conversation has become, here in this old house! You must be exhausted from your journey. Let me retire and leave you to your bed, which you will find made up and ready in the adjoining room. Tomorrow I have business to transact, and must leave you alone. It will be best if you remain in your rooms, and do not wander in the castle. It is old, and has many sad memories. I should be back by nightfall, and we will meet again for supper. I will show you the men you require, who will be ready for your inspection. And then we may conclude our business. And Dracula left me, vanishing as swiftly as the Slovaks had disappeared. I glanced up to the great mirror above the fireplace to watch him depart, but he had already gone.

My conversation with the Count having taken up much of the night, I slept late, and woke to find a cold repast set out on the dining-room table. Dracula was nowhere to be seen. As I breakfasted I began to muse on the strangeness of this house, and its even stranger master. Where were his servants? Everywhere I could see the evidence of great wealth, from the finely-wrought gold of the table service to the luxurious appointments of the furniture. Yet the Count appeared to inhabit this vast place in solitude. He must be a kind of recluse, I reflected, who has withdrawn from the world for some reason of his own: some disappointment, perhaps, in politics, or in love. He reminded me of some of our own Catholic nobility, men who prefer to sit at home, nursing their grievances, to enduring the continual shame of public life in a Protestant tyranny.

My hunger satisfied, I had nothing to do but while away the few hours until the Count's return. Though he had instructed me to stay in my chambers, I thought there could be no harm in a little exploration. So I passed the time by wandering around from chamber to chamber of the castle, finding everywhere the same evidence of faded grandeur, neglected splendour, wealth and status fallen into desuetude, brightness decayed into rust. As I explained above, the castle is set on a tall cube of rock, a thousand feet high, orphaned from the surrounding cliffs by some geological cataclysm of the distant past, and linked to the mountain-side only by that narrow stone bridge. What a fortress to resist a siege or assault, I thought! But a place better suited to the warlike days of the past than the conveniences of modern living.

Not that traces of a more sophisticated existence were entirely lacking. I lingered for a while in the chambers on the south side of the castle, a suite of rooms which had once perhaps, long before Dracula's time, accommodated the lady of the house, for here there was evidence of finer luxury, rich hangings, uphol-stered chairs, and a little writing-desk. In one sitting-room, over the mantelpiece, I found hanging a group of portraits, a type of adornment entirely missing from the Count's own rooms. One was of a man in the prime of life, and in the costume of an earlier age, perhaps two hundred years ago. Had it not been for those distinguishing features, I would have sworn it was a picture of the Count himself, so exact was the resemblance. The same aquiline face, the same thrusting chin, the same commanding eyes, even the same flowing waves of hair, a deep black in the portrait, and the strange bushy horizontal moustache. He wore the rich uniform of a *boyar,* red and black, with large gold buttons; on his head a red velvet hat, with a brim all of pearls, and above his brows a massive badge or royal insignia, set with a huge amethyst, and three very large sea-pearls. Beside the picture of this man, who clearly must be an ancestor of the Count, was a portrait, of the same age and fashion, of an extraordinarily beautiful woman. Her hair and skin were unusually dark, as if she had perhaps some gipsy blood. The features were small and delicate, but the eyes huge and luminous, like great black stars. Her full red lips were slightly parted, open in what might be understood as some kind of invitation. Beneath these pictures were two smaller portraits, both of women: one fair, blue-eyed and blonde; the other freckled, brown and with red hair. Two daughters, perhaps? There was no family resemblance. The dark lady, I assumed from the contiguity of the portraits, must have been the wife of this old *boyar,* and the lady of the castle. I wondered about their history, and what it must have been like to be spouse to the man in the portrait. Was she happy? I mused. The eyes betokened a kind of sadness, and the pouting lips some reservoir of unfulfilled desire.

I turned from the portrait, uneasy at the strange feelings it provoked in me. But try as I might, and despite the universal pall of dust that covered everything, I could not avoid sensing, in the very air of those chambers, some female presence from the past. My imagination was being led, against my will, to places I had no wish to enter. Was it here she sat, I wondered, while her lord was away at the wars, to gaze out of these windows, at the varied colours of those high mountain slopes, the dark greens and browns of the forests? Was it here at this writing-desk that she wrote letters to her husband, or even perhaps, if disappointed in love, to another knight who may have been her lover?

The sun was setting among purple clouds, and touching the distant mountain-tops with orange and gold. I sat for a moment in a dusty armchair, and admired the view. The sun declined. For a moment, by some trick of the light as the shadows lengthened, I thought I saw a glimpse of that beautiful young woman, with her dark hair and skin, and her unfathomable dark eyes, dressed in the alluring immodesty of the middle ages, beckoning me into a painted bedchamber. I felt irresistibly impelled to follow her, though my vows of chastity in the service of Christ held me back. My ears hummed with a strange sound, of an intolerable and intoxicating sweetness, like the sound of a finger-tip running around the rim of a wine-glass. I looked for her reflection in a large gilt-framed mirror on the wall, but there was nothing there. In spite of myself, I half rose to go to her, but at the same time grasped for aid at the crucifix on my breast. Straightaway, like a phantom, the shape seemed to disintegrate into motes of dust, leaving nothing but a wide smile of bright red lips, and sharp white teeth, hovering maddeningly in the empty air. Was it my imagination, or was the place haunted by the shade of its mistress? Did her spirit wander these rooms, waiting to trap an unwary pilgrim in the sweet snares of her sinful embrace? I heard faint sounds like words, drifting on the lightest breeze. *Ajuta ma! Salva ma!* If words they were, I understood them not, except as cries for help, for salvation. But their sounds penetrated through me like fear, or lust.

Intrigued and apprehensive in equal measure, I thought I would sit for a little while longer in this more comfortable and congenial spot. I came however to regret my inclination, since shortly thereafter I must have fallen asleep, and my slumber was haunted by terrible dreams. I thought I awoke, still seated in the same dusty armchair, to find the chamber in darkness, with only the light of the moon, flitting through scudding clouds, penetrating into its shadowy interior. Before me stood the figure of a woman, not the dark-haired beauty, but one younger, fairer, with a mass of blonde hair. Behind her stood another, even younger, pretty rather than beautiful, but this one had long hair of a reddish brown. In the dream they seemed strangely familiar to me, since I did not at the time recall their faces from the portraits on the wall. Both had bright red lips, and the prominent canine teeth I had noted in Dracula himself, and glimpsed for a moment in that vision of the dark-haired lady, as she vanished from my sight. Who were these three women? Their voices were low and metallic, as they spoke softly to one another in their unfamiliar tongue. *Tu du-te în primul rând,* said the redhead, as if to say to the blonde one, you are first. *Există suficient pentru doi,* replied the blonde. Did she mean there would be enough for all? Enough of what?

They laughed together, laughter like sweet bells jangled out of tune. As the fair one spoke, I saw her, through the fringes of my eyelashes, kneel down before me, and bring her face close to mine. I could neither move nor speak, chained down by some dreamlike spell. I smelt her breath, sweet as flowers, but underneath a scent of something bitter, like the taste of iron in blood. She licked her lips with a bright red tongue, leaving upon them a thin filmy gloss. Her face bent lower. Her lips approached my throat. In my dream I was paralysed, quite incapable of movement or resistance. Supposing, that is, I had wanted to resist, for I confess my feelings were more of desire than of fear. I longed to feel the touch of those red lips. The skin of my neck tingled as that voluptuous mouth drew near.

Suddenly I was aware of another presence in the room, and the girl who knelt at my feet was thrust aside by an arm of extraordinary power. There, between the two girls, was the dark-haired lady of the portrait, her face white with anger, her eyes flashing red with a demoniacal rage. *Lasă-l în pace!* she cried in a reverberating, sibilant whisper. *El nu este pentru tine!* Somehow I knew that she meant leave him alone, he is not for you. The other two hissed at her, but crouched away in a kind of petulant resistance. *Il vrei pentru tine*, said the redhead accusingly, as if to say, you want him for yourself. *Nu!* said the dark lady. *Aparține comandantului*. He belongs to the master! At this the other two shrank and cringed backwards, as if in fear. *Nimic pentru noi?* asked the blonde, with a plaintive, discontented whine in her voice. Are we to have nothing? As if in answer, the dark lady pointed to a bundle, lying hitherto unnoticed in the corner. Something lay under a kind of rough blanket, something that moved. At once the redhead swooped upon it, and held it tight to her breast. A thin wail came from the bundle. It was a child. She held it to her breast with a kind of maternal delight. She has given suck, I thought, and knows how tender 'tis to love the babe that milks her! Perhaps she has lost her own child, and will take this one in its place?

No such matter. For to my astonishment, the woman plucked the baby from her breast, and held it aloft, with a dreadful look of triumph on her face. The baby cried loudly, clenching its little fists, showing its boneless gums. Then to my horror, she sunk her sharp teeth into the dimpled flesh of the baby's neck, and began, with an awful greediness, to lap the infant's blood. The child gave a strangled shriek, and was silent. The blonde also fell upon the tiny form, snatched with her teeth at its flesh, and drank its blood. Still unable to move, caught fast in the web of my nightmare, I had no choice but to lie back and watch the carnage being enacted in this chamber of horrors.

And then, thank God, I awoke, to find myself back in my own bedchamber, with the morning light streaming through the dusty window-panes. How I came there, I had no idea. My breakfast was set out on the table by the fire, exactly as it had been yesterday. Again there was no sign of my host. I rose and dressed, eager to shake off the spell of that terrible dream. Cured of all curiosity and inclination to explore, I resolved to spend the whole of that day in my own room. I prayed, wrote up this letter, and then read the *Little Office of the Blessed Virgin* until, a few minutes after sunset, I heard the steps of my host returning.

Dracula again excused himself from eating or drinking, since he had been obliged, he said, to take refreshment on the road. I had been there two days, and had not yet seen him take a bite of food, or a drop of liquor. He was however his usual courteous self, and prepared, he said, to introduce me to the men who would be entering my service. Taking up a lantern, he led me from the room, back down the great stone staircase I had ascended two days before, and along a flagged passage that led towards the back of the house. We reached a small door set under an archway, which Dracula opened to reveal a flight of stairs leading downwards into darkness. He led the way, his lamp casting fantastic shadows, down and down to an enormous depth. At the foot of the stairs a low passage-way sloped steeply downwards. As far as I could tell, we had descended deeper than any cellar, and must have penetrated right into the heart of the great rock on which the castle stands.

The end of the passage-way opened out into an area that was clearly an excavation, even perhaps a mine. The space was brightly lit by a number of lamps, held in brackets around the walls. Their combined light was focused on a high wall of rock, composed of the most obdurate granite, whose opaque surface was flecked with iridescent specks of brightness that sparkled and twinkled in the light. And there, in that vast subterranean cavern, quietly working at the face of the rock, was the strangest company of men I had ever seen.

There were twenty of them, all dressed in rough smock and trousers such as our own miners wear. They were clearly strong and active men, taking turns to strike resolutely at the rock-face with small picks and hammers. Some chipped away, while others knelt and shovelled aside the fragments of stone. But their faces! I had never in my life seen men who, though clearly alive, looked as dead as any corpse. Their skin was as pallid as the Count's, but not like his, smooth and barbered, but creased and crusted with a semblance of decay. The skin of their arms and legs hung loose on their limbs, like the dead skin that sloughs away from an ulcerated wound. Their lips were ragged and frayed as worn sacking around their protuberant canine teeth. Their eyes were fixed and expressionless, discs of deadness like the eyes of a shark. A faint odour stirred from their bodies as they worked, less like the smell of human sweat, than the smell of a gangrenous abrasion, or the rank odour of decaying teeth.

As we entered, the men glanced back at us, but exhibited no reaction, staring fixedly ahead with those eyes that seemed dead in the midst of a blank, decomposing face. So these were the men I was to transport with me back to England! Thank God they would be content, if the Count was to be believed, to exist in the confines of an underground prison-house! For never had such beings walked the earth, unless they had been demons released from Hell.

Some of them began to show interest in the stranger amongst them, and to steal covert glances in my direction. Most of them continued to focus on their work, but one creature began to utter a strange mewing sound, and rock to and fro on his knees. Then he stood up, and began to sidle towards me, without looking, with a peculiar rat-like motion of indirection. Within two yards of me he hesitated, and snuffed the air around me like a hunting dog. His face contorted in a kind of spasm, and his ragged lips began to champ around his jutting teeth. For the first time he looked at me, and stopped in his tracks, evidently struck with fear at some aspect of my person. It occurred to me, remembering the Count's words, that the object of his fear might be the crucifix I wore round my neck. So I disentangled the chain from the folds of my shirt, and held it out towards him. The effect on him was astonishing. He was literally forced back, like a man trying to stand in a strong wind, as if impeded and baffled by the power of the cross.

Dracula, who had been watching this pantomime, suddenly

uttered a strange sound, somewhere between the snarl of a wild-cat and the bark of a dog. *Cobori!* he snarled, his dark eyes flashing red with a terrible anger. *Caine! Sporcaciune! Dute la munca!* I needed no translation to know that he was calling the man a dog, or worse, and ordering him to work. Evidently terrified, the man slunk back towards the rock face, and hid himself behind some of his companions. Presently all were back at their work, as if nothing had happened. I was left wondering which had had a more potent effect on the man, the charisma of my holy *signum*, or the hellish rage of his *boyar*.

I had seen enough. The Count could see that I was shocked by the appearance of the men, and sought in his urbane way to reassure me. They are not a pretty sight, he admitted, but what does that matter, since there is no-one to see them? They exist in darkness, they work in the bowels of the earth, they feed on rats and mice, they sleep on the sour and stagnant earth of their homeland. What do you expect them to look like? If they resemble the fiends of Hell, their appearance conforms to their nature, which is to dwell eternally in the nethermost pit. But their ugliness in no way diminishes their usefulness. The labourer is still worthy of his hire.

We retraced our steps back to the upper levels of the castle, and over a bottle of wine, from which the Count poured two glasses, though he never once raised his glass to his lips, we sealed our bargain. I handed over to him the agreed sum of gold. He could not conceal the pleasure he gained from this acqui-sition. Unable to resist the promptings of my curiosity, I asked him what kind of work these men were doing for him. I will tell you, he replied, though I have asked nothing of you about the work you intend for them. This castle is built on a rock that was carefully chosen by my ancestors for its rich mineral deposits. Everywhere within its folds and fissures lie precious stones. These men, and the men I will bring in to replace them, work at those deposits, and extract the gems. Forgive my curiosity, I said, but you seem, if I may judge from so brief an acquaintance, to have very little use for wealth? His eyes took on a cunning expression, and his mouth displayed his teeth in a wolfish grin. I have on foot a venture, which as it happens, involves a major investment in your own country, England. The project will entail the conveyance of property, the purchase of land, the buying of services, and many other legal and administrative arrangements. All these measures will require, to capitalise them, a huge fortune. I estimate, on current projections, that sufficient wealth will have been amassed within – roughly you understand – about three hundred years. I gasped in astonishment. Three hundred years? How is it possible to plan so far ahead? Oh, Master Fawkes, he said, we Draculs measure time not in years, or lifetimes, even generations, but in centuries and millennia. My family has been engaged for many years in building towards this great work, a work that will not be accomplished in my lifetime, or even that of my successors. (Did the Count have children, I wondered? If so, where are they, and why has he never mentioned them? Who does he mean by "we"?) It is possible, he continued, that in a small way you, Master Fawkes, will make a contribution to this master plan. Though neither of us will live, of course, to see its fruition – since, as your scripture observes, man that is born of woman hath but a short time to live – we may take satisfaction from knowing that we have played our part.

Now, he said briskly, let us discuss practicalities. You have bought your men, and must now transport them safely to the crowded streets of your mighty London. For your assistance I will provide you with a company of Szganys. These men are the gipsies of these parts, sometimes known as Roma. By an ancient bond of servitude they belong to me, and claim my name as theirs. The Szgany affirm that their ancestors came here from India, and they are certainly very dark of complexion. (I thought of the dark lady in the portrait, wondering if she too came of a similar exotic race; but was sensible enough not to mention this to the Count, who I felt would disapprove of my unlicensed roving through the rooms of his ancestral home). You will need a wagon capable of holding twenty coffins, and enough Szganys to handle them. You could return by land, the way you came. But the road is perilous, and over such a long journey the men might become restless by night. A wagon wheel jolts on a stone, the lid of a box shifts a little, and your man has slipped off into the darkness, where you will see him no more. You have lost your investment.

Now there is one other peculiarity of these men about which I have yet to inform you. And that is that they cannot bear water. They cannot cross a river, they cannot venture into the sea. Confine them to a boat, and you have them pinned down body and soul, with no possibility of escape. My advice to you, my young friend, is to take your cargo back by sea. I have included in the price the hire of a vessel from Muscovy that will carry you to England. The Szganys will transport you to the port of Varna on the Black Sea coast, where your ship and crew will be waiting. These Russians have a longstanding debt to me, and will obey you in every particular. Your boxes will be loaded and stored below, and you will set sail for your homeland. The Muscovites will steer you safely into the Bosphorus, and through the Dardanelles. You will need plenty of what the Turks call *baksheesh* (and he clinked some of my gold coins in his palm, to signify what he meant). I predict that you will enjoy fair winds and convenient tides, at least until you reach the Aegean, where my influence does not reach. (Did he think he could control the winds and waves, I wondered?) Through the *Mare Nostrum*, round the coast of Spain, into your English Channel. Round the coast of Kent, into the estuary of the Thames, and safely disembarked at Tilbury, whence you may make your own arrangements.

I complimented the Count on his knowledge of English geography. Oh, he said, one never knows when such knowledge may become useful. Will the men be able to breathe in these boxes, I asked? Oh, yes, he replied disarmingly, everything is properly ventilated. And how will they be fed, how will they drink? They will sleep through the entire voyage, and need no sustenance of any kind, until you have them safely ashore, and in your mine. Then you may let them out, and they will be ready to do your command.

And one last thing, said Dracula. I have taken an additional precaution, hardy necessary, but enough to make all safe and secure. I have commanded the Szganys to nail, into the lid of each coffin, a small silver cross. This device will, without fail, keep your labourers safe for the duration of your voyage. And at no extra cost! I will bear the expense myself. All will be ready for you in the morning. I will not see you, as I have business elsewhere. I take my leave of you, Master Fawkes, and I wish you every good fortune in your expedition. I hope to hear great things of you in the future. And again the Count vanished, as suddenly and invisibly as he had come, leaving me wondering how much he could know, or guess, of the work we have in hand; and what long-term plans he might have for his dynasty's investment in my country.

He was as good as his word. Early in the morning a team of Szganys was waiting for me, with my twenty boxes already loaded onto one of their long leiter-wagons. The load of black boxes was neatly stacked and secured, and the little silver crosses nailed into their lids glinted brightly in the morning sun. Then we were away. As my driver expertly inched his horses slowly over that perilous crossing, I took my last glance of Castle Dracula, which looked as desolate and forlorn in the rays of the rising sun, as it had appeared the night before by sunset, during my strange twilight sojourn. I could not help thinking about the strange dark lady I thought I had seen in the southern wing of the castle. Surely she had been a ghost, or some fantasy of my fevered imagination. Yet her presence had seemed substantial.

Could she have been a real woman, perhaps some neglected mistress of the Count's? I looked closely to see if any of the vacant windows framed a lovely dark face, that might perhaps be watching, with a pang of regret, my departure. But they stared blankly back at me, reflecting nothing but their own vacancy.

And so we reached the port of Varna, where my Muscovites were awaiting me with their ship. She is a beautiful vessel, built in Sweden, and named the Vassa. Swiftly my boxes were embarked and stored below, the crew cast off, the sails were set, and out we sailed onto the Black Sea, borne on a freshening northerly breeze. It is some five hundred miles to Constantinople, so in the course of the voyage I have taken the opportunity of compiling this report for your information, and perhaps education. Certainly many strange things have happened to me since my leaving England.

Indeed the voyage becomes stranger with every day that passes. It was abundantly clear to me, from the moment of departure, that there was something about the ship, or its cargo, the crew did not like, though I could not fathom what it was. They seem afraid of something, and are often to be found whispering together between decks. They are reluctant to go below, even when ordered, as if unwilling to be anywhere near my cargo of coffins. The captain, who speaks only Russian, keeps them to their work with strict discipline, and has more than once shown them the whip as an earnest of the proper punishment for disobedience. The weather is fine, the winds fair, and the boat sails smoothly through tranquil waters. Yet still I am surrounded by disquiet, by anxiety, by fear …

This morning, as we are sailing past the city of Burgas, or Pirgas, something of this covert trouble has at last broken out into the open. There has been a theft. One of the officers, chancing to go below deck, noticed that a silver cross was missing from the lid of the nearest coffin. The captain was clearly enraged, and determined to make an example of the thief by hunting him down, and exacting a cruel penalty. I learned this from a midshipman who speaks some German, and asked him to urge the captain to let the matter lie, lest it delay our progress. But my remonstrance prevailed nothing. A thorough search was conducted of the whole ship by his officers, who eventually found the cross hidden beneath the mattress of a seaman's bunk. The poor wretch was dragged out onto the deck, and pinioned for the captain's inspection. I feared that the most extreme punishment – flogging, or keel-hauling – would be visited on this fellow for a petty theft that had injured no-one. In the event, however, as far as I could understand the proceedings, the only penalty to be exacted was to have the man tied to the main-mast, and exposed to the elements through the course of the night. This seemed to me the gentlest of punishments, and my mind was set at rest. I asked if the silver cross could be replaced on the lid of the coffin, but was assured, perhaps a little evasively, that it would be done first thing in the morning. The man was lashed to the mast and left there, while the remainder of the crew retired to rest. No watch was set on the upper deck, which seemed unusual to me. The wretched thief cringed and whimpered in fear as though some unseen terror lay in wait for him, but I could not imagine any great harm would come to. Reassured by this thought, I managed to shut out the man's terrified moans, and get to sleep.

Whether it was the anxiety of this shipboard crisis, or the unease I had felt while roaming around Dracula's castle, I know not, but my sleep was haunted by vivid and disturbing dreams. I seemed to sense again that presence I had felt in the southern wing of the castle, and to feel again the stirring of those unwanted and impure thoughts. There were no images in my dream, no vision, only an utter and absolute darkness, and a heightened and intensified realm of sensation. I dreamed that I heard, rather than saw, someone enter my cabin: the motion of a sinuous body, a rustling of silk, the sound of light breathing. There was that strange odour, intoxicatingly sweet, yet somehow suggestive of badness, like rotten fruit, or a decayed perfume. I felt a cold hand touch my head, and gently caress my cheek, and the tips of cold fingers begin to explore my lips. Then all in a moment the phantom withdrew, the dream was gone, and I was startled awake by a horrible screaming from the thief on the deck. As I struggled to rise, strangely paralysed by the effects of my dream, I heard the scream strangled into a choking sob, and a loud splash like a body fallen into the sea. I rushed out onto the deck, and the man was gone. Nowhere to be seen. As the sun rose brightly over the soft waves of the Black Sea, I could hear a hammering from the hold, that I guessed to be the cross being nailed back onto the lid of the coffin. The crew were once again going about their everyday business. The incident of the night was not even mentioned. I could only assume that the poor wretch, driven to distraction by the thought of his crime and the shame of his penance, broke free from his bonds and leapt overboard.

And so I have reached Constantinople, the holy city of Byzantium, where the starlit dome of Hagia Sophia, now a Mohammedan mosque, stands as mute testimony to the lamentable fall of Christendom in these eastern lands. And here I must break off this narrative, and consign it to a courier, who will speed on swift horses across Hungary and Germany to bring it before your eyes. By the time you read it, I will by the grace of God, be so much nearer to home.

Your beloved brother in Christ,
Guido Fawkes

2 August 1605. New Place, Stratford

What a bizarre tale! thought William, as he put down the letter.

And where was Fawkes now? A journey through the Mediterranean should take a few weeks, barring accidents of flood and fortune. Something must have delayed him.

Jack was fast asleep on the couch. William envied him his slumber of exhaustion, so unlike his own perturbed unrest. Let him stay awhile. The best of rest is sleep. Then why fear death, which is no more? The letter from Fawkes required no answer, no action. Between the acting of a dreadful thing, and the first motion, all the interim is like a phantasma or a hideous dream. He had put that into the mouth of his Brutus, as he endured the long anticipation of tyrannicide. Once the secret anguish of a tormented republican, it had now become his own state of mind. The night was bitter cold.

Back to the play. A few more lines of *Measure*. The young man is condemned to death, for fornication. The disguised Duke seeks to persuade him life is not worth living.

Thou hast nor youth nor age
But as it were an after-dinner sleep, dreaming on both.

His own youth was now little more than a memory, a dream of ardour and passion and burning zeal. The prospect of old age was equally fantastic, a condition impossible to realise, something he might never attain. Between them was this unbearable interim, this hideous dream. Soon the day would dawn, the shadows of night recede for a time. The day was for business; the night for fear. History was a nightmare, from which he was trying to awake.

15 August 1605. New Place, Stratford

Wright had gone back to London, advised of the content of Fawkes's letter by a brief précis from William. Wright had asked him to keep the letter, to hide it among his papers. There was nothing to be done. Fawkes had not been heard from again. William understood from Wright that everything else was in place for the Plot, the powder and armaments gathered and stored at the house in Lambeth, the details of the execution worked out and rehearsed. No progress had been made on obtaining premises beneath the Palace: nothing was available. Everything depended on the tunnel. And so the great Cause hung in the balance, while the Plotters awaited the return of Fawkes and his miners.

William had remained in Stratford, while London blistered in the August heat, getting on with *Measure for Measure*. He began to feel an acute nostalgia, as he prepared to take leave of the old town, perhaps for the last time. As he walked the streets, he was continually haunted by the spectres of his old life, people and places, neighbourhood and community; a recusant world of Roman Catholics co-existing uneasily with Elizabeth's Protestant regime. Most of the common people were still papist at heart. Their faith lay hidden from the searching light of day, sleeping through the Protestant centuries in a mediaeval sarcophagus, of antique design, that housed the relics of buried Catholic piety.

He walked past the old grammar school in Chapel Street, and saw himself once again a child, at his desk, poring over a Latin text. He recalled his teachers, many of them Catholics. One was a Jesuit in the making, who ended up at Douai. Another, John Cottam, an executed Jesuit's brother. Over there was the house of Hamnet and Judith Sadler, godparents to his twins, obdurate recusants. His own children bore Catholic names.

He walked through Eley gardens, round by Meer Street into Henley Street, to pause and stand in front of his childhood home, where his mother still outlived her husband. His parents had been born into the aftershocks of Henry VIII's Reformation. His father had lived through the brief and zealous reign of Protestant Edward, and the even briefer regime of Catholic Mary Tudor, a dawn of hope aborted like a still-born child. By the time William was born, Elizabeth had restored the Protestant faith to the Church of England. Attendance at Protestant services was obligatory, and absence punishable by fine. His father, a holder of civic office, had to swear an oath of allegiance to the queen as supreme head of the church, though it wounded his very soul to do so.

In 1592 his father was identified in a government report as a recusant, a Catholic who refused to attend the services of the Church of England. He pleaded that his absences were to avoid being arrested for debt. William smiled to himself. His father was always in debt, but never arrested. The defence was a transparent excuse.

He thought of his mother Mary, proud to be an Arden. The Ardens were prominent among the old Catholic families who kept the faith alive in the West Midlands: the Treshams, the Wintours, the Catesbys. The names were a roll-call of dissidents: they were the names of his comrades in the Plot. His mother's kinsman, Edward Arden, had been executed by hanging, drawing and quartering, for plotting against the queen. His severed head was impaled and displayed, a grisly trophy, on London Bridge.

Something drew him back along the High Street, past his own house, and down to the churchyard of Holy Trinity. Reluctantly he paced the path around the church to where his only son occupied his tiny resting-place. A little, little grave. Poor Hamnet.

* * *

He was back in September 1601. He shuddered as he stood by the insignificant plot. The small pile of earth, thick black loam and yellow clods of clay overturned to the air, seemed obscene, as if the exhumation were exposing the flesh under the earth's skin. He shivered, not from cold, though there was a small chill in the autumn evening, but to imagine those frail bones, respectfully composed now and tightly sheathed in their winding sheet, but so soon to disunite, as the fragile flesh corrupted and dissolved. My son.

He had not been there to nurse the boy in his illness; had not laid a cool hand of ineffectual blessing on the febrile forehead; had not seen the little limbs folded together, or paced behind the bier as it was borne to the churchyard. He had taken for granted Hamnet Shakespeare as his son and heir; but he had scarcely been any kind of father to the boy.

He asked himself what was he doing there now, paying unnecessary respects, enduring his wife's bitter and majestic silence, condemned by the reproachful incomprehension on the faces of the little girls, as they stared at him with their mother's eyes. Looking down he saw that mud was caked onto his patent leather pumps, and he fastidiously stepped back from the grave. Many miles from there, he wrote and acted death every day. But nothing had prepared him for the climbing sorrow induced by this modest little exit from the world's great stage.

Beside him stood his father, whose copious tears shamed the flinty self-command of his dry-eyed son. John had been the first to rush out when Will stumbled wearily from his horse outside the house in Henley Street. The old man was crying when he flung his arms around his son's neck, and clung to him in a passion of grief, and a smell of stale beer and old age. He was crying as they walked through the High Street, accepting commiserations from friends and neighbours. He was crying as they stood by the grave, tears running down the white stubble of his face. Inconsolably he wept for his little grandson, gone inexplicably before him into that great void dark.

And all the while, Will knew, there was something the old man wanted to say, something that must out and be spoken, though the father was as unwilling to utter it as the son reluctant to hear. Gently he took his father's arm, and turned him from the grave, an open wound in the torn earth, and towards the church.

"What was it like? The funeral?"

"Oh beautiful, beautiful," said the old man, his sobs subsiding. "He looked so peaceful you know, all his pain washed away. Poor little lad. 'For He shall wipe away every tear from their eyes.' He said that, the Vicar. Beautiful it was. Beautiful service. But Will ...."

"Go on."

John Shakespeare glanced behind him and came close, confiding, pleading, hanging on William's arm.

"*What ceremony else*, Will? Is that all, for your only son? A few words from Cranmer's prayer book; a handful of dust scattered over his little face?"

Will tried to draw his arm away. "What could I do? You ask too much."

"You could pray for him, Will, as our Saviour taught us. You could find a priest to say Mass for his little soul. You could cheer him on his way with bell, book and candle. You could give him the words of intercession. He's out there now, lost in some great grey limbo, alone and crying for his mother. We can speak to him, Will. Through the church. We can send him our prayers. Through a priest. We can help him ..."

Will was walking away, thinking of Tyburn and the Tower. Of his cousin Edward, nothing left of him but a blackened skull, grinning at the crowds on London Bridge. Of Southwell, left hanging by his hands while his tormentor casually went about his business. Of Campion at his trial, his broken hands wrapped in a linen cloth, too enfeebled by torture to lift a cup of drink to his own lips.

The old man called after him as he strode quickly back towards the house, away from Stratford, back in the direction of London where he could hide in plain sight.

"What will you do for me, when my time comes?" he shouted after his son, indifferent to whoever might hear him. "Will you leave me burning in Purgatory, without a drop of mercy to cool my tongue?"

* * *

The old man's words echoed in William's memory, and startled an unfamiliar tear from his eyes. On his way home he stopped in at the Guild Chapel. He remembered, strange incidence of anamnesis, that today was the Feast of the Assumption of the Blessed Virgin. The bodily taking up of the Virgin into Heaven. Of course there were no observances of so Catholic a rite in Protestant James Stuart's reformed church.

The chapel was empty. He sat in a blackened old pew and stared at the wall above the altar. Whitewash. By its very blankness the wall gestured at something unsaid, mute witness to an invisible meaning. Just a bare surface, creamy off-white, rough-textured in patches where the lime had run, a piece flaked off and yellow underneath, strands of hair from the plaster tangled with hog's bristles from the workman's brush. Why did it seem to speak to him? Was it an invitation, a blank canvas waiting to be coated with all the colours of his fancy? Or was there some picture lying concealed beneath, some defaced image slackly slubbered over with whitewash, some pigment of palimpsest, latent, veiled, waiting only to be disclosed?

He knew. In 1559 an iconoclastic royal injunction had demanded the removal of all signs of "superstition" and "idolatry" from places of worship. Before this the Guild Chapel had been decorated throughout with religious paintings, including a magnificent "Doom," a depiction of the Last Judgement, above the rood-screen. All such images were required to be defaced, covered over with whitewash. The job had been supervised by the Chamberlain of Stratford. Shakespeare's own father. "Item payd for defasyng ymages in ye chappell ij^s."

* * *

He was a boy again, sitting next to his father in the Guild Chapel at Evening Prayer, one later afternoon of summer. An assiduous observer, Will had noticed that members of the congregation, alternately pious and bored, devoutly attentive or irritably fidgeting, tended to look round in all directions during the service: now at the priest and the communion table, now up at the ceiling, now down at their feet, now at the church door. He had observed, however, that his father only ever looked in one direction, staring continually at the whitewashed wall above the nave. His eyes remained constantly fixed on that mark, while he kneeled and stood, while his lips moved soundlessly in prayer, while his hands were lifted frequently in supplication.

"O Lord, open thou our lips," sang the priest.

"And our mouth shall shew forth thy praise," raggedly responded the congregation.

Will had thought for a long time this was merely an idiosyncratic habit of personal devotion, but realising how different was his father's physical attitude from that of his fellow-parishioners, curiosity at last moved him to speak.

"Father," he asked. "What is it that you see there?"

John's eyes were bright with tears. But he only sighed, and shook his head.

"I see nothing. Nothing but the light of the setting sun as it moves across the wall."

And yet he continued to stare at nothing, to bend his eye on vacancy.

The choir intoned: "My soul doth magnify the Lord ..."

Will asked him again: "Father, what is it you see there?"

"I see nothing. Nothing but the shadows of evening gathering round about us."

"Please, father, tell me. You can tell me. I have to know."

John Shakespeare heaved a great sigh, that seemed to shatter all his bulk and end his being. He leaned very close to his son and whispered, thrillingly, in his ear.

"It is not nothing I see, child. It is everything. I see Christ in majesty, seated on a rainbow. I see Him judging all the peoples of the earth, the quick and the dead. The righteous he assigns to his kingdom, and the unrighteous he sends down to the pit. It is all there, on the wall, just behind the whitewash. We have covered it over because we had no choice. But God forgive us the deed of that day. God forgive me."

He sat back in the pew and put an arm round his son's shoulders.

"Now it is all I can see. One day we will see it, with our own eyes. For yet in my flesh, shall I see God."

The service was ending.

"Now lettest thou thy servant depart in peace, according to thy word. For mine eyes have seen thy salvation ..."

* * *

On his return to New Place, William went to his study, and locked the door behind him. Searching at the back of a shelf behind a pile of books, he found, and removed a small yellowed pamphlet. Spreading it on his desk, he examined it carefully. It was a six-page, hand-written testament of Catholic faith, in fourteen articles, each page signed in the name of John Shakespeare. Composed by Carlo Borromeo, Cardinal Archbishop of Milan, thousands of copies were distributed to Catholics by travelling Jesuits, with the intention of reinforcing, and encouraging them to make public profession of, their faith. William knew this document had been brought to England by Jesuit missionaries Edmund Campion and Robert Persons, who travelled from Rome via Milan, where they met with Cardinal Borromeo. Campion stayed with Sir William Catesby, Robin's father, only twelve miles from Stratford. The pamphlets were distributed to Catholic believers, including John Shakespeare, at secret masses and clandestine home visits.

The pamphlet was an illegal and heretical declaration of faith in Catholic doctrine, in the sacraments and in Purgatory. It was plangent with long-prohibited prayers to the Blessed Virgin and the saints.

I, John Shakespeare, do protest that I will also pass out of this life, armed with the last sacrament of extreme unction: the which if through any let or hindrance I should not then be able to have, I do now also for that time demand and crave the same; beseeching His divine majesty that He will be pleased to anoint my senses both internal and external; with the sacred oil of His infinite mercy, and to pardon me all my sins committed by seeing, speaking, feeling, smelling, hearing, touching, or by any other way whatsoever.

Holding the pamphlet in his hand, William was overwhelmed by a vision of his father's death. He had been summoned back to Stratford from London, and arrived at his father's house to find it full of mourners. He had run up the stairs to his parents' bedroom. The room was full of smoke. The air smelt sweet. On the bed lay the old man, already sunken in death. Around the bed, he saw the familiar faces of his family and neighbours. But someone else was there, a stranger. The room was filled with burning incense. A surplice; a stole; a rosary. Gently the priest took a phial of oil, dabbed it on a bit of cloth, and softly wiped the oil into the palms of John's hands, the soles of his feet, the lids of his eyes, his nostrils, his lips.

"Per sacrosáncta humánae reparatiónis mystéria remittat tibi omnipotens Deus omnes praeséntis et futúrae vitae paenas, Paradísi portas apériat, et ad gáudia sempitérna perdúcat." (1)

William did not know which was more fearful, the certainty of his father's death, confirmed by this black-robed harbinger, or the fear of all that beauty and horror from the past, sweeping over him again. It all came back, the chanting, the lovely old prayers, the taste of bread and body, *corpus Christi*, lying on the tongue. The piety and the pain; the rack and the scavenger's daughter. Thumbscrew and manacles, brazier and gallows. A burning, all-consuming love, inseparable from a crippling fear.

"*Per istam sanctam Unctiónem et suam piisimam misericórdiam, indúlgeat tibi Dóminus quidquid per visum, audiotum, odorátum, gustum et locutiónem, tactum.*" (2)

John Shakespeare had died in the love of Christ, in the arms of the church, and in sure and certain hope of the resurrection to eternal life. He lived, and died, a papist.

His son honoured his memory: too much, perhaps. Some debts exceed the debtor's capacity to pay. He must hide the pamphlet. It would be enough in itself to incriminate him. He thought of the fear he had felt when Wright had knocked on his door, bringing under his house's eaves the thrilling anxiety of terror. He was a conspirator. The Powder Plot was here, with him, inside the house. He could be apprehended, and the house searched, at any moment.

He put it away again. He would conceal it in the loft-space of the old house in Henley Street. No-one would think to look for it there. If it were discovered, it would be long after his death. For nothing is secret, that shall not be made manifest; neither *anything* hid, that shall not be known and come abroad.

20 August 1605. The Globe Theatre, Bankside

William was back in London, rehearsing *Henry V* for a court performance. The play remained popular, though he was bored to tears by its unrelenting patriotism, its militantly protestant heroism, its beefy Englishness. The Agincourt scenes were proving difficult, with actors coming on and going off at the wrong times. If Henry's army had been so refractory and disorganised, we'd all be speaking French.

Out of the corner of his eye, William caught sight of a figure standing on the edge of the stage, a form that made him involuntarily flinch. The man was wearing a costume, though he was not involved in the play. It was the kind of dress William had seen in the Venetian carnival, when he travelled there in the company of Harry Wriothsley. Clad from head to foot in a loose robe, with a hood like a monk's cowl, and voluminous long sleeves, the man wore a bizarre white mask, shaped like the beak of a bird. The costume was completed by a large broad-brimmed round hat. The man's face was invisible, but his eyes peered owlishly out from holes in the mask. William recognized the character from the Italian *commedia*: it was the uniform of the Plague Doctor. The figure crooked a finger at William, as if to beckon him.

William strode over to him. "Who the hell are you?" he demanded, with some asperity.

"Come with me." The voice sounded familiar, but orotund and distorted into a hollow echo inside the beak-like proboscis of the mask. It was like talking to the oracle at Delphi.

"You must be joking. Come where?"

"You must come."

"It's not my time, friend. I haven't got the plague. Go find somebody else to play your games."

The man came closer, and the long beak nuzzled clumsily into William's ear. "It's me, you fool," the voice intoned, in a harsh, sibilant whisper. "Percy."

"Trying not to attract attention, I see, as usual. Can't you see I'm busy?"

"Guido is back," explained Percy. "We have to go fetch him."

"From where?"

"Foulness."

William had heard of Foulness, but only as a God-forsaken east coast promontory, nest of windblown seabirds, haunt of migratory wildfowl. What was Fawkes doing there? So the rehearsal was over for the day. William signalled to the cast and crew to knock off, and followed Percy, in his bizarre disguise, out of the theatre, and into the street. There, waiting for them, was a long black cart, with railed sides, of the kind used to gather the corpses in time of plague. Percy jumped lightly up into the driving seat, and urged William to join him. Jostling the big cart uneasily through the narrow streets, they crossed the river, and took the road to the east.

Once they had cleared the city's precincts, Percy stripped off his hat and mask to reveal, beneath the monastic hood, a grimed and sweating face.

"Why?" asked William simply, genuinely nonplussed.

"Answer me two questions, Will," Percy cheerfully replied. "One. Did you recognise me?"

"You know I didn't."

"And two. Would you have gone anyway near this cart without a damn good reason?"

"Point taken," said Will.

"Well then," said Percy. "I'd call that a result." He rummaged in the folds of his costume cloak, and produced a letter. "Here. Read this."

William took the letter, again written in French, and read it, as the big cart lurched and creaked and bumped along the dusty road to Colchester.

From Foulness, Essex
19 August 1605

My dear brothers in Christ

This letter is an urgent summons for your assistance. The fellow who brings you this knows exactly where I am, and you may trust his guidance. Come quickly, bringing enough wagons and men to transport the cargo I have told you of, on to London. I am stranded on the island of Foulness, off the Essex coast. As the place is forlorn and deserted, and separated from the shore by narrow creeks, so far we have not been discovered. Make all dispatch to join me, and we can get our miners safe home, before any alarm is raised. As you travel you may, at your leisure, read the rest of this account, explaining how I arrived here, so far from my intended destination.

Once we had cleared the Dardanelles, my voyage through the Mediterranean proceeded without further impediment. Soon we had passed the rock of Gibraltar and entered the Bay of Biscaya. The weather there is often vexing and foul, but we found a smooth passage ahead of a fortunate wind. Likewise our journey through the channel. You can imagine my exhilaration, on my first sight of those chalk-white cliffs of Dover! But our course was set for London, and so the Vassa continued to sail round the heel of Kent, and into the mouth of the Thames. We were home and dry, or so I foolishly imagined.

For without warning, a terrible tempest blew in from the North Sea, and broke violently over our heads. The sails flapped madly before the contrary winds, and the rigging creaked in the storm. Straightway the ship was blown off course, pushed north towards the Essex marshes. The behaviour of the crew was even more inexplicable than the vagaries of the weather, for they began to run about the vessel, screaming in fear. In the lurid blue flares of the lightning I could see their faces, distorted in terror, like the faces of the damned in Hell. Some of them, without hesitation, vaulted the ship's rail, and plunged headlong into the sea. Experienced sailors, driven to madness by a simple storm at sea? Something else was afflicting them, but I knew not what.

The ship plunged and heaved, as if driven onwards by some ulterior force, beyond the control of human hands. After some hours of sheltering in my cabin, and watching the deck lashed with torrential rain, I crawled off in search of the captain. Pulling myself along the deck by ropes, I found him clutching the steering wheel, as paralysed by fear as his crew. Then I observed that he had lashed himself to the wheel with a rope, and tied around his hands the beads of a rosary. He too seemed completely mad, unable to communicate anything save a torrent of gibberish, which I took to be prayers. So high were the seas, and so heavy the rain, that we could see nothing on any side of the ship, and had no idea where the land was. Knowing the shore here to be flat and marshy, I did not fear that we would drive onto rocks and split, but felt acutely the danger that we would founder and beach on some mud-bank. Just as I began to consider this likelihood, with a shock that ran through the whole vessel from stem to stern, the Vassa ploughed into the sandy silt of the Essex shore. The impact brought down the main-mast, and a great heavy spar fell directly onto the captain at the wheel, killing him instantly. The ship heeled violently over, as its hull came to rest on the shoal. As for the crew, all I heard were screams of terror and splashes, as they plunged into the water to escape from whatever nightmare it was that was riding their distracted brains. Some maybe reached the shore, and ran off into the storm; others perished in the weltering undertow of the surging, sucking tides. Soon I was the only living soul left on the ship, except for my cargo of miners, sleeping quietly below decks on the soil of their homeland.

And then, as quickly as the storm had broken, it died away, leaving in its wake a huge healing calm. It was almost nightfall. The low sun broke through swirling grey clouds, and touched the marshes with gold. I shinned down a rope, on that side of the ship that lay closest to the bank, to feel the firmness of earth beneath my feet, and walked a little way towards the shore. Looking back across the low-lying mud-flats, I saw her standing black and angled against the light of the setting sun, which gilded the maze of creeks and runnels that ran and puddled over the shallow banks and shoals. Then to my astonishment I witnessed – if it was not another dream – the most extraordinary incident of my entire journey. Standing on the deck of the ship, gazing towards me over the flat marsh, was a horse, a coal-black mare with a long wispy mane and huge nut-brown eyes. I had never seen so beautiful a mount, nor one I so desired to ride. What was it doing there? Surely there were no horses aboard? I started towards the ship, and it watched me as I ran. But as I came closer, the horse gathered its haunches for a spring, and in a beautiful fluid motion, vaulted the gunwale where the ship's heeled side lay closest to the shoal. Once its hooves touched the shore, it sped off into the gathering twilight, and disappeared like a wraith.

I scrambled back on board, and went straight below to inspect the ship's hold. What other mysteries might it not contain? I found nothing else unusual, except that one of the coffins had been dragged by the storm from its position in the hold, its lid smashed and torn away from the box. It was empty. I could not understand how this had happened, since all the boxes were equally firmly secured. At any rate I had lost only one of my men, while the rest still lay quietly and at peace. For me, it seems, though not for the captain and crew of the Vassa, it will have proved a most happy wreck.

By the will of Providence, before darkness fell I discovered, working a fishing coracle down one of my neighbouring creeks, the dependable young fellow who brings you this message. In return for a little gold, more than he would earn in a year, he has agreed to carry my post to you, and to point you the way back to the wreck. For God's sake make speed, and come to me. All now depends on our peremptory conveyance of these miners to the safe house in Westminster. Make all haste.

Your loving brother in Christ,
Guido.

20 August 1605. Essex Road

"Enough wagons and men," William quoted. "Do we qualify?"

"Look in the back," said Percy.

William craned his neck round to peer down into the body of

the cart. Again he recoiled in horror at what he saw. Slumped in a corner of the cart was a corpse, swathed in a winding sheet. Over and around it was a light sprinkling of quicklime.

"Good Christ!" William yelled, half minded to jump off the moving cart. "What is it?"

"Calm yourself, man," said Percy cheerfully. "It's Jack. I think he's asleep. He's playing the part of a plague-stricken corpse. What do you think of his performance? From a professional point-of-view?"

"He shows an admirable economy of movement," said William, recovering from his shock, "and a certain pleasing understatement of gesture. He needs to work on his vocal delivery, though."

The corpse began to stir and utter a low, spectral moan.

"Get out of there, Jack," said Percy. "You must be hotter than Hell."

Wright's head snaked itself free from the shroud. He too was sweating in the afternoon sun.

"I was doing the Ghost of King Homelaicte," he said. "Did I frighten thee, Will?"

"No more than usual," said William glumly. "At least I'm not really driving to Colchester with a bubonic corpse and a mad Plague Doctor."

He made to hand the letter back, but Percy insisted he keep it. "You're our bookkeeper, William," he said. He slipped it into his doublet. He was, after all, a man of letters. And now a librarian of regicide, an archivist of treason. He must write a play about all this one day, he thought to himself, if he lived. Some of the scenes of this tragedy seemed to possess a natural theatricality.

They reached Foulness in the afternoon. The ship was still there, resting on the gravelly silt, its remaining masts sloping at an angle from the heeled hull. On the deck stood Fawkes, grateful to see them, and eager to unload his cargo. The three of them got the boxes off, and onto the cart fairly easily. Though each contained the heaviness of a little earth, their occupants seemed to weigh very little. They stacked the coffins neatly inside the rails of the cart, and lashed them together with rope from the ship. William noticed that the last box, as described in Fawkes's letter, lay in the hold empty, with its lid wrenched off and lying by its side. He peered into the interior, and shivered. Inside there was nothing but the thin layer of Transylvanian soil, black and soft. His imagination brooded vividly on the experience of being confined in an earth-lined coffin, for days on end. Buried alive! Sightless eyes staring at blackness. A constant rocking from the motion of the ship. The lapping of the waves, the creaking of spars, the flapping of sails, the shouts of the mariners. Bound for a strange land, and a life of subterranean servitude. A slave ship. He jumped when Fawkes came up behind him.

"Shall we leave this one, Guido?" he asked.

"No, bring it along," replied Fawkes. "You never know, the fellow may turn up again, looking for his bed."

The day was drawing in, and the sun westering over the marshes, as the long cart, with its sinister cargo, crunched and slithered across the Foulness gravel and mud. All four crowded onto the front seat, since no-one wanted to sit atop the pile of coffins. On the road Percy lit lanterns to guide their way, as the darkness gathered round them. William thought he could hear noises coming from the boxes: a soft whisper, a creak like the turning of a restless sleeper. He glanced at Fawkes, who seemed morose, and was largely silent.

"Did you ever see that horse again, Guido?" William asked.

"There was no horse," answered Fawkes shortly. "A trick of the imagination. A man escaped, that's all. Forget it."

They reached London in the middle of the night. Very few people were abroad, and those who were gave the grim conveyance a very wide berth. At the house in Westminster they unloaded the boxes and carried them, one by one, into the room containing the mouth of the tunnel. There they were lined up around the orifice of the shaft, five on each side. The empty coffin lay with the others, its detached lid leaning against its side.

Despite the successful accomplishment of their mission, the four men were silent. A kind of melancholy enveloped them like a fog. The room seemed unusually cold.

Fawkes broke up the hiatus with a peremptory set of commands. "Right then. You can leave these fellows to me. They must be set to work immediately. Tomorrow I'll rest with them through the day. We must dispatch. Thomas, Jack, make sure all is fast with the powder, and prepare it for transporting here. We will need it as soon as we break through the wall. William, bring me some food and drink before nightfall tomorrow. If I'm still asleep, rouse me. Now farewell to you all." And then he added: "May God and his angels defend us against all perils and dangers of this night."

William sensed an unusual sincerity in Fawkes's conventional Evensong prayer, and left with an uneasy mind.

21 August 1605. Westminster

William returned to the house the next night after sunset, carrying a basket of food and drink for Guido. The door was unlocked, so he let himself in. In the room where the shaft had been excavated, the coffins were gone. He could hear the subdued sounds of labour at the bottom of the shaft and further down the tunnel: the soft chink of a pick against rock, the slurring of sand and gravel shovelled into a bucket. No sound of human voices.

He peered down into the well of the shaft. At the bottom Fawkes appeared, and called cheerfully to him. "Stay there, Will, I'll come up."

Gratefully Fawkes took the basket of provisions. William noticed he was wearing a huge pectoral cross, on a chain round his neck. A cumbersome accessory for underground working.

"Does it go well?" William asked him.

"Excellent well," mumbled Fawkes through a mouthful of bread. "They are superb workers. Give me a moment, and you can come down and see."

At the shaft-bottom William could immediately see the changes in the shape and scope of the excavation. Five tunnels had been dug outwards from the circular hole, like the arms of a five-pointed star. In each one lay four of the boxes, now all lying empty with their lids leaning against the sides. From inside the mine he could clearly hear the noises of the work progressing.

"Are they tunnelling through the wall?" he asked.

"They are," replied Fawkes, "and making speedy progress. We shall have all done in a matter of weeks. Just enough time to prepare for 3rd October."

"Can I see?" William asked, unable to suppress the curiosity he felt from his reading of Fawkes's account of his journey to Transylvania.

"Let them be for the moment," said Fawkes smoothly. "They've come on a long voyage, to a strange country. And they are just getting used to the work. Best not to distract them at the moment."

William shrugged. Perhaps it was better for him to know as little as possible. Fawkes hunched his shoulders and made to return down the tunnel to the face.

"One thing, Guido," William could not forbear asking. "These men. Your description of them. You made them sound – unusual."

"Unusual? Let me remind you, William: we are digging a tunnel beneath the Parliament House, in order to blow up a king. We left the usual behind a long time ago. Don't concern yourself about this aspect of the operation. I will take responsibility, and deliver the tunnel as I promised."

Fawkes began to retreat along the excavation. His lamp lit the darkness beyond. William strained to see what lay there, beyond the swinging lantern's ambit of illumination. He caught a glimpse of one of the miners, crouching in a bend of the tunnel, and holding something to his mouth. It looked like the body of a rat, the long tail lashing from side to side. Then Fawkes's bulky form interposed, and the man vanished from his sight.

William ascended the shaft, left the house and walked quickly away towards his lodgings. Beneath his feet he could feel the earth moving.

Love

10 September 1605. Wood Street, London

At this point everything changed. William fell in love.

Rumours had been circulating for some weeks, through the entertainment districts of the South Bank and Clerkenwell, through the theatres and bear-pits, through the inns and taverns and brothels, through Paris Garden and the Liberty of the Clink, of a new and exceptionally beautiful whore, who had swiftly established herself as the Empress of the London stews. She was a Princess from Muscovy, some said, as cold as the snows of Siberia, as fierce in passion as the Russian wolf. She was a Persian houri, veiled and voluptuous, a devoted priestess of profane pleasures. She was a mujra dancer from the deserts of Arabia, escaped from some sultan's seraglio.

Her black hair dispersed an exotic perfume that drove men insane. She was of complexion dark, black as the tents of Kedar, as the curtains of Solomon. Her eyes were like the fishpools of Heshbon, by the gate of Bethrabbim. Men who had been with her grew pale and wan, seemed to lose all their will to live, and were found at night loitering aimlessly beneath her window. There was even gossip that a man or two had been killed about her. But William heard this from a fellow who clearly could not afford her exorbitant fee, and so his narrative was suffused with the bitterness of disappointment. She was known as the Countess, and she worked only at night.

He heard that she was holding court at a tavern in Wood Street, only a stone's throw from his lodgings. That same evening William threaded his way through narrow lanes and alleys that crooked and dog-legged deep into the red-light district of Love Lane, looking for a tavern called, obscenely, The Swan with Two Necks. The place looked sufficiently insalubrious, but within it was brightly lit, and from the open windows came the noise of boisterous singing. He entered, avoided eye contact with the ruffianly clientele, and ordered a drink at the bar. In the corner there were a couple of whores, one fat and red-cheeked, the other emaciated and sickly-looking, with the face of a death's head. But there was no sign of the Countess.

Will was acquainted with the fat prostitute, a country girl from the north. "How's business, Doll?" he inquired.

"Slow, Will. Slow. Fancy a tumble?"

"Not at the moment, Doll."

"This is my friend Bianca."

"Delighted to meet you." Bianca extended her hand in a parody of gentility.

"Bianca! How delightfully inappropriate," he replied.

"You could do us both," said Doll helpfully.

"No, thanks. I'm looking for someone."

"He's looking for *her*," Bianca interjected, with obvious irritation. "Everybody wants her these days."

"Do you mean the Countess?" asked William eagerly. "Is she here?"

"She will be," said Doll, sucking loudly at a mug of ale. "But not until after dark. You want to watch out for yourself, Will. She's dangerous."

"She's foreign," added Bianca.

"She's skinny," said Doll.

"She's expensive."

"But is she not beautiful?" he asked.

They both shrugged noncommittally. "We all look the same in the dark," opined Doll.

But William was no longer listening. A woman had come in through a door at the other end of the room, and her entrance caused a hush of stillness to descend over the raucous noise. She stood for a moment, with all eyes upon her. When she moved, abruptly the row began again, but in the lacuna of that pause,

William had fallen hopelessly in love.

She was unusually tall, and stood out from the crowd, like a glossy-feathered raven trooping with common doves. She was indeed dark, with soft black hair cascading over her shoulders and down to her waist, and black eyes that shone like moonlight on the waters of the Thames. A dark lady. But she taught the torches, or at least the guttering tallow candles that lit the dingy bar, to burn bright. She wore a red, low-cut gown that revealed smooth, olive-skinned breasts. Her eyes were large and almond-shaped, her eyebrows oddly tilted upwards at a sharp angle, and the eyelids heavy with some dark red colouring. But William could not take his eyes from her glossy scarlet mouth, and the gleaming white teeth, with strangely prominent canines that rested coquettishly on her lower lip. There was some unearthly charisma about her, some powerful charge that electrified him with an alternating current of desire and fear. Unthinkingly he stood up, and began to move towards her, as if drawn by a magnetic field.

"There he goes," said Bianca.

"He'll be back," said Doll. "With his purse empty." They both giggled salaciously.

William presented himself to the Countess. "My lady," he said. She extended her hand for him to kiss. He took it, and was astonished at its icy coldness.

She seemed intrigued by his courtesy, and replied to him with an unplaceable foreign accent. "May I retrieve my hand, good sir? I may need it tonight."

He let go of her hand. Her laughter was like broken glass. He gazed deep into her black eyes, and saw within them the stirring of a red flame, like burning magma in the core of a volcano.

"Do you wish to introduce yourself?"

He could hardly speak. "My name is William Shakespeare."

The name seemed to mean nothing to her. "I am the Countess." Her pointed tongue was as red as her lips. The prominent white teeth dazzled him, and made him feel faint. "Do you have money?" He jingled the gold in the purse at his belt. "Come then." She led the way, out of the bar and up some stairs to a chamber on the first floor. It was furnished like an ordinary brothel room, with red curtains and hangings, a big bed with untidily tangled white sheets, an armchair, a basin and a jug of water. He took the purse from his belt and laid it on the bed. "Would you like to talk with me first?" He was literally speechless, his voice stuck in his parched throat. She sat on the edge of the bed. "Afterwards then. Come here." She extended her arms, and with what seemed like extraordinary strength, drew him towards her. He bent down to kiss her, and for a moment was lost in her mouth. Then her face slid down his chest to his waist, and with deft fingers she untrussed him, releasing his engorged penis from its confinement. Gripping its base, she slipped her bright red lips over its head. Her mouth seemed achingly cold around the burning shaft of flesh, though her breath was hot, and her cold fingers flickered around his balls. His mind dissolved into blackness. There was an earthquake underground, a volcano erupted, a league-long tidal roller thundered on a Pacific beach. When his eyes opened, he lay spent in the armchair, and she was sitting on the bed, hugging her knees and smiling at him.

"Who are you?" he asked her. He had recovered his sensibilities and was almost himself again.

"You know who I am," she said. "I am the Countess."

"Where do you come from?"

"From a land far away. You would not know its name."

"I have an extensive knowledge of world geography. Try me."

"You are too curious. Perhaps you are a government spy. You would have me deported."

"Not for all the world," he replied fervently. "I would have you stay here for ever."

She seemed touched by his ardour. "You are young. You do

not know how long for ever is."

"Young! I'm pushing forty."

"Young in the ways of the world." Her voice seemed wistful, touched with regret. She stared out of the window at the darkness outside. The moon was rising over the rooftops. The clock was striking midnight. When her glance returned to him, her face had changed. There was a kind of anger in it that tinged her cheeks with red, and smouldering in her eyes a red flicker of hate. Her lips lifted away from her teeth in an expression of malevolence, or disdain. He lifted himself from the armchair, sat by her on the edge of the bed, and laid his hand gently on her knee.

"You want more?" she asked. Her face contorted with a kind of hunger. The red tongue ran around her protuberant teeth, and noisily she licked her lips. Her voice hummed in his ears. He felt a hectic tingling in his blood.

"I have no more money."

"Then what can you offer me?"

"Only my heart."

"Perhaps I will take it."

He lay back on the bed beside her. She bestrode him and bent over him, her long black hair falling like a curtain around them. Slowly she brought her face down to his, and he urged his lips towards hers for the longed-for kiss. But her face slid lower, and her lips began to caress his neck. The sensitive skin of his throat tingled as he felt the touch of that bright red mouth. Though the lips were cold, he could feel hot breath against his skin, as her tongue licked and lapped noisily round his jaw. The hard points of two sharp teeth pressed lightly against his throat. He melted into a mist of voluptuous longing.

Then words and music came to him, cadences forming a rhythm, phrases coalescing into lines. He began softly to whisper them. He had nothing to give her but his own dark gift.

Let me be obsequious in thy heart,
And take thou my oblation, poor but free ...

Abruptly she stopped what she was doing, listening, but kept her mouth against his neck. "What did you say?"

"I'm a poet," he said. "I want to write for you."

"Say it again." She sat back and looked at him.

The lines of the sonnet formed quickly in his mind.

Let me be obsequious in thy heart,
And take thou my oblation, poor but free
Which is not mix'd with seconds, knows no art,
But mutual render, only me for thee.

"That's beautiful," she said. The expression of hunger had gone from her face, the lightning of hatred disappeared from her eyes. "Is that yours?"

"Of course," he said, proudly. "I'm William Shakespeare."

She inclined her head, as if to acknowledge the name, to remember it perhaps. "Can you write so quickly?"

He grinned. "Not always. For you, yes." It was the one thing he could do. What he thought, he wrote. His mind and hand went together.

She seemed to decide on something. "You may come and see me again," she said. It was not a question. "Tomorrow night. But you must bring a poem. A new one."

"What if I can't?" he asked.

"Oh, you will come."

"Write a poem, I mean."

"Then," she said, mysteriously, "I cannot answer for the consequences. Goodnight, William."

It was his dismissal. He went down the stairs, his mind lost in a turbulent dark dream.

11 September 1605. Wood Street, London

The next night William was back in the bar of The Swan with Two Necks, with a new poem in his pocket. His hand trembled slightly as he reached out for his drink, and he had difficulty swallowing. He was expected. The barman signalled to him to go upstairs, and a servant ushered him down a corridor. A different chamber this time. He sat on the bed and waited for her.

She appeared at the door, and the sight of her beauty stopped his heart. He offered her another purse of money, but she waved it away. "You have the poem?" she asked.

"I have it here," he replied, drawing the paper from his pocket.

"Not yet," she said. "Later. Lie down."

Again she began to untie his points. He took hold of her wrist. So cold! "May I not make love to you?"

She shook her head decisively. "No. My body is – different. I am unable to take a man inside me. If you wish to love me, then you must be satisfied with this." She cupped her cold hands around his genitals, and kissed the tip of his penis with her soft red lips.

"Oh well," sighed William, leaning his head back against his folded arms, and thinking of England. "I'll just have to reconcile myself."

Afterwards he reached out for the poem, but again she deterred him. "Let us talk a little first. Tell me something about yourself."

"I'm a writer. I write plays for the stage, and poems for my friends. I used to act, but not so much anymore."

"So that's your profession. But what about you, yourself?"

"Oh, there is little to tell," he said, evasively. "I don't find myself very interesting."

"Ah. Then let me tell your fortune. In my country the gipsies can read a man's life in his palm."

"Are you a gipsy, then?"

"No," she laughed. "But I lived among them long enough to learn some of their ways. Show me your hand."

He held out his hand, palm upwards, for her inspection. She pored over it, tracing the ingrained lines and puckered creases in the skin. Great long lashes swept over her downcast eyes, and a small frown wrinkled her forehead. "You are a very complicated man."

"Am I?"

"Yes. You are very successful, but you doubt yourself. You can play a part convincingly, but you do not know who you are. You care more about your writing than about the people who love you."

He shivered slightly at the accuracy of her observations. But a quick wit could have gathered such knowledge merely from what he had already told her. He did not believe in gipsy wizardry.

She seemed startled by something, and tilted her head back to see more clearly. "You are married."

"Yes," he said.

"But your wife is far away."

Not far enough, he thought regretfully.

"You have children."

"Two daughters."

"Do you love them?"

Her questions were so direct as to disarm him. "I suppose so."

"You should cherish them. They will keep your name alive."

His name was already a living thing, that had no dependence on a couple of querulous wenches, or a dead son who had taken all his dynastic hopes to the grave with him.

He tried to take his hand away, but she held it fast, with a new intensity of interest. "Wait. You are involved in some great enterprise. I see danger, darkness. Men working in a pit … a king with a sad face … he is afraid of something."

He had heard enough about himself. He closed his hand

decisively. "You see nothing but dreams. The children of an idle brain. My mind is full of sad-faced kings. What you see, I have invented. But now, you must tell me about yourself. I have no second sight to read your thoughts. Where were you born?"

She sat back on the bed, arms around her knees. "In Arabia," she replied. "A city in the desert. But I was taken from there as a young girl."

"To be married?"

"Yes."

"Where?"

"A kingdom in the east, by the Black Sea."

"Your husband? He lives?"

"Yes. But he is old. Very old. I do not think of him."

"Does he not miss you? Will he not come to find you?" He, William, would go to the ends of the earth to fetch her back.

"Oh, no. He has – much business to attend to. He will forget me. We were not – happy together."

"And is there anyone else in your life? Another man?"

"There is someone. The man who brought me here. He saved me from my old life. But he does not know I exist. Still, I feel I – owe him. I would like one day to make amends."

A pang of envy lanced through him. It must have showed on his face.

"You are jealous?" Again that silvery, metallic laugh. "But I am a whore. A bay where all men ride. You have me now only because any man can have me, for a purse of gold. This body is not your personal plot, but the wide world's common thoroughfare."

The church bells struck the hour. It was dead midnight. On the final stroke of twelve, he saw again the change come over her. She looked out of the window at the great yellow moon. Her face took on that strange expression, somewhere between hunger and rage. The one emotion inspired pity in him, the other dread. He felt some danger in her, some unidentifiable violence that she could barely control. Her tongue ran noisily over her teeth, making a churning sound. She panted like a dog.

"Now," she said, "quickly. The poem. Read it to me."

He picked up the paper and read her the sonnet.

In the old age black was not counted fair,
Or if it were, it bore not beauty's name;
But now is black beauty's successive heir,
And beauty slander'd with a bastard shame:
For since each hand hath put on nature's power,
Fairing the foul with art's false borrow'd face,
Sweet beauty hath no name, no holy bower,
But is profaned, if not lives in disgrace.
Therefore my mistress' brows are raven black,
Her eyes so suited, and they mourners seem
At such who, not born fair, no beauty lack,
Slandering creation with a false esteem:
Yet so they mourn, becoming of their woe,
That every tongue says beauty should look so.

As he read, a calm descended on her. Her face lost the look of angry desire, and resumed its serenity of expression. She did not look directly at him, but askance, the long lashes fringing her lovely eyes.

"Exquisitely done. You are a poet. But also clever. I like that. Explain it to me. You say that here, only fair women are counted beautiful: those with white skin and blonde hair? While I am black …"

"… but comely," he quoted.

"Ye daughters of Jerusalem …" she continued.

"You know the Bible? You are a Christian?"

"I was born a Muslim. But I became a Christian when I married. I do not care much for religion. I have seen too many men kill one another over articles of faith, and there is no joy in it."

"Is there ever joy in death?" She looked at him strangely. "Do you believe in God, then?" he asked.

"Of course," she replied, as if the question were beyond dispute.

"And in eternal life? In Heaven?"

"Yes," she nodded, almost sadly. "There is life eternal."

"And Hell?"

"Oh yes. Hell. Everlasting pain. Torment. Punishment for the adversaries of God."

"So the book says. But do you believe it, here in your heart? That we will be tormented for love?"

She raised her lovely eyes and gazed into his. "Are you not tormented now, William? Are you not in Hell?"

My God, he thought to himself, who is she? Such knowledge, such honesty. A kindred spirit. But so cold! Was he like that to others? A man who knew too much, with an icicle buried in his heart?

"Tomorrow night," she said, and turned away from him.

Again he felt dismissed. He obeyed the arbitrary mandate of his dark lady.

12 September 1605. Silver Street

I am in Hell, he thought, as he dipped his pen in the inkwell. And she has put me here.

His new nocturnal existence was beginning to tell on him. He slept late into the afternoon, and woke with the urgent imperative of a poem pressing upon him. He was getting no work done. *Measure for Measure* lay half-finished on his desk, and he had made no contact with his fellow-conspirators in the Plot. Yet he seemed to have no choice but to obey this strict lady's imperious command. He was her minion, his will in thrall to hers. But this was not the age of courtly love. This was the modern age of commerce. Everything had its price, including her. Tonight he would make demand of her, to test the real extent of her hegemony.

He finished the poem, and as darkness fell, made his way back to the tavern. She was waiting for him, on the bed in the same chamber as before. She seemed pleased to see him, but as always cold and aloof in love-making. He sat on the bed and kissed her, pushing her back against the pillows so she could not assume control. Her mouth opened to his, and his tongue met the softness of hers. He laid a hand tentatively on her left breast, which seemed, to the touch, warmer than her cold hands, closer perhaps to her heart. Did she have some illness that restricted her circulation? She placed her hand over his, and together they pressed and fondled the breast until the nipple grew hard.

He sought to find the key to her desire. She moved gently beneath him, sighed, and twined her arms about his neck to pull him closer into the kiss. Her tongue lashed softly at his between her canine teeth. He reached down to take the hem of her dress and began to lift it upwards over her knees. He could feel the skin of her legs cold under the black stockings. His hand slid higher, past her knee, to caress the silky skin of her inner thigh. He felt her legs part slightly, as if opening for the entrance of his questing fingers, and her mouth widened beneath his kiss.

But then suddenly she gripped his right hand in her strong, cold grasp, and pulled it away. A jet of rage spurted in his veins at this thwarting of desire. It was like being sixteen again: foreplay without consummation. He recalled a dozen pretty Stratford lasses: "I can't go all the way. Don't 'ee get me with child, William." Until he met Anne … He fell back on the bed, mentally pushing her away with a cold, hard-edged anger.

She sat up and looked at him. "Don't be like that," she said. "I told you I cannot take a man inside me."

"What would happen?"

"Death," she said shortly. "You would not survive."

So she had a disease! That explained everything. A man or two killed about her. She was protecting him from a deadly infection that would inevitably destroy him.

"I want you so much," he said, pleadingly. "But you withhold your passion. It is cruel to keep me away from – there."

"Very well," she said. "Let me show you my passion."

She made him sit on the end of the bed and watch her. She pulled the dress over her head, revealing to the full the astonishing beauty of her body: the sleek olive skin, the soft, pendulous breasts with their dark aureoles, and between her legs a thick matted bush of black hair, cut close like a spaniel's fur. She lay back, her long dark hair spread on the pillow, raised her knees, and opened her legs. The dark bush of her pubic hair was bisected by a bright pink slash that opened like a wound. She parted the lips gently with her fingers: the inside of her was like the lining of a seashell, iridescent with orient pearl.

Then she did what William had never, for all his experience, seen any woman do. She slipped the fingers of one hand into the soft pink channel of her vagina, and with the fingers of the other caressed her clitoris till she brought herself to a shivering, yelping orgasm. Then she held out her cold fingers, glistening with moisture in the moonlight, and put them into his mouth. They tasted like the sour lick and tang of the salt sea-spray. His mind went dark, and on his knees above her he pressed his cock into her passive, receptive mouth. Her red lips expertly peeled back his foreskin, and her pointed tongue encircled the sensitive skin of his penis. He could feel her sharp teeth rubbing maddeningly along his shaft. He rocked and undulated inside her mouth on a wave of desire, like a man being swept helplessly down a dark river. The coiled energy of life itself sprang open from the base of his spine, her lips tightened around him, everything burst and exploded as a great bright stream arced across the space between them, like a waterfall in sunlight. He could hear her lapping eagerly at the semen that filled her mouth, as if she found some nourishment in it. Then he was drowned in darkness, his head slipped beneath the black enveloping waves, and he was gone.

He must have slept. When he woke she was sitting in the armchair across from him, the moonlight from the window silvering her features. Her eyes gazed at him with the look of hunger. Her lips drew back from her protuberant teeth in a kind of snarl. Her voice had changed to the breathy metallic whisper. "The poem," she said.

He held the page to the white light from the window, and read her the sonnet.

> Thine eyes I love, and they, as pitying me,
> Knowing thy heart torment me with disdain,
> Have put on black and loving mourners be,
> Looking with pretty ruth upon my pain.
> And truly not the morning sun of heaven
> Better becomes the grey cheeks of the east,
> Nor that full star that ushers in the even,
> Doth half that glory to the sober west,
> As those two mourning eyes become thy face:
> O! let it then as well beseem thy heart
> To mourn for me since mourning doth thee grace,
> And suit thy pity like in every part.
> Then will I swear beauty herself is black,
> And all they foul that thy complexion lack.

She was silent for a time. "It is a long time since I saw the morning sun of heaven," she said. "I live in a world of darkness. A lady of the night. Is that not what they say? 'Two mourning eyes' … who do they mourn for? The living or the dead? It's not only my eyes that pity you, William. My heart is sorry for you too. But my heart is not my own. If you knew the whole story, you would think differently …" Then suddenly she broke off, and turned away from him, as if she had said too much. "You must go now."

"May I not stay?"

"It will be morning soon. You slept too long. How would you feel if you could never see again the grey cheeks of the east? The glory of the sober west? To live for ever in darkness? If my eyes wear black for mourning, it is myself I mourn for, as well as you. The day is for living, the night for death. Do not choose death, William. Not yet."

He guessed she was talking about her illness, the contagion she was loath to inflict upon him.

"One day I may offer you a choice. But only when you know all there is to know. Now go. I scent the morning air."

As William walked back through the narrow streets, the all-cheering sun was rising in the furthest east. But it was away from light he stole, back to his lodgings. Private in his chamber he penned himself; shut up his windows; locked fair daylight out, and made himself an artificial night.

22 September 1605. Silver Street

And so it went on, night after night, until William began to feel himself trapped in the intricate interlacings of a fatal web, from which there was no escape but death. Softly, inexorably, the silken threads had spun around him, their filaments reaching out and touching him with a disarming gentleness, slowly but surely wrapping him around, cocooning him into reckless abandonment and subjection. He was a minion of her pleasure. Night after night, poem after poem, sonnet after sonnet he penned, and laid in propitiation at the feet of his dark goddess. Every day he slept till afternoon, then rose to commit to paper the words and music of his slumbers. Every night he followed the same path to her bed, to find his delicious but frustrating relief at the tips of her cold fingers, or between the soft ridges of her red lips. Each time they talked together for hours, exchanging secrets more intimate than any he had ever shared with a woman, an endless conversation that brought him no nearer to any understanding of the mystery of her being. Invariably, at midnight, she would exhibit that alarming condition of desire or hunger, in which her face was transformed from its serene, ageless beauty, to the mask of a vicious animal lusting for its prey. Again and again he would read to her his new poem, and the great rage would die within her. And every morning the whole eerie pantomime would break off, abruptly, at cock-crow. He would find himself again on the bald street outside, watching the breaking of another blank day. He felt like a man who had sold his soul to the Devil, and was beginning to wonder who had the better part of the bargain.

There was no day-time reality to his life any more, since she was the only thing that mattered, and he saw her only in the night. She was his lady of darkness, perceived only in the moonlight that silvered the contours of her brown skin. He made love with her, after a fashion, though it was not the love he truly desired. She was always in control, and he was a victim, crucified on the rood of his passion. She never let him in. She seemed to him less and less a person, more as some dark goddess who kept him in her thrall, or as some exotic wild beast who had chosen to lie with the prey she could easily devour.

His condition of subjection to her inexplicable power began to alter his perception of her. He observed her closely as they talked. Were not her features a little coarser than he had initially thought? Her long hair grew like black wires. Her mouth seemed disproportionately big, the lips a bluish colour in the moonlight, the large canine teeth almost a disfigurement. Her breath was sour. Her skin smelt of sweat, with an acridity that obscured the musky scent of her perfume. There were fine black hairs growing on her legs, under her arms.

Still he went on with it, trying to rekindle a dying flame. He still wanted her, and the want could still make him feel sick and faint when he thought of it, but there was no pleasure in it. His yearning for her would irritate and exacerbate his temper to madness. He felt himself becoming a seething cauldron of extreme emotions, savage and cruel. He trusted no-one, and lied to everyone, even to those who had previously held all his confidence. Towards her he felt violence and cruelty, not love. Sometimes it crossed his mind that he might murder her, in that sordid room, so he would be free of guilt and shame. Could he commit such a crime, and get away with it? Who would mourn over the loss of another London whore?

When he made love to her, it was as if his spirit were merely expending itself in a waste of shame. As soon as he had had her, as much in hate as in love, he wanted her again. It was as if, in draining his bodily fluids, as she so avidly did, she injected some subtle poison capable of driving her victim to a frenzy of further desire. He looked forward to these violent delights with an aching of desire that once got, became a long forgotten dream. Looking at the pale, drawn faces of the men who haunted the low tavern, and loitered idly in the sordid streets, he was convinced that they were in the grip of the same dark obsession. Bloodless, enervated, drained of life and energy, they passed him silently through the night, without speaking, each one with his eyes fixed upon his feet, seeking some satisfaction he would never find. They knew the secret: but they were as uncommunicative as the dead. Not one of them could tell him how he could escape from this abjection. Not one of them knew.

30 September 1605. Wood Street, London

Then one night his deliverance arrived, and with his freedom came the breaking of his heart. He retraced his usual journey to The Swan with Two Necks, entered the low-ceilinged bar, and ascended the stairs to their usual chamber. It was empty. Not just empty of occupants, but eloquent of a significant absence, vacated, emptied. She must be elsewhere in the tavern. He hunted around in the adjoining rooms and corridors, eventually found a manservant he knew, and asked him for the whereabouts of the Countess.

"Gone," said the servant, simply.

"Gone? What do you mean, gone? Left?"

"Aye," said the man. "One minute she were there, and the next – gone. Vanished."

"I can't believe it."

"Oh, it happens all the time with these girls. They run up a bill, you know, rent and drink and food, promise to pay the Master his share of their business, then just scarper into the night. She were a good whore, too. Good reputation. Brought in a big clientele. Not much repeat business, though. You're the only one who kept coming back for more."

And yes, thought William to himself, I kept coming back for more. Yet somehow the more always eluded me. And now she's gone. Maybe he would find her again … But he knew in truth that he would not. She was gone for ever. Returned to her old husband, perhaps, in his eastern kingdom. Or become reunited with the man she had mentioned, the one who brought her to England, the one to whom she felt indebted. Or just moved on, to another town, another country, another world, where he could never reach her. The affair was over, and he ought to be grateful to have his own life back again. So he told himself. But never had liberty been bought at so high a price. Never had freedom been earned with so much heartache, so great a penalty of pain.

Powder

1 October 1605. London

And so, in a desultory way, he drifted back into his old life again. He checked in at the theatre, but they had given up waiting for his new play, and were rehearsing an old one. In his profession people did temporarily disappear, sometimes: into prison, into the country, into hiding, for one reason or another. Somehow the absence was always managed. The show must go on.

He realised with a shock that it was already October, and the date of the Plot was almost upon him. In a matter of days his world might be ending in an apocalyptic conflagration. So he trudged round to the house in Westminster to re-connect with his fellow-conspirators, and rejoin the Plot, before it was too late.

If she had not disappeared, he reflected, it probably would not have occurred to him to seek reunion with the conspiracy at all. He had found enough love and death in her cold arms to last him a lifetime. But without her, he needed to feel again the frisson of peril, the intoxication of absolute faith, the thrill of terror. He knocked on the door, but no-one answered. He thought he could hear sounds of movement from inside the house, but though he waited for some time, there was no sign of life. Was everything ready in there? Was this the calm before the sudden blow, the lull before the storm? Or another silence of vacancy, like the stillness of her empty chamber? Had the Plot been abandoned? Perhaps, after all, the attempt had failed, and they had decided to pass no further.

William decided to seek out Catesby. He crossed the river and walked towards Lambeth, where he knew Catesby's house to be, though he himself had never been there. He passed the warm red-brick front of old Lambeth Palace, with its white fig tree planted by Cardinal Pole. In a tavern he was provided with directions to Catesby's house, and before long found himself standing at the gate. The house was a substantial manor, with a view of the river, surrounded by elegant grounds.

This was a different world from the underground in which he had met with Catesby: this was a world of wealth and privilege, in which a scion of the Catholic gentry lived his daytime life. No-one would guess, thought William, as he walked down the drive, between the fruit-trees and the flowering bushes, that this luxurious façade concealed the means by which an entire society was to be destroyed, and raised up again. For somewhere in Catesby's mansion they had concealed the barrels of gunpowder that had perhaps already been shipped over the river to Westminster, and which now lay beneath the Parliament House, awaiting their fatal ignition.

At the door a servant received him, and told him to wait in the hall. After a few minutes Catesby came down the stairs, and greeted him with a comradely embrace.

"Where've you been, William?" he asked. "We'd almost given you up."

"Better late than never," William replied, conscious of his dereliction.

"Not so late, in fact. Parliament is to be prorogued until 5th November."

"November? I hadn't heard." In truth for weeks he had heard nothing at all about anything that did not affect his nocturnal devotions to his strange dark lady.

"Yes. We heard it from a friend in the House. A pity in a way. We had all ready. And I'd got used to thinking of 3rd October as a historic date of the future. November the 5th doesn't have the same ring to it."

"So the tunnel is completed? The Westminster house seemed to be empty."

"Yes, Fawkes got it done, as he said he would." A slight frown furrowed Catesby's handsome brow, but he shook it away. "The powder," he whispered, pointing to the floor, "is still here."

William felt a sudden unease at the close proximity of such destructive power. He was literally standing over a powder-keg.

"Your arrival is opportune, though, William, since we are planning to transport the barrels across the river to Westminster. We hoped you would be able to find us a boat."

"Yes, of course." He was back in it again now, with a vengeance. He felt a thrill of the old excitement, shadowed by a spectre of doubt, or perhaps just fear. The touch of anxiety made William think for some reason of the men Fawkes had imported from Transylvania. "So Fawkes is still at the house, with his miners?"

Again the little frown creased Catesby's frank and generous features. "Yes. To tell you the truth, William, we've been a bit worried about Guido. He's spent so much time in that house, alone with those men, digging and tunnelling in the darkness. The rest of us haven't been allowed in, so we've never even seen them. He says all is well and the tunnel completed, but … I don't know what it is. Something. You know he's taken to wearing a mask?"

"A what?"

"A mask. Over his face."

"I know what a mask is. I work in the theatre, for God's sake. But what kind of mask? A disguise?"

"Well that's the oddest thing. The mask he wears looks exactly like his own face. He must have had it made to look like himself. It has his nose and cheeks, his moustache and beard, those slanting eyebrows … with a kind of fixed smile. Uncanny. And the eye-holes are lidded, so you can't really see his eyes."

"How bizarre," William replied. "Who on earth would wear a mask that just made him – look like himself?"

"I don't know. He won't explain it. Do any of us show our true faces to the world, William?" Catesby came very close to him, placing his hands on William's shoulders, and looking down into the other man's eyes. "Some seem like the innocent flower, yet prove to be the serpent under it."

Was he talking about the Plot? Or did he suspect William of treachery? The moment passed, and Catesby embraced him again. A warning? William's doubts about the Plot were perhaps written in his face. Maybe he too should start wearing a mask.

Catesby resumed his brisk and authoritative manner. "Fawkes has asked us to come and view the excavation tomorrow night. If all is well, we plan to begin taking the barrels over the river. Go and talk to your boatmen in Southwark, William. Hire a craft for a couple of weeks. Big enough for our purposes. We can row and pilot her ourselves. We are almost ready. For the great day, when history will change for ever. People will always recall the 5th of November."

"Remember."

"Remember what?"

"It rhymes. Remember, remember, the 5th of November."

"So it does! Never occurred to me. How felicitous!"

And Catesby wandered off back into the house, repeating the phrase like a mantra. William was moved, as always, by the stimulating energy of Catesby's charismatic leadership. But as he walked back along the river towards Southwark, his doubts persisted. If the Plot could encompass the desired end; if it could bring, with the king's surcease, success; if this blow could be the be-all and the end-all; then surely the means would be justified? But he could not help brooding on the means, and wondering if they would not inevitably colour and contaminate the end they were meant to serve. A new Catholic monarchy; toleration and freedom; restoration of the true Faith – surely all this was worth a few deaths, and the wrecking of a building or two? The end would justify the means.

But what if that pure, unstained vision of a new world rising, like the Phoenix of Arabia, from the ashes of the old, were in practice to be stained and sullied by the dust and violence of its compassing? Reckless, desperate men, whispering in low taverns of murder and treachery; a dark subterranean tunnel, dug by invisible strangers with hideous features; the cloaked and hooded figure of Fawkes, his identity hidden behind a copy of his own face; a blue flame, a hissing train of powder, a huge earth-shaking blast, a man falling from a burning tower. Was this, truly, the way to change the world for the better?

2 October 1605. Westminster

Fawkes opened the door to William and Percy with the largesse and magnanimity of a landed proprietor showing guests around his stately home. He wore the mask Catesby had described, white with black features, and was otherwise dressed entirely in black, even to a pair of black leather gloves. Not an inch of his skin was showing.

"Welcome, welcome," he said. "It's so good to see you again." His voice rang hollow inside the visor. "Come in, come in."

They entered to find the others already there, standing and sitting around the room: Catesby, Wright, Wintour, and other men William did not know, who had been recruited more recently into the Plot: two recognisable by family resemblance, Tom's brother Robert Wintour, Jack's brother Christopher Wright; and a nervous-looking man Catesby introduced as Frances Tresham. Catesby and Wright were talking amongst themselves. The newcomers seemed ill at ease, stealing covert glances at the visored Fawkes, who offered no explanation of his eccentric disguise.

Without further ceremony Fawkes took up a lantern, and beckoned them all to enter the excavation. One by one they shinned down the ladder into the shaft. At the bottom William noticed that the twenty coffins were all still in place in the five ante-chambers leading off from the main shaft, each now firmly closed, with its silver cross nailed in place. The miners were back at rest, then, so the conspirators would not be meeting them. Fawkes led the way along the tunnel, his lamp illuminating the contours of the excavation, which had been enlarged as well as extended, high enough now to enable a man to walk upright. Soon they reached the old palace wall, the point where William had last seen the tunnel abruptly terminated. But in place of the blank obstacle that had formerly arrested their progress, the tunnel now ran straight through the foundations. The ancient stones had been expertly cut through, shaved and polished, smoothed and rounded off to form an easy access. The wall was indeed, as Catesby had guessed, some twenty feet thick. But its stones now provided a triumphal arch for the victorious entrance of the Gunpowder Plotters under King James's defensive battlements.

The tunnel continued in the same direction for some distance, into the underground cavities of the Palace of Westminster. At last its progress halted, and ended in another vertical shaft that rose into complete darkness. Fawkes waited for the company to form into a circle at the foot of this shaft, and then pointed upwards.

"Above here," he said proudly, "is the cellar beneath the Great Hall." Another ladder stretched up into the gloom, and Fawkes lost no time in ascending. They climbed to the mouth of the shaft, which disgorged them onto the stone floor of a large vaulted undercroft. Fawkes lit several more lanterns to light the place. It was cobwebbed and dusty with neglect, littered about with piles of firewood and broken barrels.

"You see," said Fawkes, raising his lantern to reveal the shadowy corners of the vault. "This is the cellar I spoke of. It is quite cut off from the surrounding chambers. We found a couple of doors that had been bricked up to secure the place. There is no access to it. Except, now, from below, and for us. And we can easily conceal this shaft with planks, so even on inspection, this cellar will seem empty and deserted."

Fawkes set his lantern on the floor and from behind his mask proudly surveyed his subterranean domain, like Satan gloomily perusing the fields of Hell. The devil of the vault. Nobody else spoke. Torchlight flickered across all their shadowy faces, their eyes quick and bright with excitement and fear. Except for the mask of Fawkes, which showed white in the lamplight, offering for decipherment nothing more legible than those immobile, inscrutable features.

Catesby felt the hiatus of hesitation that had paralysed the company, and quickly moved in to break it. "Excellent, Guido. A superb achievement. He is to be congratulated, gentlemen. And now the rest of the work falls to the remainder of us. Tomorrow night we will start to bring the powder across the river from Lambeth, and store it here. William will procure us a boat. Someone must guard this place. Do you want to take a break, Guido? Leave it to the remainder of us for a couple of days? Get some fresh air?"

"No, no," Fawkes replied quickly. "I'm content to remain here. All you need to do is get the barrels into the house, and my men will do the rest."

No-one argued with him. He seemed at ease in his nocturnal, underground world, which no-one else was particularly disposed to share. One by one the conspirators descended the ladder, passed through the tunnel and climbed up at the other end. William paused at the bottom of the shaft, peering through fitful darkness at the neat rows of coffins stacked around it. Something was different.

"Guido," he said, with his foot on the bottom rung of the ladder, "all the coffins are closed. When we brought them here, one was empty. Why is that?"

"Oh," said Fawkes non-committedly, "you wouldn't believe it! That fellow we lost at Foulness found his way here after all. It seems he missed his comrades, and wanted to be reunited with them."

"I see," said William thoughtfully, suspecting the glib explanation. "Resourceful chap."

"So are they all. Consider what they've accomplished," said Fawkes, gesturing back down the tunnel.

By the time William reached the top of the shaft, all the other men had disappeared into the night. He lingered a little, waiting for Fawkes to follow him up.

"I have to ask, Guido," he said as the other man heaved himself over the lip of the excavation. "Where did you get the mask? I could use craftsmanship like that in my own work."

Guido laughed softly at William's apparently innocent inquiry. "Sit a while, William," he said, lowering himself into a chair. "I haven't had anyone to talk to." Then as an afterthought, "Apart from my men, of course."

All around them the night was still and silent. Outside a church clock told the hour. A huge brown cockroach scuttled out of the empty fireplace, followed its questing antennae to rattle and zig-zag across the room, and disappeared into the shaft. William instinctively lifted his feet from the floor. Fawkes paid no attention.

William was ready to listen. Fawkes was silent for a time. Then he spoke, hesitantly, as if something obstructed his speech.

"God," he began, unexpectedly, "has chosen a strange path for me, William. When He created the heavens and the earth, He divided the light from the darkness, and the land from the sea. He made the earth's surface as a home for man, and for the creatures that serve Him. But there are other worlds, alien to man: the depths of the sea, where we cannot go; the spaces beneath the earth; the kingdom of the night. Each world has its proper inhabitants. Who knows what monsters dwell beneath the waves? Seamen tell stories of the Kraken, the giant squid, the sea-serpent. Perhaps they are true. Many creatures make their home under the ground: the worm, the mole, the shrew-mouse. And there are beasts that move easily in the darkness, where we are blind, to hunt and to kill: the cat, the wolf, the bat, the owl. Creatures of the night.

"I was born, like all men, to live in the light of day, to dwell on the surface of the earth. To feel the sun on my cheeks, the wind in my hair. To show my face to the world, to other men and to God. All this has been taken from me. Now, to serve God, I must dwell in the darkness, like the souls in Sheol; toil under the ground, like the slaves of Egypt; and like Moses when he spoke with God, hide my face behind this mask."

"But why?" demanded William impatiently. "I still don't understand. Why the mask?"

"Working here, underground; dwelling in darkness; co-habiting with the creatures of the night – all this has changed my appearance, William. I have no vanity, God knows. I was never handsome like Catesby. A rough soldier's visage was all I ever displayed to the world. But God made me in His image, and it is His image I would not profane by revealing myself in this – altered state."

For a moment there flashed through William's mind the description, in Fawkes's letter from Constantinople, of the men he had brought back to England: the dead eyes, the glistening yellow skin, the corrupting flesh.

"Will you – recover?" asked William. "When this is over?"

"I have a sure and certain hope," replied Fawkes steadfastly, "in God's Providence. At times, to work His will, He will turn His most faithful servant into His greatest adversary."

"How can that be?" asked William incredulously. "St Paul said you cannot serve God and the Devil."

"Come, William," Fawkes retorted. "Think what God did to his servant Job! And the cruel torment He practiced on His only begotten Son, whom He nailed to a cross. Did not Christ Himself, in His agony in the garden, beg His father to release Him from his Passion? And among His last seven words from the Cross, did He not cry out against His Father who had forsaken Him? I have suffered. I suffer still. But I will rise again, as Christ rose on the third day."

William listened in silence. At the window the darkness thinned. "It is time for you to go now, William. Thank you for talking with me."

Methinks I scent the morning air. William suddenly remembered his dark lady, and her infallible matinal valediction. "Have you ever been in love, Guido?" was his impromptu question.

"With a woman?" Guido said, clearly startled by the inquiry. "No. I have loved God, though He has forsaken me. And a few men, like Catesby. I have taken many women, as all soldiers do, in carnal lust. But love? I do not think so ..." His reply tailed off, as if he did not quite know how to answer.

Was he dissimulating? Another mystery. And one not to be resolved that night, as Fawkes was urgent in ushering William out of the house and away.

William's mind spun like a Catherine wheel. Twenty coffins. A man so disfigured as to hide his face, even from his friends. The devil of the vault. Forty barrels of powder. I will rise again, on the third day. The be-all, and the end-all. He crossed the river and made for the moorings of the Southwark boatmen.

4 October 1605. Lambeth

The night was bitter cold. Somewhere in Catesby's garden a rabbit screamed pitifully from between the teeth of a fox. William stood in a group with the others at the back of the house, all cloaked, hatted, booted. Their breath fogged white in the moonlight. A back door opened: Catesby with a dark lantern. Barely audible, whispered instructions. A hooped cask rolled slowly down a ramp towards them. William and Tom Wintour took one end each, and began to trundle it gingerly across the lawn, towards the river and the waiting vessel.

Earlier that day William had secured the loan of a craft from a boatman of his acquaintance. A flat-bottomed barge, of a type commonly used for transportation on the Thames, it was in truth little more than a raft, that slewed and dipped precariously in the swells and eddies of the river. It was far from ideal for shipping barrels of gunpowder, but it was the best he could do. Now he stepped cautiously from the end of Catesby's garden onto its bobbing deck, and took the weight of the first barrel from Wintour. Gunpowder was notoriously unstable. Sliding the cask onto the vessel's low gunwale, he tried to ease its descent into the bottom of the boat, but Wintour lost his grip, and it fell with an audible thud into the shallow hold. The flat barge ducked, and a dark Thames wave slopped across the bows. Both men stood stock-still, like characters in a dumb-show, legs bent at the knees, arms outstretched, waiting for the explosion that would blow them precipitately through the gates of Hell.

The cataclysm did not come, and the barrel lay peacefully on the deck. Both laughed nervously. William leaned his weight on the end of the barrel, and using a technique remembered from his boyhood labours, twisted it on its curve and flipped it over to stand upright. The first cask, safely aboard. Only thirty-nine to go. And in the thrilling moment of terror, William realised, he had forgotten about the dark lady.

The barge took ten barrels without difficulty, but the weight of the cargo set it low in the water, and the tide was running. They judged it safer to make the crossing with what they had. The casks were securely lashed to the boat, and four men – the Wright brothers, Tom Wintour and William – boarded along with them. Wintour took a long paddle at the stern, and steered the barge, while the burly Wrights each manned an oar. William stood in the stern as pilot. Percy pushed them off, and they were running before the tide. A full moon silvered the black waters of the Thames, the softly dipping oars stirred white circles of phosphorescence, and Wintour's improvised rudder traced behind them a glittering wake. They showed no lights, and the river banks were dark and deserted, so William's job as navigator was far from easy. If they missed their destination in the dark, the strongly-flowing tide would carry them on down the river, and it would be the devil's work to row back up again. But soon the grey bulk of the Palace rose from the north bank, and in the glimpses of the moon, William could see the little landing stage that gave access to the garden of their safe house. He signalled to Wintour to steer across, and in minutes the barge was bumping the wooden piles of the jetty. William jumped ashore, and making fast a rope, moored the sinister craft, with its fatal cargo, firmly to the Westminster shore. Glancing up from his concentrated knotting, William flinched to see the white mask of Fawkes hovering in the darkness above him.

"Christ, Guido, you frightened the life out of me," he grumbled, as he gave the mooring rope a last twist round the stanchion. They threw a plank from the barge to the deck of the jetty, and one by one trundled the barrels across. Not a soul was abroad, and nothing stirred. Eventually all ten casks were stored in the front room of the house, and Fawkes had taken charge of them. "Let me take it from here," he said. "By morning we will have them under the Parliament House."

Obediently they left Fawkes to his subterranean labours, re-boarded the barge and pushed off for the south bank. Rowing against the tide was harder, but the craft was now empty, and the muscled arms of the Wright brothers bore them speedily across the river to Lambeth. Back at Catesby's house, a servant opened the door to them, and showed them to chambers where they could sleep.

It occurred to William that this man, whom the others addressed as Bates, would be adjudged in the eyes of the law as culpable together with the master who commanded him, equally guilty of the highest treason. Should they be caught, he would not be spared merely on the grounds of his menial status. And neither would I, thought William, though I am but a poor player, who struts and frets his hour upon the stage, and then is heard no more. In fact, so strongly was the law prejudiced in favour of rank and wealth, that common men like himself and Bates were more likely to feel its most extreme rigour than the gentlemen who were their natural leaders: more likely to be tortured, more likely to be imprisoned, more likely to die. Well, we all owe God a death, William thought, quoting his own line to himself. A good line. But little comfort to him in this extremity.

26 October 1605. Silver Street

On two more successive nights, the same procedure had been repeated. Ten barrels drawn from the cellars of Catesby's mansion; rolled down the garden and loaded onto the barge; shipped across the river, and delivered into Fawkes's keeping at the house in Westminster. On the fourth night they had six barrels aboard, when a word of alarm swept through the company. Each man stopped what he was doing, and held his breath. Percy had spotted a boat, lying low beneath the bank upstream, showing no light, and close enough to observe them. It could have been anyone: fisherman, smuggler, scavenger, spy. Presently the craft slipped away from the bank, and disappeared into the river-mist. Still they were taking no chances. Quickly they secured the six barrels and cast off. Thirty-six casks of powder would be plenty for their purposes.

Everything was ready. The powder was in place beneath the Great Hall, with Fawkes standing by to ignite it when the moment arrived. The others had dispersed to take up their stations and lead the insurrection. Now there was nothing to do but wait. Once again William was alone with his thoughts. Action had absorbed him, and stilled the clamouring of his imagination. Inactivity re-opened the wounds of his passion for the Countess, and they began to bleed again. He sat down to his work, hoping to lose himself again in the cold snows of his dream.

William was struggling with a structural problem in the source he was using for his play, *Measure for Measure*. In the earlier versions of the story, all based on an Italian tale by Cinthio, the heroine, model for his Isabella, is raped by the Duke's deputy, who has her brother executed in any case, and is then forced to marry her to repair her honour. William disliked this denouement, which would require his audience to set aside their natural distaste for Angelo's exploitative lust and rapacious opportunism, his forcing of a holy nun, his judicial murder of an innocent brother; and accept him as a suitable mate for the woman he has violated. All very well for the looser morals of Italy, but a problem for the respectable burghers of Cheapside.

He had been working on a solution to the difficulty, in the form of a new plot-twist, and an additional character. Consider the possibility that Angelo had previously been betrothed to a woman who had, by some means, lost her dowry, and thereby earned his self-interested rejection. Let Angelo's lust be targeted, by some stratagem, on the woman he has jilted. The pious custodian of morality would then find himself in a situation identical to that of Claudio, the young man he has sentenced to death for the same offence: carnally united, albeit unwittingly, to the woman to whom he was affianced. The solution was elegant, exquisite the irony. But how to engineer the predicament?

Think. Think. He had it! The old bed-trick. Crude, but effective. Let Angelo arrange to meet Isabella at night, under cover of darkness, in cloistered secrecy to over-master her. Let the Duke cause Angelo's former betrothed to be supplanted in place of Isabella. There let her lie, cocooned in silk and lace, prone in a reckless abandonment of maiden surrender, a soft sweet dew beading the immaculate rim of her virginity. There let Angelo ravish her, thinking her someone else, thrusting himself into the moist, innocent flesh, his fierce member throbbing and thrilling with the pleasure of violation. And despite himself, all unconsciously, as the flood-gates of his dammed desire burst and drenched her pale pink skin with the thick white spawn of lechery, planting his seed, lawfully, in his own unoccupied and untilled plot.

Now, a name for the woman, for Angelo's betrothed. Something mellifluous, musical. Marina? No. Too aquatic. Too maritime. Nice, though: he would use it again. But he liked the melody. Mmm. Ma. Ah. Maybe three syllables? Yes. Mariana.

Mariana. Young, beautiful, epitome of man's desire, but cast off and abandoned by a man's casual cruelty. What would she do with her life? Why, very little. Sit. Wait. Wait for some anticipated, unexpected eventuality. Something feared and hoped for. A letter. A message. A knock at the door. Good news or bad. Something, anything, other than, different from, this endless waiting for what may never come; and if it comes, when it comes, may be more unwelcome even than this rigorous statute of waiting.

And where would she reside? Somewhere remote, insular, off the beaten track. A house in the country, an isolated homestead. A castle? No, she was too poor. A manor house? Too populous, too connected. Something abandoned, neglected, left alone, like her. A grange! That was it. An old grange, fallen into disrepair. A roof of ancient thatch, weeded and worn. Somewhere on the dreary fens, marshland. A waste of wildfowl and water. Nothing visible for miles across the flat, wet land.

Around the house, an unweeded garden, grown to seed. Tendril and filament of fruit and flower, wild, profuse, drooping despondent with the weight of their own unchecked growth. Branches of pear-tree fallen from the rusty nails that pinned them previously to the gable wall. Unpruned luxuriant vegetation, clustered with blackening moss, home for a hundred flitting flies. Things rank and gross possess it. A wooden gate, sealed with cobwebs. An unlifted latch.

She should be enclosed, insulated, cloistered like Isabella in her convent. Some barrier must sunder the grange from the outside world. A moat! Perfect. A reed-fringed, water-lily-surfaced, carp-harbouring, mayfly-rippling trench, encircling the house. He had her. Mariana. Mariana in the moated grange.

And last, her state of mind. How would she feel, this lovely, lonely woman, from day to day, from year to year? Everything she sees from her window is an occasion of melancholy. The dreary dawn of yet another uneventful day. The dewy eve of yet another sleepless night. Bats flutter across the violet sky. She peeps around her curtains. He cometh not, she says. And then through each long day she flits aimlessly from room to room, all through the dreamy house, without hope of change. Sunbeams lie athwart the rooms, thick with motes of dust, and William thought, for some reason, of the woman Fawkes had described in Dracula's castle, a presence diffused, lightly suspended between sunset and moonrise. As she passes the foxed and tarnished mirror on the wall, her being registers no reflection, but shows as a faint reverberation in the atmosphere, like ripples in water. Barely disturbing the air, except as a taken breath, a soft exhale; then lapsing from solidity into a fluid stream of particles, chased by flickering moonlight from the empty room.

Mariana's world realised itself to him with shocking clarity, with acute precision of sensation. Every door in the old house creaked and groaned on its rusty hinges. A trapped blue-bottle buzzed and sang in a corner of the window. A mouse squeaked shrill from behind the mouldering wainscot. Why such detail? Was this truly the topography of a lonely mind? Or was it rather he, the poet, supplying unsolicited the décor of her interior world with objects, images, things that he could see, and feel, and hear, and smell and taste?

The poet and the dreaming woman. Was there truly any distinction between himself and Mariana? Was he not, like her, a soul cut off, seceded, isolated inside the castle of his own imagination? Did he not instinctively retreat into that secluded fastness among the fens, brooding on what was, what has been, what might have been? All his plays were set firmly in the past: old plots, old societies, old relationships. His fellow playwrights greedily absorbed and reproduced the contemporary scene, establishing a fluid traffic between stage and world. He alone elected to dwell inside that moated grange that represents the past, sealed off from the present by that shimmering, circumambient ring of bright water.

He had written of England in exactly the same figure, a precious stone set in a silver sea. That was what old John of Gaunt had said, in his *Richard II*. This blessed plot. Around it the swelling seas severed and sundered, rose and fell. As a moat defensive to a house. This England. And what was the Gunpowder Conspiracy, but a reactionary attempt to restore that England of the past: its quiet farmsteads and ancestral homes; the piety and dignity of ancient church ritual; the sound of church bells floating across the waters?

He closed his eyes, and thought of Mariana. Once more she drew her curtains by, once more she gazed upon the glooming flats. Would he come today, that looked-for, unexpected stranger? A thunderous knocking echoed through the house. Was it for her? Was this the call? The knocking persisted. Moss-blackened thatch shook as the rafters trembled. Waterfowl noisily rose and clamoured from the reedy moat. Behind the wainscot, a scuttling and squeaking of mice. He comes? He is dead? He will come, but not today? Tomorrow, perhaps? Tomorrow. And tomorrow. This petty pace.

His eyes opened. It was the grain of the wood of the door of his lodgings that rattled and resounded to this importunate rapping of knuckles, that muffled thudding of fist in glove. A summons. An appellation.

"In the name of the king!"

The message was for him.

Examination of William Shakespeare

29 October 1605. The Tower of London

William sat down and looked across the table straight into the eyes of his interrogator. The eyes were cool, composed, nonchalant in a long, strong, confident face. A large chin, and a well-shaped mouth lined with a thin moustache. William had never met him, but knew who he was. Sir Edward Hoby, highly-placed at court, well-connected by family and marriage. His father had translated Castiglione's *Courtier*. His father-in-law was late patron to the Lord Chamberlain's Men, the Earl of Hunsden. He could scarcely be an accidental choice of inquisitor for William Shakespeare.

"Is your name William Shakespeare?"

"It is."

"Repeat it, for the record."

"My name is William Shakespeare."

"You stand accused of conspiring with persons unknown to encompass the king's death. This of course constitutes high treason. What do you have to say?"

"I know nothing of this."

"Nothing? You plead both innocence and ignorance? But we have here a report that puts you under suspicion, barely four years ago, of conspiring to overthrow the late queen's majesty. Your patron and friend the Earl of Southampton was a ringleader of that revolt. Your play, Richard II, showing the abdication of a king, was played twenty times in streets and houses to provoke insurrection. The men of your company were questioned on that matter by the Privy Council. How can you say you know nothing of this?"

"Had I been proven guilty of such treason, My Lord Inquisitor, we would not be having this conversation. A man may live next door to a murderer, yet he is not guilty of his neighbour's crimes."

"Very good. Yet he may be guilty by association, if he fails to alert the authorities to some danger in the state. If he fails to divulge information that might lead to the murderer's arrest. He may be guilty by concealment. You know what the word conspiracy means?"

"Of course I know. I am a writer. Yet still I am not guilty."

"You are suspected now of conspiring with others to assassinate the king's majesty in the Parliament House."

"You cast me as an inveterate regicide. Queen, King, Tudor, Stuart, are they all the same to me?"

"Many kings have died in your plays. Some deposed; some slain in war; some poisoned by their wives; some sleeping killed. All murdered. You have often told the sad stories of their deaths."

"I am glad you know my work. But these deaths are fictional. But fantastical. Poison in jest. My kings are played by actors, mere walking shadows. They are creatures of the imagination. Poetry makes nothing happen."

"This may be so. We are beyond the pale of our inquiry. Did you write this letter?"

"What letter?"

"This letter to my Lord Monteagle. 'Yet I say they shall receive a terrible blow this parliament and yet they shall not see who hurts them.'"

"I know of no such letter."

"But it is in your handwriting."

"How do you know that?"

"We have compared it to specimens of your own hand."

"How do you know they are genuine?"

"They bear your signature."

"Show me."

"Here. And here."

"The hands are not even the same. And the names are spelt differently. This is a forgery. It means nothing."

"I ask you again: did you write this letter?"

"I did not. But I do know something about writing. Let me give you a supposition. Is it not the case that a man might, in certain circumstances, write a letter, and yet the letter be not of his writing? This is a paradox."

"Then resolve it."

"It is for the reader to interpret, not the writer."

"Then let me interpret. Shall I say that you – or someone else – placed these words on paper, but the words were not yours? Or his?"

"I commend your wit."

"If such a man say he did not write it, irrespective of the source of the words, would he not be lying?"

"Not necessarily. He might be equivocating."

"Ah, yes. We know all about equivocation. You palter with us in a double sense, and lie like truth."

"I am a poet, sir. I do not use words as they are used in ordinary language. Double sense is my domain. The truest poetry is the most feigning. I lie to render truth."

"So there is no connection between the writing, and the man who writes?"

"In the case of my art, none. Plato would have no poets in his Republic, for he held them liars every one."

"I see. Tell me, do you recognize this poem? It is a sonnet, I believe."

"Where did you get this from?"

"From a gentleman whose house we had occasion to search. Is it one of yours?"

"Yes it is."

"What does that line mean, you see there: 'every word doth almost tell my name?'"

"Yes, but not literally, 'tell my name'. Only if the reader

already knows who it is. You cannot identify a man from his poem."

"Really? 'Showing their birth, and whence they did proceed'. I put it to you that there can be only one meaning here: that the poem does identify the man. That his words express his meaning. That the poem is a confession. You do not agree?"

"Still, I did not write that letter."

"Master Shakespeare, if we are to proceed in this way, I may as well give your answers myself. You will say that you – or your imaginary friend – were compelled to write those words. That you – or he – were in fear of your life. That the man who forced them to be written would have killed the writer had he – you – refused. That he will kill you now, if you admit to me his true name. Then we will torture you, until you reveal his name, and the names of his associates. Do you wish to be tortured?"

"Does any man?"

"You have seen, as I have, in these strange latter days, many men, even women, willingly place themselves in certain peril of torture, execution, dismemberment, all the grievous penalties of the law. Why do you think they do this?"

"They love, and hate. As the poet says, *odi et amo.*"

"Catullus. Another paradox. This one you will expound, I think."

"Gladly. They love what they have lost, what they believe has been taken from them. And they hate those they hold responsible for the taking."

"Call it love or hate, such passions have burnt men and women to cinders. Do you love and hate, Master Shakespeare?"

"I am not talking about myself."

"No. You do not seem to me of the stuff martyrs are made."

"It is true. I lack both the fortitude and the courage. The fortitude to withstand torture; the courage to die for an ideal. I am both weak, and a coward."

"In this case weakness is loyalty, and cowardice obedience."

"Then in obedient weakness, I offer my cowardly loyalty to His Majesty, if he will have it. I have done nothing wrong. You have no evidence against me. I have powerful friends to vouch for me. Your threats of torture are mere bugs to fright boys. You simply hope to glean from me some stray husk of information that might accidentally fall from my verbal reaping-hook as it slices through the grain-field of your questions. I know your game, Master Inquisitor. But it is over. Let me go, or charge me with some offence. The choice is yours. Now may I, by your leave, return to my cell? I have a play to write."

Hell

30 October 1605. The Tower of London

Back in his cell after his examination by Sir Edward Hoby, William placed his hands on the embrasure of the window to stop them from trembling. Fear shook him, as a terrier shakes a rat. The effort of retaining his composure throughout the interrogation had been almost too much for him. Now the reaction was enough to shatter all his bulk, and end his being. He kept his face towards the window, in case anyone was watching him from behind the door.

He had been arrested at his lodgings in Silver Street the previous morning, and brought straight to the Tower. No charges, no accusations, no explanation. He was shown to a cell that surprised him by its relative opulence of light, and air, and modest though not uncomfortable furnishings of bed, and chair and table. It was very like the cell Harry Wriothsley, Earl of Southampton, had occupied during his long sojourn in the Tower after the fall of Essex. A nobleman's quarters, rather than a dungeon for a peasant.

He was not, it seemed, to be mistreated with the usual privations of darkness, and damp, and short and musty straw. He had no idea why, having expected the worst. Unless this apparent gentleness was simply a tactic to put him off his guard, confuse him, render him easier to break. He was not left short of food, or drink; in fact he was liberally supplied with both. There on a sideboard lay bread, and cheese, and even a flask of brandy. Why this insistent but inexplicable hospitality? The most remarkable detail was the fact that all the books and papers from his lodgings had been gathered up, transferred wholesale and neatly laid out in his cell. Even the manuscript of *Measure for Measure*, that had lain half-finished on his desk, was now placed invitingly on the table under the window. There beside it were pens, and ink, and salt, and all the appurtenances of the writer's craft. As if there were someone behind all this, who for some reason didn't want him to stop writing ...

From his interrogation he gathered that he had been betrayed to the authorities, but he could not imagine by whom. Unless it was that shifty new fellow, Frances Tresham. He had no inkling at all as to who wrote the letter, though as a "man of letters" he was the obvious prime suspect to be the conspiracy's amanuensis. The letter was apparently sent to Lord Monteagle. A Catholic peer. Warned, for his own safety, to avoid the opening of Parliament. Was not Tresham a kinsman of his? Surely he was. That explained why Tresham should tip him off, but not why he, William, should have been the only one fingered for the crime. The others should be alerted, but he had no means of communicating with them. If he *was* the only one ... Was the game up? Were the others here already, all kept isolated in their separate cells? Or was it rather a happy accident that he, the least of the conspirators, was the only one they had been able to find? In which case all he had to do was bide his time, keep his mouth shut and wait. If all went ahead as planned, his release would come soon enough.

He might as well get on with the play. It was not going well. He had reached that point in the story where the young man, Claudio, lies in prison, awaiting his execution for the crime of fornication. With the Powder Plot weighing heavily on his mind, this enforced dwelling of the imagination on thoughts of incarceration, and beheading, rendered the process of writing stubborn and intractable. Moreover, the old tale was heavy with virtuous characters, who insisted on labouring the glamour of goodness in long sententious speeches of moral probity. The night was cold, so he slung his cloak about his shoulders, and was as comfortable here as anywhere. Occasionally he would hear a door grate on its hinges, and catch for a moment a sound of someone sobbing. The claims of another's misery he put firmly from his mind. If he was to die, then let the play be his epitaph. If to live, then it would need to be finished and ready for the theatre by the time he was released.

He took up his pen. The Duke has entered the prison disguised as a friar, and is counselling the young man to accept his fate. William forced himself back to the page, and continued to dictate the Duke's long-winded celebration of death. Be absolute.

> Be absolute for death; either death or life
> Shall thereby be the sweeter.

Catesby, Percy, Fawkes, they were absolute for death. To them life was ground down to a sharp point, like a finely-honed blade. They seemed, in their very being, to feel themselves as instruments of a noble purpose, their personal destinies subjected to a larger cause. Perhaps it was a soldier's philosophy, a kind of chivalry that enabled this studied disregard for the body, this disciplined burnishing of the spirit to its full brave brightness. William had heard Spanish and Portuguese travellers speak of the Japanese *Samurai*, warriors who practised a philosophy known as *Zen*. They had spoken of a "Way of the Warrior" that was synonymous with a resolute acceptance of death. "The Way of the Warrior is death," they would say. "This means choosing death whenever there is a choice between life and death." The *Samurai* believed in a Void, a great nothingness at the centre of the universe, and tried through meditation and discipline to make contact with it. This achieved, the soul was entirely free from care and anxiety.

> Thou art not thyself;
> For thou exist'st on many a thousand grains
> That issue out of dust.

"If you keep your spirit correct from morning to night," says the *Samurai*, "accustomed to the idea of death and, resolved on death, and consider yourself as a dead body, thus becoming One with the Way of the Warrior, you can pass through life with no fear of failure." How liberating it would be, to feel that perfect detachment from mortality, to see the self as an amorphous cloud of atoms blowing on the wind! To be at one with the powers of the air, free from the cowardice of the flesh!

He, William, was neither a soldier, nor a philosopher. His genius was too closely enmeshed with the body, its appetites and desires, its pleasures and pains, its perceptions and sensations, to detach himself so completely from the corporeal realm. He could never be absolute for death: the triumph of life, the imperative to live, was too strong in him. Yet he must give to his Claudio at least the show of resignation:

> To sue to live, I find I seek to die,
> And seeking death, find life.

Why, Claudio can be as mealy-mouthed as his ghostly counsellor! But he cannot mean it: not in his heart. William poured brandy into a glass from the flask, on the table, and drank it at a draught. He was tired. Be absolute for death. Now to bring in Claudio's sister, the chaste and beautiful nun, Isabella. She too will exhort the young man to bid farewell to the flesh, and encounter darkness as a bride. She holds the key to her brother's fate: all she would need to do, to release him from his terrible punishment, is to lie with Angelo. But this she cannot do, for she too is absolute, not for death, but for her own purity. You must die, she tells Claudio.

> Your best appointment make with speed;
> Tomorrow you set on.
> Is there no remedy?

None, but such remedy, as to save a head
To cleave a heart in twain.

A woman's virtue, for a man's life. His head, or her heart. What kind of equivalence is this? What kind of woman would refuse to open her legs, if it might unlock her brother's prison cell? What kind of woman would outlive her brother, to see her white maidenhead stained with his red blood? Let her make it plain to him: all she would have to do.

If I would yield him my virginity
Thou mightst be freed.

Now, let's see how determined this young man is to embrace sharp death! Now he knows what a little thing stands between him and reprieve: his sister's virtue. Sure, he will be thinking, it is no sin. The chance of life now is working within him, like a hectic in the blood. As surely as a pulse beats in his veins, so must his very soul cry out to live.

Death is a fearful thing …

To die, and go we know not where. Claudio must imagine it, the life beyond, Hell and all its terrible punishments. But how to envisage that undiscovered country? Where to find a map, a description, an itinerary?

Of course. He reached over to his books, stacked tidily in a portable bookshelf, and pulled across a volume. A geography of Hell. Dante's *Divina Commedia*, the latest edition, done in Florence by Domenic Manzani, borrowed from his old Stratford friend, the publisher Richard Field. *L'Inferno*. He began to read. "*Nel mezzo del camin di nostra vita …*" The exquisite music of the Italian verse lulled his senses. His head lolled onto the table. Sleepy dullness in that instant weighed his senses down, and the true path he left.

* * *

He was in a wood, though he had no recollection of how he got there. It was a pine forest on a hillside, of the kind he remembered from his travels in Italy, Tuscany perhaps. The trees were so tall they shut out the light. His shoeless feet scuffed the leaf-meal forest floor. Through the trees he caught glimpses of a high sunlit pasture, and longed to be there, for the darkness of the wood struck a cold fear into his heart, but he had no idea how to retrieve the path.

Ahead he saw a clearing with a small grassy hill, and made his way towards it. Then he stopped in his tracks, for on the mound there stood a hooded figure, clad in a floor-length robe of antique design. The light was behind the other, his face in shadow. But William's inexplicable fear of the wood prompted him to seek help from this stranger.

"Have mercy on me," he cried, feeling the words to be oddly familiar, like an involuntary quotation. "Whether you be man, or spirit. Help me."

"*Non omo,*" replied the other, "*omo gian fui …*"

"I don't speak Italian," said William, immediately recognizing the angular, brown features, the hooked nose, the jutting chin.

"*Poeta fui …*"

"You can skip the introduction. I know who you are. Sorry, were. But this is my dream, and if you want to be in it, you'll have to speak English."

"Very well," replied the shade. "I will speak in impeccable seventeenth-century English."

"That's better. I too am a *poeta*, and though this may not be my story, I'm doing the dialogue. And yes, I have read your book, interminable as it was. You're going to lead me through Hell, so I'll see the error of my ways and repent. So let's get on with it."

"Yes, I am to be your guide."

"Then lead on."

Dante's ghost led the way back into the forest, down a hill that started as an incline, became a steep slope and ended in a precipice. How fearful 'tis and dizzy to cast one's eye so low. Beneath, unfathomable darkness. Here sighs, with lamentations and loud moans, resounded through the starless air. A multiplicity of tongues, fear translated into every language, universal cries of terror whirled upwards from a depth of solid darkness, like grains of sand in a whirlwind.

This was clearly the short tour, since William found himself almost immediately in the Second Circle of Hell, where the souls of the lustful are blown forever on the winds of their own passion. Here light was silent. From the air came a noise like the sea, vexed by warring winds. And there he saw them, like a flock of starlings in winter, rising and falling on the gusts; or like a skein of geese strung out upon the sky, clamouring their disconsolate song; the spirits of those who lived and died for love. There he saw all the souls he had read of in Dante's poem: Semiramis and Dido and Cleopatra and Helen; Achilles and Paris and Tristan, and thousands like them. And there he saw the murdered lovers, Paola and Francesca, riding the blast in a close embrace, happy in their mutual misery, together, as they had sworn to be, for all eternity.

"You've read this before," said Dante. "But look over there."

Riding towards them through the air was a small group of spirits, five or six, who moved together in what seemed a slow and stately dance. As they approached, he could see that one was a woman, the others men. One man played a viol, and the rest performed a courtly dance, changing hands, circling one another, keeping a music of time, yet gazing with the saddest faces William had ever seen. He fixed his eyes on the woman, a beautiful brunette with dark almond eyes and a rosebud mouth. A gold chain with a pendant 'B' almost, but not quite, concealed the thin red line that circled her neck.

"They all wanted her once," said Dante, "and now they have her, for ever. And she has them. But she has lost everything else."

It was Anne Boleyn, with the men who died for her: Smeaton, Norris, Brereton, Rochford, and brother George. William burst into tears. "She was guilty then! Yet she bore a gentle mind, and surely heaven's blessings follow such creatures!"

"A sweet new style. I think you should write a play about her."

"And show this?" said William, pointing to the long-suffering sinners, tears running down his face.

"What's the matter?" asked Dante. "Why so sad?"

Anne smiled down at William and blew him a kiss, as with her sad adulterous consort she floated slowly past. Even on the scaffold she had shown a goodly smiling countenance, and she showed it still. Much joy and pleasure in death.

"There are worse places," Dante continued, looking round him and obviously comparing it to other possibilities.

"So this," said Shakespeare, wiping his eyes, and conscious of his own unredeemed promiscuity, "is where I am to spend eternity?"

A smile creased Dante's grained wooden features, like a crack in seasoned timber, and he shook his head.

"Where then?"

Dante held out his right hand, and with his index finger pointed downwards.

"Oh," replied William. "I see. Let's hope I wake up before we get there."

And before the sentence was completed, they were there. Transport in Hell had improved since Dante's time. The Seventh Circle. Beneath their feet an arid, thick Saharan sand. William's bare feet winced at the heat from below, and Dante pulled him up onto a low brick ledge skirting the desert. The sand was covered with souls in agony, singed from below and scorched from above, for the hot air was filled with floating flakes of fire, raining continually down like snow in a windless Alpine storm. Some sinners lay supine on the sand, others sat with heads between their knees, while many walked and hopped about in vain attempts to escape the heat. Their hands were never still, as they flapped and swatted at their burnt bodies to shake off fresh brands of torment that fell continually from a blazing sky.

They paced along the wall, and William saw the spirits of many he had known, and many he had read of, all condemned for the one apparently universal sin of sodomy. A group of souls came skipping past, flailing with their arms to brush away the angry sparks. One of them scrutinised William closely, then reached up and grabbed him by the hem of his garment. William bent down to examine him closely, and though disfigured so, he knew him: within that scorched, baked countenance he recognized the beauteous face of one he had loved, and long lamented. A fallen angel.

"Kit!" he cried, "you, here!"

"The same," replied the shade, his old smile breaking through cracked, parched lips. "Go on without me," he called to his companions.

"Hell's not a fable, then?" suggested William, unable to resist the jest, even as the tears fell for his suffering friend.

"I'm still not convinced," said Marlowe, knocking away a redhot flake of fire. "That's the power of scepticism. Hell may be just a state of mind. But does it make any difference? You're only dreaming, but I can see sweat pouring down your face. Or is it tears? Don't you feel the heat as I do? Don't you feel the pain?"

"Not quite," said William, keeping to the safety of his ledge.

"Or shall we say not yet?"

"All this, just for loving tobacco and boys?"

"Yes. And I did say that St John the Evangelist was bedfellow to Christ, and leaned always in his bosom, and that Christ used him as the sinners of Sodom. So I asked for it. Oh, it could have been much worse. They could have got me on blasphemy, or even murder. Accessory. Every time I gave secret information to the government, people disappeared. They must be down here somewhere, though fortunately I haven't met any of them."

"You were a spy, then?"

"Aren't you? You must be crazy. The pay's much better than you get for writing."

"But your work, Kit; your work lives for ever. You were the father of all of us, though you died so young. None of us would have done anything without your mighty line, your exquisite music."

"Yes, yes, I know. I did make something of myself. The thought keeps me going, even down here. And at least this is a social circle. I have plenty of friends. Nobody cares any more what we do. I'm quite a favourite with some of the lads, even with these unhealing sores."

"Well, to be honest your skin was never that good."

"So you'll be joining us before long? I look forward to it. It'll be like old times."

"I really don't know. My guide, there, he's not especially communicative. He talks in Italian and riddles."

Marlowe peered through the hot air to observe Dante, who was keeping to the other side of the wall. "Oh, him! That was always his way. Master of the cryptic conundrum. 'He shall not feed on neither earth or pilfering/But upon wisdom, and on love and virtue;/Betwixt two Feltros shall his nation be.' Who the hell was he talking about? Has anybody managed to find out?"

Dante signalled to William that they should proceed. "I'll pray for you, Kit," William said with genuine feeling.

"Won't make any difference to me, I'm afraid. But it might make you feel better. I should have prayed when I could. I had the knowledge, and the gift. I saw, with my own eyes, the firmament, streaming red with Christ's blood. One drop would have saved my soul. Now I'm like the rich man in Hades: I'd settle for a drop of moisture."

"But like Lazarus, covered in sores. Is there anything I can do?" pleaded William.

"Give me a kiss," said Marlowe. "Quickly, while he's not looking."

William bent down to plant a kiss on the burnt forehead.

"No you fool, a French kiss, on the lips."

He placed his open mouth on the shade's searing lips, and briefly felt the flickering touch of a cauterized tongue. Spittle was sucked out of him like so much steam.

"That should ease me for the next thousand years," said Kit cheerfully. "Now be on your way. Remember me to the old gang. I have to catch up." And he ran off into the desert, as if running a fast race, looking more like a winner than a loser, with the speed of an athlete chasing a prize.

William watched him go. And in an instant, he and Dante were again somewhere else. After the stifling heat of the Seventh Circle, William's skin was flayed by the stinging of an intense cold. As he turned around, he saw in front of him, under his feet, a lake made all of ice, that seemed more glass than water. Veiled in a shroud of mist, yet thicker by far than any that, in the harsh winter-time, wreaths Austrian Danube, or the Russian Don. Beneath the glacial surface William could see the blurred shapes of dolorous souls encased in frost. Each one concealed his face in the thick-ribbed ice; each mouth smoked with cold; and every eye gave witness to the sadness of the heart.

As Dante led him across the ice, William peered through the distorting gelatinous prism to see if he could recognize any of the agony-contorted faces buried beneath. But he knew no-one here. This was the Ninth Circle. Caina: the final resting-place of the murderer. This was no place for him. He had murdered no brother, and knew no-one who had. Why then was it being shown to him? They reached a kind of edge, like the brink of a frozen lake, and he saw, leading downwards, steps cut into the ice as if with some sharp tool. Following his guide, his bare feet raw with pain, he limped and slid down the brittle grey steps, slippery with melting ice. Finally they emerged into a kind of cellar beneath the glacier, a huge chamber completely empty of any sign of life, or after-life. Here Dante stopped, and stepped aside to let him observe.

The walls of the cellar were constructed from some material William had never seen. It was like stone, but softer and more featureless; like plaster, but harder and more porous. It seemed man-made, yet bore no trace of any human skill or artistry. Yellow and grey by turns, it exuded a strange hopelessness, a mean and sordid acceptance that even bare survival was hardly worth the effort. The roof of the chamber was formed from the thick-ribbed ice of the great glacier of Caina, and from its edges melting water trickled in places down the walls, adding a sensible frigidity to their inhospitable coldness.

William had never seen, or felt, in reality or imagination, so dreadful a place, so deep and despondent a pit of despair. To be held hostage here! A place helpless, hopeless, raw, unfinished. All hope died within him as he looked at it. To be imprisoned here, with no hope of rescue, no prospect of escape, was the most awful fate he could imagine. A cold fear snatched at his heart.

"Master, what is this place? I read nothing like this in your book. Is this a new addition to the mansions of Hell?"

"It is," said Dante, his voice soft and serious. "From the birth of the human race, the nine circles of Hell have served the cause of justice. All sins, with their punishments, could be contained within them. But a new kind of sin demands a new kind of punishment, a new place of penance. This is the Tenth Circle. As yet it has no inhabitants. It is reserved for a special kind of sin, committed by one who deliberately slaughters innocents in the prosecution of a cause. The sin has a new name too, since it contains a multiplicity of crimes – theft, betrayal, blasphemy, murder – and yet is worse than any of them. It bears the name of Terror."

"But why is there no-one here?"

"They have yet to arrive. They will be here soon."

"And what will be their punishment?"

"Only this: to be held hostage here, in continual dread of violence. Their hands and feet will be bound fast. They will be hooded, or blindfolded, so they can see nothing. At every moment, demons will torment them, threatening to beat, or torture, or behead them. Or they will promise them release, and then renege on the promise, and laugh out loud at their disappointment. There will be no hope of reprieve: only an eternity of fear. From time to time their hoods will be removed, so they can see the awfulness of this place. They chose it for others; now Justice has chosen it for them."

William stood in the midst of his own nightmare, and shook with cold and dread. Did he really believe, really fear, that such a fate awaited him after death? What was it Kit had said? "Hell may be just a state of mind." And if it was? Was this in fact the place he had already entered when he joined the conspiracy?

"'Why, this is Hell,'" Dante quoted, reading his thoughts: "'Nor are we out of it.'"

"Master: save me," said William, clasping his quivering hands together in prayer.

"Save yourself," replied Dante. "All you have to do is wake up."

* * *

The lights burned blue. Did he wake, or sleep? Christ Jesu, where had he been? What had he witnessed? There was still some brandy in the bottle. Quickly he poured and gulped. The drink flamed in his throat and fired his belly. His play. The page lay half-written. Claudio's speech: his fears of death and Hell. Now he had the words.

Ay, but to die, and go we know not where;
To lie in cold obstruction and to rot;
This sensible warm motion to become
A kneaded clod …

Such oblivion would be a relief to the horror he had seen this long night past. The dread did not lie there, but in the fear of something after death. The terror of unending pain:

… and the delighted spirit
To bathe in fiery floods, or to reside
In thrilling region of thick-ribbed ice;
To be imprison'd in the viewless winds,
And blown with restless violence round about
The pendent world …

Yet there was worse. The windswept lovers, tossed on the chaos of desire; the scorching sodomites, sharing the lesions of their incendiary wounds; the murderers, fixed in the frigid decisiveness of their homicidal will – all bore the dignity of their crime, together with the pain of its proper penalty. All spent eternity inside that critical moment of rapture, seduction or surrender within which they sacrificed themselves to sin. Hell was their state of mind. But those for whom the Tenth Circle waited? No dignity for them, no glamour, no consciousness of justice. Not for those who had subjected others to indignity, and blown all justice into the clouds. Only a forever of boredom, and apathy, and inertia. They were worse than worst. Bound and hooded, manacled and blind, nowhere to go but the memory of their own guilt, nothing to contemplate but the horror of their own deeds. And when their blindfolds were removed, was it better or worse? Watching the blankness of those featureless walls; staring at the restless twitching of imprisoned limbs; gazing on the flickering horror that lived in all their eyes.

... or to be worse than worst
Of those that lawless and incertain thought
Imagine howling: 'tis too horrible!

To be worse than worst. He knew now there was such a thing. To commit evil beyond the possibility of forgiveness; to abrogate God's destructive power; to seek revenge on the innocent for wrongs not of their doing. Vengeance is mine, saith the Lord; I will repay. The ravens were coughing below his window. The sky grew pale. Beyond the old stone walls, the city stirred. Bells summoned him. As soon as it was light, he would ask for an interview with Master Secretary Cecil.

Discovery

30 October 1605. Burleigh House, The Strand, London

Early the next morning after his vision of Hell, William was bundled into a boat, rowed through Traitor's Gate, and shipped up the Thames to a landing-stage by Charing Cross. There his guards transferred him to a closed carriage, which set off in the direction of the Strand. No chances were taken of his being identified. Exiting the carriage, he recognised the double-fronted, red-brick, three-story mansion, with its four corner turrets, as Burleigh House, old William Cecil's "rude cottage." He was escorted discreetly through the front door, and ushered into a long room that was full of paper.

Bundles, dockets, reams and quires. Tied with ribbon, tied with string. Sealed with sealing wax, bound in leather. Parchment, vellum, papyrus. Leaf after leaf, sheet after sheet of writing. A frozen whirlwind of intelligence, information, data. At the end of it, behind a big desk, reading, in the grey light from the rear windows, one paper, and writing on another, the large-headed, tiny-bodied, hunchbacked figure of Robert Cecil, Earl of Salisbury, Secretary of State to his Imperial Majesty, King James the Sixth of Scotland, and the First of England.

The usher who preceded William whispered in Cecil's ear. The little man nodded, and without looking up, gestured with his quill towards the opposite side of the desk. William did not know whether to stand or sit, but as Cecil himself seemed to be seated, he chose the latter position.

After a few moments, to his horror, without any discernible elevation, Cecil walked round the desk to greet him. The Secretary had been standing. He was little taller than a dwarf. William tried to rise, but Cecil with open palms indicated he should stay seated. William knew all about body language, submission and dominance, superior and inferior positions, and was impressed by Cecil's instinctive mastery of the dramatic arts. With one simple trick he had discomposed his visitor, characterised himself as gracious and tolerant, and avoided the embarrassment of standing next to a much taller man.

Cecil drew up another chair to the corner of the desk, and perched on it, across from William, his legs failing to touch the floor. Again the physical placing was strategic. Then he listened carefully to everything the other man had to say.

William confided a synopsis of what he knew, naturally diminishing his own role in the conspiracy, and avoiding the naming of his co-conspirators. He protested that he knew by hearsay about the Plot, but was not directly acquainted with the perpetrators. All the information had come to him by random and accidental circumstances. He mentioned nothing of the tunnel, or the Westminster house, or the Thames crossing, all of which led of course straight to Catesby's house. He omitted the more bizarre features of the plot, such as Fawkes's journey to Transylvania, the shipwreck, the miners. He described the vault beneath the Parliament House, but admitted nothing of how they had gained access to it. Let the king's guards hack their way into the cellar from the adjoining apartments. The more detail he admitted to knowing, the more likely it was that he had been directly involved. The cover story was as flimsy and transparent as gauze, but he hoped the value of his intelligence would go some way towards ingratiating himself with the authorities.

Even before he had finished his confession, however, the feeling grew on him that all this circumlocution, aimed at exculpating him, was a waste of time. The Secretary's face remained impassive and indecipherable. There seemed to be no way of penetrating Cecil's knowledge, or outflanking his intelligence. By the end of their conversation, William had no idea whether the Secretary knew everything, or nothing; suspected everyone, or no-one; had already taken steps to crush the conspiracy, or would be very surprised if it proved to be true at all. He seemed in no hurry to inform the king, who was out at Royston on one of his frequent hunting trips, even though the Plot was a manifest threat to the king's life. He seemed quite incurious as to the identities of the traitors, and only mildly concerned with the powder.

If anything, he was more interested in William's poetry and plays, of which he claimed to be a passionate devotee. He preferred to talk of *Julius Caesar* and *Hamlet* than of kingship and treachery. Cecil's large, liquid eyes betrayed no hint of fear, anger or even anxiety over what William had told him. Does this man know everything? William thought to himself. Has he been privy to the Plot all along, merely waiting for it to ripen, like a snake's egg, before swooping on the viper's nest? In which case William had perhaps decided to turn king's evidence not a minute too soon.

Though it was difficult, in all honesty, to guess at what Cecil had in mind for him. The Secretary seemed genuinely uncertain himself. Thoughtfully he toyed with a paper-knife, spinning it on his desk, as if to see which way, when it came to rest, the blade would point. Does my life hang on the final direction of that spin? thought William to himself. The point towards my breast? Or the handle towards my hand?

Cecil seemed to come to a decision, and stayed the dagger before it stopped spinning, its tip safely pointing away from either of them. "You are wondering what I intend to do with you," he said, looking up at William with an inscrutable expression. "Clearly, Master Shakespeare, you have got yourself mixed up in a very dangerous business, and with some very desperate characters. You are guilty of high treason. You deserve a cruel and violent death."

He rose from his chair, went over to the window, and looked out across the parterres and ornamental fountains of Covent Garden. Again William was shocked by how short he was.

Majesty shrunk to the size of a child! My power is vested in weakness.

"But you have clearly repented of your crime, and thrown yourself upon our mercy. You have offered us information that may prove useful in apprehending some of these villains, whose names we already know. And above all, Master Shakespeare" – and he turned back towards William with a smile – "we all love your plays. His Majesty finds them particularly delightful."

William was privately surprised to hear that the king had ever been sober enough to notice what play was being acted before him, but he held his peace.

"Nobody wants you dead. There's not enough good entertainment in the world for us to kill off our best poets. But we will need to keep you in the Tower for a while. You are housed there quite comfortably, I believe? Good, good. Your stay will be extended, for perhaps two or three months, while we arrest, try and execute these traitors. It will be far too dangerous for you out there. And in any case, we may need you to identify someone, or corroborate some evidence, or expand upon your confession. Hopefully not. I'd rather keep you out of it as much as possible."

"You are very gracious, my Lord," said William sincerely. "I am forever indebted to your mercy."

"Oh, let's not talk too much about mercy. Mercy is for the weak. For the moment we must appear ruthlessly strong. And you can't hope to get off scot free, you know, if that's what you're thinking. Can you? Your life is being exchanged for your loyalty."

Oh God, thought William, he wants me to be a spy. A double agent. Put me back into play. Like Kit. Haven't I had enough of all this? Will I have to hang round filthy taverns in Deptford, take it up the bum from hairy Spaniards, end up getting a dagger in the eye?

Cecil seemed to guess his thoughts. "Nothing excessive, Shakespeare. We don't want to waste your talent. On the contrary, we want you to write a play for us. A royal commission. While you're a guest, staying with us at His Majesty's pleasure. Think of it as a sabbatical, a writing retreat. A play, dealing with these late events. Showing the evils of ingratitude, and the chaos that dogs the heels of disobedience. A wise, tolerant and gracious king, threatened by a violent and unprovoked assassination. The plot discovered, and the traitors brought to justice. You seem to be in a good position to undertake such a commission, do you not?"

"I have a play half-written, which I must finish," said William. Was it a mistake to suggest reluctance? Quickly he added, "But it won't take me long."

"Ah, yes. You may complete that first. You will have plenty of time. *Measure for Measure*, I believe it is called? An appropriate title, if ironic in the circumstances. For while those disloyal ingrates will taste the true measure of their treason, you will be saved from your deserts, by an entirely undeserved act of clemency."

"That's actually the point of the play, Your Excellency," put in William hesitantly. "True justice is not an eye for an eye, but the free gift of grace. St Paul. Epistle to the Romans."

Perhaps the time was ill-chosen for either literary criticism or theology. Cecil's eyes hardened, just a fraction. "We'll see about that. And talking of eyes, I do have one outing planned for you, to relieve your confinement. An early morning visit to the Old Palace Yard at Westminster, where you will be able to use your eyes to full advantage. What you see there, you will perhaps bear in mind, next time you feel inclined to be drawn into a treasonable conspiracy to assassinate your king."

Cecil rang a little bell, and picked up his pen. The usher appeared at William's elbow. "And start thinking about that new play," the Secretary called after him, without looking up from his writing, as he was led towards the door. It was not a request.

30 October 1605. The Tower of London

William was led back to his cell in the Tower, where he began to think about Cecil's instructions. Clearly he had no choice but to write the play.

The Gunpowder Plot was over. The conspiracy was betrayed, by others long before him; the plot was discovered, the perpetrators proclaimed; they were already arrested, or on the run. William had no means of knowing exactly what was happening outside the perimeter of the old stone walls that immured him. How could he begin to write a play about it, without any direct knowledge? Though even in so secure a prison as this, the whispering tongues of rumour blew like the wind, scattering truth and half-truth, fact and speculation, documentary narratives lavishly embroidered with the embellishment of fantasy.

Still, was this a sound basis for authorship? Perhaps it was, indeed, the right way for a writer to engage with history: trapped in a stone-walled cell, his only freedom the exercise of imagination. Listening attentively to every hushed conversation, every tapped message, every door that opened and closed, every footfall in every echoing corridor. Piecing together what he knew, with what he perceived, and what he conjectured. Crafting the epic story of the Gunpowder Plot as if it were a legend from the past, an old tale in which he had played no part. He took pen and paper and started to write. A title? *November the Fift*. He liked that. But was it to be his play, or Robert Cecil's? The Secretary would want it called something like *The Devil of the Vault*. All right. He could come back to the title. It was his play. He could still find ways of saying what he wanted to say.

Could he write it? He had written nothing before that documented the present. Unless you count that frolic about the horny housewives of Windsor. He had only written that to please the queen, who had asked him to give Falstaff another outing. His plays were all set at a distance, in the past, in some far-off land. Nothing too near. He doubted if his gift extended to a dramatization of today.

And in any case, if he wrote a contemporary play, was this the play Cecil had commissioned? It would be received as too real, too true, too even-handed, too sympathetic towards the enemies of the state. They would want something much more black and white, something about the polarities of good and evil. A perfect king, who was a father to his people: generous, tolerant, loving. A murderer devoured by envy, goaded to violent madness by ingratitude. An assassin with no motive; a rebel without a cause.

It was no use. Perhaps he would give Ben Jonson *November the Fift*. He owed him a favour. The seed of his Gunpowder Play would need to be sought further off, in the dark backward and abysm of time. He would need to travel back to the king-killing *medium aevum*, and find there an appropriate story. One he could thickly encode with his own deepest feelings, without ever betraying them to the authorities, or the multitude. A play of darkness, and horror, and blood. He would look into his Holinshed.

31 January 1606. Old Palace Yard, Westminster

In due course William found himself a spectator at the fifth and final act of this strange, eventful tragedy. By this time he had learned the whole story of the foiled plot and its aftermath. The Monteagle letter, its contents shared among a few frightened Catholic nobles, and then dutifully reported to Cecil, had divulged the plot to common knowledge, and triggered the state's hasty and violent crackdown. The Catholic nobles, many of whom, William knew, had covertly promoted the insurrection, stood aside and denied any complicity, leaving their sons to the state's mercy. It was as if Abraham had given Isaac the knife, bid him sacrifice himself, and then run ignominiously away. Many of William's informers were convinced that the authorities had a complete knowledge of the plot, perhaps even from those same recusant lords, long before the receipt of the letter, and were merely waiting for it to "ripen." They certainly knew the identities of the ringleaders, since their names were immediately posted as wanted men, a proclamation that precipitated their flight from London.

The various narratives that came to William's ears tended to dwell naturally on the dramatic. At midnight on the 4th of November, the king's guards had marched straight down to the cellar beneath the Parliament House, smashed through one of the bricked-up entrances, and discovered Fawkes, booted, cloaked and spurred for travel, tinder-box in hand, standing over the barrels of powder. The news spread quickly to the other conspirators, Catesby and Percy, the Wintours and the Wrights, who mounted their swift horses and fled to the north. For the first time William heard the names of other men who had been involved with them in the conspiracy, but whom he had never met: Sir Everard Digby, Ambrose Rookwood. He knew poor Bates was among them. But there was another hapless servant, named Grant. And someone called Keyes. How many more?

Not many. Though they were nothing more than a band of fugitives desperately trying to evade inevitable capture, the plotters had apparently persisted in their delusions, hoping to raise rebellion among the Catholic gentry of the Midlands. They had never doubted that in the revolution precipitated by their deed, the greater part of the kingdom would take sides with them, either from a desire for change, or out of hope of better fortune. But every door was closed to them. They made their last stand at Holbeach House in Staffordshire. Catesby and Percy were felled by the same shot, and died, like Spartans at Thermopylae, in one another's arms. The Wright brothers were also killed, the rest captured.

The eight survivors had been tried in Westminster Hall. An eye-witness told William that while some of the plotters hung their heads in doggedness, and others tried to muster a stern look, the demeanour of Fawkes throughout was dignified and unyielding. He was, it seems, allowed to retain his mask: perhaps someone had decided that his face would terrify his judges. Tall he stood, and proud, gloomily surveying what was to have been his kingdom. Even the king, it was said, who had spied upon the whole proceeding from behind a curtain, saw in him something of a Roman resolution.

The trial was of course nothing more than a prelude to execution. And it was to witness the ritual slaughtering of the last of the plotters, Tom Wintour, Rookwood, Keyes and Fawkes, that William had been temporarily released from his imprisonment. Digby, Robert Wintour, Grant and Bates had already been dispatched, in St Paul's Churchyard, on the previous day. Taken from his cell, in the early hours of the morning, to the Palace of Westminster, William was positioned by his guards next to a window directly overlooking the gallows. From here he could observe, without being seen. The executions were to take place before sunrise: apparently the authorities still feared some measure of civil disobedience, and it was common knowledge that the mob could not get up in the morning.

Lit by lanterns and torches, the scene was even more macabre. The gallows rose tall at the end of a long raised platform. The dais was reached by wooden steps, the gallows ascended by means of a ladder propped against it. Spread around the platform were the gruesome tools of the executioner's trade, ropes and baskets, knives, cleavers, barbed hooks. A brazier flickered with a low, white-hot flame. In the centre stood the hangman himself, in a black vest that left his muscled arms bare, his face concealed behind a black mask, waiting with folded arms for the arrival of his victims. Behind him were his assistants in butchery, the lowest of the low: sadistic perverts grinning at the prospect of blood, ready to sup full of horrors.

During this pause, William surveyed the small crowd that

congregated around the platform. One had to arrive early at such occasions to secure a ringside place. For the most part, they seemed the usual mixture of grieving friends and relatives, court observers, government spies, drunken idlers, prostitutes and thieves. But at the very front of the crowd, William noticed a group of a dozen or so spectators, pressed against the edge of the platform, nearest the gallows. They were all dressed alike, in long black robes, like the cassocks of priests. But their most distinctive feature was that each wore a white mask, identical to that assumed by Guido Fawkes. The same tilted eyebrows, the same vacant eyes, the same high cheekbones, black moustache and beard.

Who were they? Apprentices engaged in some form of collective mockery? Sympathisers wearing the mask of Fawkes as a sign, a badge of protest? He had no time to consider further, since a shout from the crowd heralded the arrival of the four condemned men, drawn into the yard on hurdles.

Tom Wintour was the first to mount the scaffold. William could clearly see his face, very pale and of a dead colour. He had always liked Tom, and felt sorry for him. Urged to make a speech, Tom merely crossed himself, and replied with extraordinary firmness: "This is no time for discourse. I am come here to die, a true Catholic." Weakened by wounds and torture, Wintour made it no more than half way up the ladder, and was pushed off to endure only a swing or two of the halter. Barely injured by the hanging, his dangling body was expertly caught as it swung, and quickly dragged to the executioner's table for butchery. His genitals were sliced off with the edge of a sickle. Sharp cleavers hacked open his abdomen, and the hangman scooped out his bowels. William could not look at Tom's face, but nothing could defend the ears against his unearthly shrieks of agony. His entrails were cast into the fire, while the hangman broke into his ribcage, and pulled out his heart. Then it was off with his head, which was held aloft, and triumphantly displayed to the crowd, before being tossed into a tub of scalding water to be boiled and blackened. The elevation of the head, that monstrous monstrance, was the climax of the show. The subsequent lopping of the limbs seemed spurious: the man was gone. For all their enthusiasm and professional pride, the executioners were hacking at nothing more sensate than dead meat.

The execution of Rookwood was less savage. His manifest contrition earned him some degree of mercy. He was permitted to hang almost to his last gasp, and could have felt little during the subsequent brutal indignities. Keyes too was dispatched relatively quickly. There was a sense that the stars of the show were the major conspirators, Wintour and Fawkes; and that the execution of Guido was the main event, what everyone had come to see.

And here he was at last, standing taller than the hangman, dressed all in black, his chiaroscuro mask displaying to the spectators a strange impersonal expression of mockery. Boldly he confronted the executioner, mask to mask, in faceless common-ality. A Roman resolution. William glanced at the crowd of Fawkes look-alikes who stood beneath the scaffold, their white faces tilted up to him like so many mirror-images. What were they up to? Fawkes stood at the foot of the ladder, where the noose was slipped over his neck. Step by step he ascended, taking his time, oblivious to the shouts of the executioners. When he had reached half way, one of the hangman's grinning lackeys tried to push him off. Fawkes gripped the side of the ladder with one hand, and with the other dealt the fellow a tremendous blow that sent him toppling to the platform. The crowd roared with appreciation. This was what they had come to see. Drama! Fawkes continued his ascent, reaching the very top of the ladder. He turned his mask to look around him. For a moment the blank eyes with their strangely tilted eyebrows came to rest on the window where William stood. Could he see him? Then without hesitation, Fawkes flung himself headlong from the ladder. The rope tautened, and when it reached the end of the drop, the sharp sound of a breaking neck echoed like a pistol-shot round the Old Palace yard. The body jerked back upwards, fell again, and the impact of Fawkes's heroic leap was enough to snap the rope. His body plummeted, feet first, into the crowd of masked figures below him.

William had a clear view of the group, but still he could not see exactly what had happened. The body disappeared among them. The white masks momentarily vanished, leaving only a swirling darkness of black robes. For a moment William thought Fawkes had disappeared. The hangman stood at the edge of the platform, shouting to the onlookers to deliver up the body. The crowd bayed.

Then with a surging movement, Fawkes's body was lifted out of the crowd, and shoved back onto the platform. The executioners seized it and dragged it to the block. But it was a stiff, unfeeling corpse they were butchering, their vain blows malicious mockery. The corpse did not bleed, even when decapitated. The hangman ripped away the mask, and held the severed head aloft to the crowd. "Behold where stands the accursed traitor's head!"

And then silence. Not a word, not a whisper. The face revealed was a face so disfigured – by imprisonment, by torture, by the trauma of a violent death? – that it looked scarcely human, let alone like the Guido Fawkes William remembered. It looked like the face of a plague victim. Yellow skin, blackened by ugly blotches. Horribly disfigured by unhealing lesions and sores. Blank, pitiless eyes, like the eyes of Death himself. The crowd recoiled, petrified. It was as if the face of Medusa had been unveiled and displayed to them.

The first light of dawn began to illuminate the blood-boltered shambles of the yard, for a moment touching the gruesome trophy of royal justice, which showed even more hideous in the light of day. But then as suddenly the head seemed, at the touch of the rising sun's rays, to wizen, pucker, crinkle and turn black. Quickly the hangman dropped it into the boiling water, where it hissed and steamed.

As William was bustled away by the guards, he observed that the crowd of doubles had vanished. He was bundled into a closed carriage to transport him back to the Tower. On the way his imagination was troubled by the dreadful images he had been forced to witness. The one that stayed with him, impossible to shake off, was the face of the severed head the hangman had held aloft, after it had been struck from Fawkes's body. He had told William his face was changed. If it were not for that inside knowledge, William would never have believed the hideous visage he had just seen to be the face of Guido Fawkes.

7 February 1606. The Tower of London

After the executions, William expected to be released. There was no reason for the authorities to hold him any longer. So he busied himself packing up his books and papers, ready to depart at a moment's notice.

Thomas, the gaoler in charge of his corridor, seemed to like William, and would come in on cold mornings to light a fire in the little grate. William had no money to give him, but the man clearly hoped to be immortalised in one of his plays. While arranging the kindling wood in a neat criss-cross pattern, he would keep up a constant flow of conversation, a little of which William (who did not speak Cockney) was able to understand.

"Bloke were reading one of your poems in the tavern last night, Master Will." (He pronounced it "Wiw"). "*Venus and Adonis*. Hot stuff, eh? We all liked the bit where she pulls him down on top of her, you know? 'He on her belly falls.' Phoar. I tried to get my missus to do it. 'Red and hot as coals of glowing fire.' Made her red in the face, at least. As for me, well it put my back out. Worth it, though. You know what? I says to 'em. You know what? I've got that Master Shakespeare, 'ere in one of my cells! That showed 'em. You ain't got no more poems like that, have you?" He looked around the cell, as if hoping to discern piles of unpublished pornography.

"Not really," said Will. "But I am writing a play about a man who wants to have sex with a nun."

"Phoar! Can't wait to see it."

"Well, the sooner I get out of here, the sooner it'll be showing. A free ticket for you, if you make it quick."

The man seemed confused. You've not 'eard, then?"

"'Eard what?" asked William, unable to resist his instinct of mimicry. "Heard what, I mean?"

"There's plague. Theatres is closed."

"Plague? Good God. Nobody told me."

"I'm really sorry, Master Will. I thought you'd 'eard."

"No, I hadn't … heard."

"So the safest place for you is – well, in 'ere."

"So it is," said William ruefully. Better to stay alive in prison, than die horribly on a plague-stricken Bankside.

By now the fire was crackling in the grate. "You can get on with your writing, then," Thomas said hopefully. "The one about the bloke having sex with the nun sounds good."

Plague

14 February 1606. The Tower of London

A key grated in the lock.

"Visitor to see you, Master Will."

"Dr Forman? What on earth are you doing here?"

Simon Forman was a doctor, physician, surgeon, quack, magus, astrologer, herbalist, necromancer, alchemist, and notorious lecher. Though continually being struck off, and even imprisoned, for practising medicine without a licence, he had an extensive patient list among the upper ranks of society. He was a handsome man, with a long straight nose, beautifully shaped mouth, and very large, charismatic eyes. He had a dark, swarthy complexion, and wore a big, rough beard that gave him a piratical, buccaneering look. He carried a long leather bag with two handles.

As a doctor, he tried to have sex with every woman he treated. His idea of doctor-patient confidentiality was to ask the women to keep quiet afterwards. His large forehead was symmetrically creased with deep lines, acquired, so it was said, from looking upwards while his face was busy between some woman's legs.

William knew him, as Forman had treated his landlady, Marie Mountjoy, a middle-aged but still attractive Frenchwoman, for some kind of woman's complaint. William had had her a few times in lieu of rent. Forman had made several house calls to Silver Street, and the muffled gasps and regular mattress-bumping William heard from the master bedroom left little to the imagination as to his clinical methods. Forman was also an avid playgoer, and a great fan of William's work. None of this however explained what he was doing here in the Tower.

"William, William," he began. "So good to see you! We've missed you at the playhouse. So this is where you've been? Very pleasant, very pleasant. Is this what they feed you on?" Forman inspected a half-eaten bowl of oatmeal, put his finger in and tasted it. "Very nutritious. Excellent roughage. Should keep you regular, despite the lack of outdoor exercise. Ingenious. Would you mind if I examined one of your stools, William?"

William glanced at the chamber pot, which Thomas had emptied earlier. "Sorry, all gone," he replied. "You'll have first refusal on the next one though. It's got your name on it."

"Good, good," said Forman, peering out of the window. "Ravens. Of course. The Tower. Dismal. Beat the windows of the dying, they say. Doesn't happen in Lambeth. Do you worry about them, Will? I suppose once you're in here, it's usually too late for bad omens." He turned around, leaned against the embrasure, and for the first time looked at William. "How I do run on! Can never seem to stick to the point. You're wondering why I'm here."

"I knew you'd get there in the end."

"Yes. Well, it won't surprise you to know that occasionally I'm called in to undertake some government service."

"If that involves inspecting turds," said William, "I wouldn't exactly call it government service."

"No, no. Well, yes, sometimes. But I'm talking about politics. I know a lot more than you'd think about this recent trouble in the kingdom. For example, I know why you're in here." The big, mild eyes turned a little shrewder.

"Oh, really," said William, noncommittally.

"Yes, really. They called me in last November to cast a horoscope. To find out where Thomas Percy was hiding."

"And did you find him?"

"Of course not. You think I believe that mumbo-jumbo? I'm an experimental scientist. I told them I could see him, in my mind's eye, riding north, with three other riders, mounted on a pale horse."

"'And the one who sat upon him was called Death.' Very apt."

"I thought so. You'd be surprised how easy it is to make the obvious sound like a 'revelation.'"

William winced at the bad pun. Though it was no worse than one of his own. "Where do you stand on matters of religion, then?" William asked curiously.

"Never in the same place for very long. I find it safer. Officially I'm an Anglican. But I have been accused of Catholicism."

"Really?"

"Yes. I had a long affair with a married Catholic woman, Avisa Allen."

"Oh, I didn't know. When was that?"

Forman consulted his notebook. "Let me see. I fucked her first on – here it is – Saturday 15th December, 1593, at 5 pm."

"Perhaps that's a little too much information."

"Oh, my case-notes are always very thorough. It was beneath a picture of St Theresa in ecstasy. Avisa was hot as hell. I'd never realised the erotic potentialities of Catholic martyrology."

"It's a well-kept secret. Otherwise everybody will want some."

"I got to know a lot of people in her circle, and as you know, papal mud sticks fast. Then in 1602 I was accused in Plymouth of being a Jesuit priest. Conducting secret masses. And at the same time, of black magic. And conjuring the Devil. They couldn't really tell the difference. Maybe there is no difference? I don't know. Anyway, emotionally I'm an atheist. I believe in nature, not the supernatural. As a scientist, I'm an agnostic. I don't rule anything out. God just happens to be a hypothesis for which I have no need.

"And now, as a scientist, I've been asked to look into this new plague. They always call on me, because I survived the plague. I caught it, in 1592. Did you know that? Felt a swelling in my groin. Took to bed, with the plague in both my groins, and some time after that I had the red tokens on my feet, as broad as halfpence. But it was for the best, as I seem to have acquired some sort of natural immunity."

"Very convenient."

"Certainly. I wrote a little book about it – I've got it here somewhere." He rummaged in the depths of his capacious bag. "Here it is. *A Discourse of the Plague*, written by Simon Forman, practising physician and astrologer 1593. Would you like a copy? No? Please yourself. The following year I lived through another outbreak, and emerged uninfected. I wrote a little poem about it. Do you want to hear it?"

"I'm sure I'm going to."

"Then came the plague in ninety three
Whence all the doctors fled;
I stayed to save the lives of many
That otherwise had been dead."

"Whatever you do," said William dryly, "don't give up your day job."

"So I starting making my inquiries, examined some of the live sufferers, inspected some of the dead bodies, interviewed various people to gather data. Did you know I've devised a method for mapping an outbreak of plague? I count the numbers of plague deaths, disaggregate them from natural and violent deaths, and locate them in their place of residence. Then I draw concentric circles, capturing the differentials in death rates. A pattern emerges as the circles increase in density. At the centre we find the source of the outbreak."

"And then what?"

"That's as far as I've got. It's a new science. I'm thinking of calling it 'epidemiology.'"

"Catchy. I still haven't got a sense of where I fit in."

"Take a look at this, then."

Forman extracted from his bag a chart, which he unfolded on the table in front of William. It displayed a map of London, overlaid by six concentric circles.

"It looks like a map of Hell," said William, recollecting his dream of Dante.

"Have a look at the centre."

There could be no mistake. The circled area was the district where lay William's lodgings. The centre was the site of The Swan with Two Necks. "It *is* a map of Hell," William said. He raised his eyes, and looked directly into Forman's.

"Yes," said the doctor. "Now I have your full attention."

William sat back and listened.

"The centre of this outbreak is that tavern. Even allowing for some accidentals in the data – people don't always catch diseases where they live, for instance, so the model needs refinement – the density of plague deaths undoubtedly concentrates there. And having spoken to the landlord here, his clientele and some of the other – staff, I learned that for a considerable period of last year, one of their most persistent repeat visitors was a writer."

"I know the tavern," said William, offhand. "I live nearby. But what of it? Am I the only writer in London?"

"No. But you're the best. The landlord gave me this. A cleaner found it, in one of his chambers." Again he took a piece of paper from his bag, and handed it over.

It was the manuscript of one of William's sonnets to the Dark Lady.

My love is as a fever, longing still
For that which longer nurseth the disease,
Feeding on that which doth preserve the ill,
Th'uncertain sickly appetite to please.
My reason, the physician to my love,
Angry that his prescriptions are not kept,
Hath left me, and I, desperate, now approve
Desire is death, which physic did except.
Past cure I am, now reason is past care,
And frantic mad with evermore unrest;
My thoughts and my discourse as madmen's are,

At random from the truth vainly expressed:

For I have sworn thee fair, and thought thee bright,

Who art as black as hell, as dark as night.

William shrugged.

"Perhaps you'd like me to attribute it to another writer? Marlowe, perhaps? No, he's dead. Lord Bacon? The Earl of Oxford's available. Or as it contains so much specialised medical vocabulary, I could even say I wrote it myself?"

"No, no, no," protested William. Forman had found his weakness. "Enough with these questions of authorship. It's mine. And yes, I left it there. But I still don't see …"

"William, I want you to assist me in this work. I have negotiated your manumission. Your release papers are here, signed by the Governor. He will cut you loose, today, but only into my care, and only on condition that you help me. I'll have to answer for you. I know you to be a man of honour."

"That's wonderful news. And of course I won't let you down. But in what way can I assist you? I'm not a doctor. And more to the point, I don't have any natural immunity to plague."

"Have no fear. In confidence: this disease," said Forman, slyly, "is not plague. It is a novel sickness, new to these shores, and as yet has no name. I hope to isolate it, and call it after myself. 'Formania.' Then those bastard Barber-Surgeons will have to let me into their exclusive little club. But whatever it is, its symptoms are exactly the ones you describe in your poem."

"It's only metaphors …"

"William, I can diagnose, from that poem, that you have already contracted this disease. And recovered from it. You're lucky to have escaped with your life. Many have not been so fortunate. So you will have immunity. And I have need of an assistant. Come now, we have work to do. You may leave any time you wish. Get your stuff back to your lodgings. Today there are some things I have to do. Meet me at The Swan with Two

Necks, at seven."

The sorcerer's apprentice, thought William. Look what happened to him.

15 February 1606. The Swan with Two Necks

The streets were unusually deserted. From fear of the plague, William assumed, though he saw none of the usual signs that accompanied an outbreak. When he entered the tavern, Forman was already there, deep in conversation with Bianca and Doll. A pitcher of wine stood between them.

"William, William," he said. "Come in. Sit down. Have a drink. I'm just explaining to these young ladies the importance of regular breast examination."

William helped himself to a long drink from the flagon. Forman was focusing on Doll's substantial and largely exposed breasts. "So you see, my dear, you take both breasts in your hands – like so – the nipples cupped in your palms – and rotate your hands – like that. Yes. Good. Feel for any sign of lumps, or thickening of the tissue."

"What happens if I find one?"

"You come to me. I'll give you a poultice. Mallows, holly-hocks, rose leaves, sheep's suet, boiled all in beer together, then thickened with crumbs of brown bread."

"I can't eat that!"

"No, dear. We smear it on your breasts. To ripen the imposthume, and rid it of venomous matter. You'll be as right as rain. The important thing is to catch it early. Now slide your hands along the sides. Gently. That's it. Lift them up. Make them pert. Oh yes. That's good."

"Is he really a doctor?" Bianca asked William suspiciously.

William grinned, and took another drink. "Of sorts."

"Is there somewhere private where I can examine you properly?" Forman asked Doll. "Let's get them out and have a proper look. Dip your nipples in white wine."

"Then what?"

"Then I lick it off. We don't want to take any chances, do we?"

"You got any money?" she asked.

"Oh, I have something better than money. Free medical advice."

"Well, I do sometimes have this burning sensation when I pee."

"I can help you with that. Come along now." Forman winked salaciously at William, as Doll led him to the stairs.

William was beginning to feel a delicious sense of relaxation creeping over him. He hadn't realised how the months of confinement had affected him. As the wine softened the edges of his reality, Bianca was beginning to look again like the pretty girl she obviously once had been.

"Come upstairs for a quick one?" she asked.

Why not? It was his first night of freedom. He followed her up the stairs and into a chamber. She laid him down on the bed, and busied herself untying him. But as he looked upwards he noticed an oddly-shaped damp patch on the ceiling. He had seen it before. It was one of the rooms he had shared with *her*. The memories began to return. The tide of desire ebbed as quickly as it had flowed.

"Bloody hell," she said, "what do you call this?"

"Willy," he replied, pulling his clothes back on. "And he's not in the mood." She looked hurt. He kissed her, gently. "It's not you. Really. I've got a lot on my mind. Another time."

When he returned to the bar, Forman was back again, his bag open by his side, poring over a paper, and writing notes in a large leather notebook. There was no sign of Doll. William looked around for her.

"She's resting," Forman explained. "Most women need a lie down after I've finished with them. How did you fare?"

"Oh, badly," William replied, taking another drink. "I couldn't get it up."

"Ah," said Forman, turning to a page in his notebook. "For that I have a remedy. Here it is. 'When one would gladly be provoked, but cannot do it.' Civet, taken in a poached egg. Works like a charm. No? I also have a cure for hair loss. 'Anoint the scalp with a burnt dog turd.'"

"Fuck off," said William. "I'd rather stay bald. Anyway how else would people recognise me?"

Forman grinned. "Perhaps another time. Now let's talk about this poem." It was William's sonnet. "I'm convinced that this poem holds the key to our plague. Here, you see, you make this connection between love, and illness. 'My love is as a fever.' Then, you say, the disease is addictive, it grows along with desire. Love nurses the sickness, makes you want it all the more. 'Feeding on that which doth preserve the ill.' Interesting, interesting. 'Th'uncertain sickly appetite to please.' You see, the appetite is for the disease itself. That's one of its symptoms. Ha! Now look at this next bit:

My reason, the physician to my love,
Angry that his prescriptions are not kept,
Hath left me …

"That's very good. If you wanted to recover, you'd take the medicine, not ignore the doctor. I hate it when that happens. But the patient can't help it, you see. He loves his disease, and resists the doctor who promises to cure it.

"Now. Here's a phrase: 'Desire is death.' It works both ways, you see. The desire will kill you. But equally, the source of death is the object of desire."

William was impressed. He could glimpse the depth and beauty of his words in Forman's explications. The only time this happened was when he read, or heard, his poetry as if it were the work of another. "You may not be much of a doctor," he said, "but you're a hell of a literary critic."

"Concentrate, William. This is life and death. In the later stages the disease causes insanity: 'frantic madness;' 'my thoughts as madman's are.' The patient knows he is 'past cure' because he is 'past care.' He doesn't want to get well. His plague is love itself.

"An illness that springs from love. Its symptoms are fever, addiction, madness, a desire for death. What we are dealing with here, William, is a sexually transmitted disease."

"What, the clap?"

"No, not the clap."

"The pox?"

"No, not the pox. It is something new, never seen before. This is why we have no resistance to it, and no idea of how to treat it."

"Are you really going to call it 'Formania'?"

"No. I didn't know it was going to be venereal, did I? Not much of a legacy, is it? 'Get your mercury baths at the Forman Clinic.' Maybe we should call it 'Williamania' as you're the first recorded case. Anyway its source lies here, in this tavern. Which brings me, William, to a friend of yours. The Countess. The Dark Lady."

William feigned surprise. "Dark Lady?"

"Don't let's waste time," said Forman, and quoted the sonnet's concluding couplet.

For I have sworn thee fair, and thought thee bright,
Who art as black as hell, as dark as night.

"Now tell me all about her."

So William told Forman the whole story of his liaison with the Countess. The doctor wrote it all down in his casebook. "And after that, I never saw her again. Never heard from her. Vanished. Without a trace."

"She broke your heart?" said Forman.

"Well, it seems to be still in one piece. Definitely bruised, though."

"This is remarkably interesting. She may well be the source of the disease. She is a foreigner, you say? So she imported it to our shores. She is a prostitute, so she has the opportunity of infecting many men. She told you she had an illness? And that you would die if you caught it. That seems conclusive. And she would not let you inside her? Perhaps she was protecting you. From the disease."

"But why doesn't she die from it?"

"She is what we call a carrier. The disease lies within her, and she can transmit it to others. But it can take no hold on her system. She may have been inoculated."

"Inoculated?"

"I have made some experiments with the sweating sickness. If you collect perspiration from a sufferer, and give it in small doses to an uninfected person, they may develop immunity to the disease. The Countess might have treated you, in the same way, with small doses of her illness. Administered orally."

"So have I had it, or not?"

"Yes and no. You have had a mild, non-fatal infection. You say yourself that you developed a kind of mania, an addiction to the source of your illness, a desire for death. These are the symptoms of the disease. But it did not kill you. Here you still are."

"And lucky to be so. I could be lying six foot under in St Saviour's Churchyard."

Forman looked at him oddly. "Not necessarily." He put his notebook and papers back in the bag. "There are still many things about this infection I do not understand. It's time for you to learn more about our disease, William. I'll call for you tomorrow night, at your lodgings."

16 February 1606. St Mary Spital

The following evening Forman collected William from his lodgings in Silver Street, and led him eastwards through the city. They arrived at an old churchyard in the Spitalfields area. William knew where he was: the site of the priory of St Mary Magdalene, dissolved by Henry VIII in 1539. The attached infirmary for the indigent poor had survived, now run by the Lord Mayor of London. They entered a ramshackle building adjoining the infirmary.

"This is the old charnel house," Forman explained. "Here were stored the bones of thousands of dead from the churchyard. An ossuary. Fascinating. I've asked them to lay out some of the plague victims, for our inspection."

William was more used to writing about charnel houses than frequenting them. The place had a sour smell of old death about it. On a long makeshift mortuary table lay a number of dead bodies, covered by white sheets. Forman lit a lantern, and placed it at the head of the table. Then he pulled off the sheets to reveal three corpses, two men and a woman. They did not seem to have been dead for very long.

"I want you to observe certain peculiar features about these corpses, William," Forman began, with the superior air of a senior doctor giving instruction, "which tell us that these people died of an unusual and mysterious illness. First of all, these corpses were discovered in state of near total exsanguination."

"Bloodless?"

"Not a drop left. Each one has a small wound, or rather two wounds, around the area of the neck."

Forman pointed out to William small puncture marks around each victim's throat. "These wounds are not sufficient in themselves to cause death. These are not homicides. How the blood escaped from them, remains a mystery. Observe also the strange expression on each victim's face. Is it pain, or pleasure?

Ecstasy, or terror? And the strangest symptom of all. Look, here."

He leaned over one of the corpses and pulled back the upper lip. William flinched. The canine teeth were unusually large and distended. They reminded him of the Countess.

"All the victims display that strange deformation of the upper canines, a symptom which seems to develop post-mortem. I have no explanation."

"So what do you think?"

"We know that our infection is a disease of the blood. It may have some catastrophic effect on the heart, causing it to pump all the blood out of a body. Perhaps through these holes in the throat. Now the heart is the seat of the passions. Driven to extremity by the love that has caused the disease, the patient's heart may burst, and shed his precious life-blood. And what of those punctures? I don't know. Some kind of strange and fatal lover's kiss." He threw the sheets back over the corpses. "There is nothing more to be learned from them." And he led the way outside.

The night air was a relief. William breathed it in. "I have not told you the strangest detail about this case," Forman continued, "which seems to take us from the world of nature into that of the supernatural. I have interviewed a number of people who swear that some of the victims of this plague have been seen again, after their deaths, apparently risen from their graves."

"Risen? Surely that's impossible."

"Is it?" said Forman curiously. "I have seen Dr Dee and Edward Kelly speak with spirits by peering into a crystal globe. And what about your own play? 'A little ere the mightiest Julius fell,/The graves stood tenantless and the sheeted dead/Did squeak and gibber in the Roman streets.'"

It was from William's own *Hamlet*. "I got that from Plutarch," he protested. "And it was a very long time ago. 'Miracles are ceased.' I never expected to see resurrected corpses squeaking and gibbering in the middle of Moorgate."

"Why, I myself have practised necromancy, and called angels and spirits. And before you say it, yes they *did* come when I called 'em. I summoned the demon Salathiel."

"Did you honestly?"

"Well, there was something there for sure. I saw fire, then a kind of shape. But I knew it was him. 'There are stranger things in heaven and earth, than are dreamt of in your philosophy.'"

"Will you stop quoting my work back at me? It's really annoying. Why would the dead want to rise again? Do they miss this world so much?"

"Remember we are dealing with an infection that arises from love. There are many stories of ghosts quitting their unquiet graves, forlornly seeking for a lost love."

"Now that I can understand. Are we finished here? 'Tis bitter cold, and I am sick at heart.'"

"Ah, Hamlet again. He is *Prince of Denmark* yet. But no, we're not done here. Tonight we will watch by this little churchyard. To test my theory. The moon will be full tonight. I arranged for one of these poor fellows to be buried here, two days ago. If he is going to rise again, I want to be there to see it."

"Couldn't you do it just as well alone?" asked William. He did not like any of this.

"You're my assistant, William, remember. I own you. It's here or the Tower."

He was not entirely sure which he preferred. They seated themselves on a bench at the edge of the yew-fringed churchyard. The ground was hollow, uneven, infirm with digging up of graves. Ancient, illegible gravestones leaned over at crazy angles. Flimsier wooden crosses lay collapsed, or broken off, splintered and rotten. A small breeze scattered faint starlight over broken tombs.

The night was still and silent. Forman composed himself to watch, furling his cloak about him. After a while William fell asleep.

Something woke him. A grey mist had seeped from somewhere into the churchyard, rolling over the low wall, carpeting the ground, gathering more thickly around the gravestones. The lamp was out, the moon behind a cloud. There was a kind of humming reverberation in his ears, as if the ghosts of the old monks were softly chanting beneath the ground. He felt disoriented, like a drunken man. The ground sloped away from him. Forman was not there. He stood, unsteadily, staggered a few paces forward. Beneath his feet lay a large patch of overturned soil, unmarked by any memorial. A mass grave of some kind, perhaps a plague pit. Wreaths of fog clung to clods of exposed earth.

Then the huge glittering moon rode out from behind its cloudy wrack, and lit the whole churchyard with a cold, hard light. The ground seemed to slope away from him again, in a different direction. His mind was unbalanced. In the centre of the grave-plot he saw a small movement. Something stirred. Some small burrowing creature, perhaps, some mole working in the earth. Flakes of soil crumbled and sheered away. And then his heart stopped, as he saw, clearly, in the moonlight, emerging from the excavated soil, the fingers of a hand.

Paralysed with terror, he watched, as the hand shook itself free and released an arm, followed by another hand and arm. Something was climbing out of the pit. The dead were rising from their graves. The surface of the soil rippled with shuddering contractions: it was like some dreadful birth. A head broke loose from the clay, shaking itself free. The dead hands grasped at the root of a yew-tree and began to pull the body out. All the while the creature was softly grunting and moaning. Soon it had delivered itself from its womb of earth, and lay supine on the soil, whimpering like a new-born infant.

William wanted to run away, but stood trapped in his nightmare. The creature pulled itself up, and stood unsteadily, turning its head this way and that, like a dog scenting the air. It was a man, who had been unceremoniously buried in his clothes. Now they were streaked with soil, stained with mould. For the first time William saw its face. It was the face of a half-decayed corpse. Desiccated skin flapped wrinkling and loose from the angular bones. The blank dead eyes stared aimlessly around. He thought of Fawkes's miners. The upper lip rose in a snarl, showing protuberant canine teeth.

Suddenly William flinched as a piercing scream broke from Forman, who had come to stand just behind his shoulder. The creature from the grave, startled by the sound, turned his head and began to lurch clumsily towards them, arms outstretched. And then they were running, Forman in the lead, racing for their lives, out of the churchyard and through the dark streets, fast as their legs would carry them.

"I don't think he was forlornly looking for his lost love," William shouted after the retreating form of the doctor. They didn't stop running till they reached Shakespeare's lodgings in Silver Street, where they pounded up the stairs and banged the door behind them.

After a few minutes they had caught their breath.

"What the hell was that?" panted William.

"Proof," replied Forman. "Proof that my theory is correct. This disease enables its victims to rise bodily from their graves, and walk the night. We have seen it, William. We have seen it with our own eyes."

"So what do we do about it?"

"This is far beyond my knowledge and expertise," Forman admitted. "I have never come across anything like it, and can offer no solutions. I need help. I will have to go abroad."

"Abroad?"

"Yes. To Leiden. In the Netherlands. I studied there as a young man. I had a friend, another medical student, a young man of extraordinary abilities, and immense promise. He may be able to help us."

"Couldn't you find someone nearer home?"

"Abraham van Helsing is the world's greatest expert on obscure diseases. And his mind is entirely open: he places no limits on the possibilities of knowledge. He is a true scientist: he makes no distinction between the natural and the supernatural. Or rather he believes that supernatural events are simply phenomena we have yet to understand. If anyone can help us, van Helsing can.

"I must take ship in the morning. I will be gone for no more than a few days. And now, William, tell me, on your honour: is there anything else, within your knowledge, that might help our investigations?"

The time for secrets was past. William unlocked a drawer in his bureau, and took out Fawkes's two letters from Constantinople and Foulness. "I am the only one who has read these in their entirety," he said. "And I confess there is much in them I do not understand. But after what we have seen tonight – well, the events described here may mean something to your friend."

"Thank you," said Forman, placing the letters in his bag. "Keep safe, William. Don't go out at night."

"Wild horses," was William's reply. But Forman was gone.

Blood

18 February 1606. Silver Street

During the doctor's absence, William had no idea what to do with himself. The theatre remained closed on account of the "plague." He had finished *Measure*, and had as yet found no way of tackling the "Powder Play" Cecil had commissioned from him. Forman had told him on no account to stir forth at night. But his restlessness became so irksome, that he decided to risk a nocturnal venture. If the danger from infection was via sexual transmission, his abortive encounter with Bianca suggested he had nothing to fear on that score. If he met one of those resurrected creatures that he and Forman had seen rise from the earth of St Mary Spital, he would run like hell again, and trust to the celerity of his heels.

So he sallied forth into the foggy darkness, and walked around to Wood Street. He avoided The Swan with Two Necks, and dropped into The Talbot, nearer to his lodgings. There he found himself a seat by the smoky fire, ordered a bottle of sack, and proceeded to do his best to get drunk. People came in and out of the bar. William spoke to no-one. The fire warmed his feet, and the alcohol his heart. He would stay here till closing time, then stagger back home and fall into bed. For a few hours, at least, he would have been able to forget his many and varied problems.

Then suddenly, just as he was thinking of ordering another bottle, he happened to glance through the window. Outside in the murky street, cloaked and hooded against the foggy air, walking regally tall and with an unforgettable elegance of gait, the figure he saw pass by the bow-window was none other – surely, he was convinced of it – than the Countess. Without a moment's hesitation he grabbed at his cloak, dashed through the bar, upsetting a table and some glasses in his clumsy rush, and ran out into the street. He could just see her elusive form, turning a corner twenty yards ahead. It could not be her! His reason forbade it. And yet the very chance that it might be forced him to hurry in pursuit.

As he hurtled round the corner he was compelled as suddenly to stop, as the figure he followed had halted, outside the door of another tavern in Love Lane. She was meeting someone. Another figure, cloaked and hooded in similar guise, but much shorter in stature, came out of the doorway, and took her hand. They spoke together. The short one threw back a hood to reveal a lovely heart-shaped face, framed by blonde hair. A woman! Her clothes were fine, her complexion fair. This was no whore, but a young lady of quality. She was smiling. Although the taller of the two wore a voluminous black hood that concealed most of her face, he saw enough – the corner of a slanting black eyebrow, a glimpse of red lips, the flash of white teeth – to conform the identification. It was her. It was the Countess. His lost love. His dear, dolorous, diseased Dark Lady.

The two turned away from him and walked arm-in-arm along the dark street. What was this? Some assignation? But with another woman? William was torn between rekindled desire, and shame at the thought of the sordid role he found himself playing. Anyone who saw him tracking them, pausing when they paused, turning the same corners, would be hard pressed to decide whether the mission he was engaged in was one of espionage or pimping. He wanted to see where she would go, that was all. Make a note of the house, and then report the infor-mation to Forman on his return. This was his duty. This was, after all, his new vocation: the pox-doctor's clerk.

The streets they traversed grew darker, and the fog a little thicker. The night was damp and raw. He knew the Countess would not feel the cold, but the other woman must surely be shivering in her fine silk cloak. Perhaps that was why they stopped, just around the corner of a garden, and stood together against a high wall, in the shadow of the branches of a tree. William clung to the wall to conceal himself. The Countess had her back to the wall, and her arms around her companion. They spoke together in low tones. He heard the echo of the Countess's silvery laughter. They were embracing! William had to get a closer look. Sidling back along the wall he found the garden gate. The house at the end of the drive seemed dark and deserted. He pulled himself up and over the gate, crept along the wall and climbed up the branches of the tree that overlooked the embracing lovers. From here he could see clearly everything that happened between them.

The blonde woman was manifestly besotted with the Countess. Looking up into her lovely face, she could not tear her eyes away. Her lips smiled, but shook with a nervous tremor. The Countess encircled her waist with an arm, and with the other hand pushed back her hood, and caressed her hair. The girl leaned back against the arm in a languorous surrender. The Countess cupped her hand around the other's head, and brought her close in for a kiss. The blonde woman's body relaxed against her. They kissed long and deep, while the Countess reached her free right hand down into the pleats of her lover's dress. The hand quested and sought, and for a moment was still. The girl pulled her mouth away and, with a trembling upper lip, gazed into the Countess's eyes with an expression somewhere between ecstasy and pain. Then the Countess's hand began to move among the folds of her dress, touching her intimately, gently, slowly, skilfully, sure. William could well imagine what those cold fingers were doing in the scalding labyrinth of the woman's febrile quim. Soon there was nothing to imagine, as the face of the girl contorted into a frown of ecstasy, a pink flush flooded her white cheeks, and her lips rose away from her teeth in a grimace of pleasurable pain. The hand of the Countess quickened its stimulation, eliciting a succession of short gasps that broke into a sobbing orgasm. The smaller woman leaned back to expose her delicate white throat. The Countess buried her own face into the offered neck. Then the sobs of ecstasy turned into shrieks of pain. The eyes that had been tightly closed in bliss, opened wide in horror. A moment's struggle from the victim, and it was over. The girl's face was again overcome with languor, her legs buckled beneath her, but the Countess held her fast. William could hear a dreadful lapping sound, interspersed with moans of pleasure, as the Countess rubbed her face into the soft receptive skin of the other's neck.

This tableau was held still for the space of a few minutes, frozen in time. Then with a shockingly casual motion, the Countess let go of the limp body, and let it slip to the ground. The blonde girl lay at her feet, fixed blue eyes staring upwards. The Countess wiped her mouth with the back of her hand, and walked quickly away. An uncertain sickly appetite.

William swung down from the branches of the tree and dropped into the street beside the body. She was dead, he had no doubt. No pink flush blossomed now in her cheeks: they were key-cold, chalk-white. On her throat he could see the two puncture marks he had seen in Spitalfields, each one raised and surrounded by a white border. One of them oozed a little blood. Poor creature. Desire is death. The Countess had murdered her, with a fatal lover's kiss. Gently he closed the staring eyes.

To follow the Countess! He left the corpse of the dead girl where it lay, and hastened after the retreating form of her killer. He could see her ahead of him, stalking through the wreaths of mist that seemed to billow away from her as she walked. Where was she headed? He knew she would seek shelter before the sunrise. Was the fog lightening? Her pace quickened, she was in a hurry. She was heading south, towards the river. A normal woman would have feared to walk such streets under cover of darkness. She feared nothing: she was an agent, not a subject, of terror.

At last they were passing through streets that seemed familiar to him. He recognised the odd landmark. They were in Westminster. Then, as he turned a corner around which she had momentarily vanished from sight, his heart stopped, as he saw her enter the door of a house, and close it behind her. It was the house of the plotters. The house that had stored the powder. The house of the tunnel beneath the Palace. The house where Fawkes had lodged his Transylvanian miners. And now it was the house of a murderess. An assassin who walked the London streets at night, drew men and women to her with her irresistible sexual charm, and drained their blood.

He had discovered the source of the plague. He had something to tell Doctor Forman on his return.

20 February 1606. Silver Street

When the doctor, returned from his travels, entered William's room, he was sitting at his desk, looking out of the window across the tiled roofs and smoking chimneys of Aldermanbury. He had been sitting in the same attitude, silent and unmoving, for most of the previous two days.

"I am so worried about 'eem," Marie Mountjoy had confided to Forman, as he ascended the stairs. "'Ee no eat, 'ee no drink, 'ee no do nothing."

Forman had caught Marie by the cunt as he passed her, and landed a wet kiss on her pouting lips. She bent back for the kiss, but then in case her husband was listening, assumed a shocked indignation. "Ooh la la!" she exclaimed. "You naughty man, you."

"French people really say 'Ooh la la'?" said Forman. "I must make a note." And he went on up. He was so preoccupied with his own concerns, that he hardly noticed William's air of melancholy distraction. "Your landlady," he began, "hath a mind to the quent. But it seems she will not be a harlot." Forman sat down to catch his breath. In truth, William was glad to see him. To whom else could he speak of what he had witnessed?

"William," the doctor began: "we are facing a dreadful adversary."

"You mean the disease?"

"Yes. And no. The disease is the enemy. But the enemy is the disease."

"You've lost me already."

"William. Listen carefully to what I have to say. Your life might depend upon it. In Leiden I met again with Abraham van Helsing. He now has a successful practice in the city. But he has kept up his old studies in necromancy and the occult. I told him what we had witnessed, exactly in every particular. He understood immediately, and was able to make a swift diagnosis. He has informed me of both the cause, and the cure, for this terrible affliction."

"So there is a cure?"

"For the disease. Not for the patients. All those who have contracted the infection must die. But the disease itself can be stopped, if we are sufficiently brave and decisive in our campaign against it."

"I see. I think. You mentioned an enemy?"

"Yes. The source of this disease is indeed an enemy. An enemy of mankind."

"Is it the Countess?" William hesitantly asked.

Forman brushed the suggestion aside. "No. I was wrong about her. I told you that van Helsing is an authority on all obscure diseases, whether caused by natural or supernatural means. You know yourself the strange things you have witnessed, here in London: phenomena that cannot be explained by any rational means. Those letters you gave me from Guido Fawkes only confirm everything van Helsing told me. He gave me this book. In it you will find a history of the foe that confronts us."

Forman drew an old leather-bound book from his bag, and placed it on the desk in front of William. The binding was ornate, graven and embossed, carefully crafted with leather-working tools. On the spine appeared the title, gilded in black-letter script. *A Natural History of The Vampyr.*

"Vampyr?" William said. "Isn't that some sort of bat?"

"There is such a creature, common enough in Africa and South America. It bites and sucks the blood of cattle. But it has given its name to something much more terrible. The Vampyr is a human being, who dies, or appears to die; rises from its grave, as we ourselves have witnessed; and like the Vampyr bat, sucks the blood of the living."

William was speechless. The Countess was a Vampyr! With his own eyes he had seen her sink her sharp teeth into another human being's flesh, and take her blood. His mind reeled at the implications. How had he himself escaped from her clutches?

"For many years it was thought that Vampyrs were the creatures of myth and legend, products of the superstitious credulity that prevails among the uneducated, slaves and peasants. There are stories of blood-sucking demons from ancient Persia, Greece, Babylon, Mesopotamia. But of late, certain genuine cases have been documented, by serious men of science and philosophy. These accounts demonstrate infallibly that Vampyrs do exist. There is an episode described here in the book, of a peasant, Jure Grando, who died and was buried, but rose again to drink the blood of the living. He was seen by many, prowling the cemetery in the darkness, feeding off the flesh of the newly interred. His widow claimed that he returned to her in the night, and importuned her for sex. She declined. See here, her words are reported: 'I may be a widow, but I'm not that desperate.' By morning Grando was gone, taking with him the rags she used to stanch her menstrual flow. He was finally laid to rest, only when the villagers dug down into his grave and exhumed his body. The priest prayed over him, then the people pierced his heart with a wooden stake, and cut off his head. You see where this happened? Look. In Croatia. At no great distance from Transylvania, where your former comrade, Mr Fawkes, travelled to find his miners. This Grando was no creature of legend, but a real man of flesh and blood, a man with a name and an address, a house and a wife. A living being, who died and became one of the Undead."

"The Undead? Are they ghosts?"

"No. The Undead is what they call them in those regions. They are neither living, nor dead. They have known both life and death, but they have risen again to enter an indeterminate condition between the two. A ghost is a spirit that walks the night, pursuing some unfinished business with the living. Like the Ghost in your *Hamlet*, who returned to tell his son about his foul and most unnatural murder. But ghosts are insubstantial as the air, invulnerable. The Vampyr is different. He inhabits his own body of flesh and blood. The body is animated, perhaps by some kind of demon. He is solid to the touch. His body retains all its functions But he is cold. Cold as the grave."

William shivered at some chill of memory.

"Every Vampyr is created by the bite of another. A Vampyr takes his victim, bites him, sucks the blood from his body and leaves him with all the appearance of death. The victim is found, and buried. But within the space of three days he awakes, and rises from his grave. In the language of Vampyrism, he has been 'turned.' Now he too is a Vampyr, and like his maker, thirsty for living blood. He walks the night, and goes on to bite others. So the contagion spreads, like a disease, transmitted from one victim to another.

"Hence we thought this at first a plague, then a sexual infection. It is neither. It is not a bacillus carried by rats. Nor is it a sexually-transmitted disease spread by your Countess, William. It is the curse of the Vampyr. And woe unto us, for to us it falls to rid the city of this foul pestilence."

"Us? How?"

"Van Helsing explained it all to me. The Vampyr preys at night. He cannot move around in the daytime, because he cannot expose himself to sunlight. God's blessed light will expose him as an unnatural thing, and kill him instantly. All day long he must sleep in the darkness of his coffin, on a bed of earth from the soil of his homeland."

"The miners!"

"The same. It is my belief that this epidemic was brought to our shores by Guido Fawkes. When he imported those men from Transylvania to dig your tunnel, he admitted this horrid infection to our land. It is all in the letter he sent to you. This Count – Dracula, I think was his name – has some mysterious power over the Undead, and can make them do his bidding. He kept them as slaves, you observe, working in the mines beneath his castle. He bonded them over to Fawkes, who inherited that same plenipotentiary power. He too was able to impose authority on them, and force them to hard labour."

"But how? Why did they not attack him and escape?"

"I do not know. It is a question of vital importance to us. The Vampyr has extraordinary strength. Think how they dug your tunnel. Van Helsing, who has made a thorough study of the science, tells me that certain signs and elements have power over these evil creatures of the night. They dread the pure and the sacramental. The cross, for instance. The body of Christ, in the form of the Blessed Sacrament. The pure element of silver.

"You remember how Fawkes in his letter speaks of quelling the Vampyr's rage with his pectoral cross? And they were kept fast in their coffins, throughout the long journey from the east, by the silver crosses Dracula had nailed to the lids. Once Fawkes released them from their confinement, and installed them in the Westminster House, he must have been able to control their blood-lust by these methods, and by the force of his own personality. But there is one thing I cannot understand: how they could exist without nourishment. They need blood, as we need food and drink, to survive."

"I think I saw one of them in the tunnel," Shakespeare said. "He may have been eating a rat." He said nothing about the Countess.

"Ah," Forman exclaimed, opening his notebook and making an entry. "That is very useful, William. It supports my theory."

"You have *another* theory?"

"Of course. I told you, I am a man of science. We investigate one hypothesis, and when it is disproved, we pursue another. These creatures need blood. But it does not have to be the blood of a human being. Like the Vampyr bat, they can feed from the blood of animals. As long as Fawkes was alive, he restrained these monsters in that subterranean excavation, and forced them to feed on the creatures of the night – the rat, the mouse, the shrew. Once Fawkes was dead, the Vampyrs were free. Free to rise from their underground lair, and feed on the blood of living humanity."

"Good God," William said, as the full horror of the plot he had been involved with began to sink in. He had not spoken of the Countess. The moment seemed to pass, and Forman was not interested in her. William would say nothing. It shall be as it may. "And how do we defeat them? Should we not inform the authorities? We will need men, arms, military force. To storm the house."

Forman shook his head. "No. Master Secretary Cecil does not want any of this to come to public knowledge. He has entrusted me with a secret mission to destroy these creatures. We know who they are. We know where they came from. We know where they live. You, William, know the location of the house. During the day they will be asleep in their coffins, weak and defenceless. We will come upon them, and take them by surprise."

"And then what?"

"We must subdue them. Bind them."

"Won't we have to kill them?"

"Eventually, yes. But first we must keep them alive – or not dead – and experiment upon them. We have to find out how they work. So first we make them fast. But we will need help. We learn from Fawkes's letters that what these creatures fear, above all else, is religion, and the sacraments of religion: the Cross, the Host, Holy Water. Van Helsing thinks the Vampyr to be some kind of demon that possesses the body of the victim. Perhaps it is introduced when the monster bites, and then operates to animate the corpse with the semblance of life. Nobody really knows. But if the creature is a demon, then we can put it to flight, and send it back to Hell whence it came."

"We can?"

"Yes. By the ritual of exorcism."

"Exorcism? Really? How much do you know about the church today, Simon?"

"Not much, I admit. I'm a scientist. Why?"

"You might have some problems getting a priest to do an exorcism. That's all."

"Why? I have already secured the services of a priest from my local church. Tomorrow he will accompany us to the Westminster House, and attempt to cast out these devils once and for all. My theory is that the body will then return to its state of natural death."

"Did you tell him *exactly* what we require of him?"

"No. Just in general terms. What's the problem? The practice of exorcism has authentic scriptural justification. Van Helsing showed me a biblical text from St Mark's Gospel. I made a note of it. Wait a minute. Ah, here it is:

And when Jesus was come out of the ship, there met him incontinently out of the graves, a man which had an unclean spirit: who had his abiding among the graves, and no man could bind him, no not with chains: because that when he was often bound with fetters and chains, he plucked the chains asunder, and brake the fetters in pieces, neither could any man tame him. And always both night and day he cried in the mountains, and in the graves ...

"You see? 'Abiding among the graves.' Notice the superhuman strength. And the inhuman sounds. But Jesus commands him: 'Come out of the man, thou unclean spirit!' The demon releases the man, takes refuge in a pig, and throws himself off a cliff. Van Helsing believes this man to have been a Vampyr, come 'out of the grave.' And Jesus was one of the first Vampyr-slayers."

"Never thought of it like that," William admitted. "But exorcism has had such a bad press. The church regards it as a typical Catholic scam, an egregious popish imposture. Some woman with attention-seeking behaviour problems starts screaming and howling. The priest says a few prayers over, her and she's quiet. Then he sends you the bill. All a fraud."

"Really? But it's there right in the *Book of Common Prayer*. I looked it up. In the rite of Baptism. 'Begone, unclean spirits ....'"

"That's an old book you're using. The 1549 version," William replied. This was one of *his* specialist subjects. "It was abandoned in the 1552 edition. Replaced with the injunction to 'forsake the devil and all his works.' It's all down to us, you see, not the mediation of the priest, to resist evil. Sound Protestant doctrine."

"Does it really make that much of a difference?" asked Forman. "These controversial niceties? Is the body in the bread, before the bread goes into the body? Does it really matter? Surely there's only one God. At the very most."

"Shhh!" hissed William. "For Christ's sake. Don't bring your damned atheism round here. No doubt in a hundred years or so there'll be a big enlightenment. But right now, most of these reformed ministers are theologically hard-core. That's all."

"Put it this way," said Forman. "One look at one of our undead friends, crawling his way out of his grave plot, and

Archbishop Bancroft himself would be grabbing for the Holy Water. I'm sure our minister will find it in his heart to lay aside his theological scruples, when confronted by a newly-risen Vampyr."

Exorcism

22 February 1605. Westminster

The Reverend Mr Saywell was a tall, thin man with a white, pinched face. He wore a long black cassock, and carried a book. Not a trace of ornament or iconography. No cross, no stole, no rosary beads. A minister of the Reformed Church of England, bearing in his hands the only weapon he expected to need: a prayer book, the word of the Lord.

William and Forman had arranged to meet him at two o'clock near the Westminster House, but the priest was over an hour late. "My apologies, brethren," he said in a thin voice. "One of my parishioners was taken in adultery. She has been receiving reprimand from the elders of the church since six o'clock this morning."

"Nine hours! That should do the trick, then," said William.

"Oh, no. I have left them at it, and will rejoin them later. Now, where is this house of unclean spirits?"

William led the way. Saywell fastidiously held up the hem of his cassock to keep it from the ubiquitous mud, and lifted his nostrils to keep them from the pervasive stench. They reached the house, and stood at the front door. It had not occurred to William that they would have no means of entrance. But Forman took from his bag a small instrument, that looked like a surgical implement, but proved in fact to be a skeleton key. With this he picked the lock, and they were inside.

The house was dark, cold, and smelt strongly of damp and disuse. They listened carefully for any sound of habitation. Only silence dwelt within. William led them through into the room where the shaft still yawned open in the middle of the floor. It was just the same. Forman lit a lantern from a tinder-box in his pocket, and one by one they shinned down the ladder.

Accustoming his eyes to the subterranean darkness at the foot of the shaft, William peered around. All the coffins were gone. The five short corridors that led off from the central shaft were empty. But they were no longer so short. William could see, at a glance, that the miners had continued to burrow their way into the underlying soil, creating a honeycomb of underground passageways. A Daedalian labyrinth, that held in its shadowy recesses and coigns something far worse than the legendary Minotaur.

"Any ideas, William?" asked Forman.

"It's all changed," William replied.

"Then we must search. One corridor at a time. They have to be here somewhere."

And so the three men tried each passageway in turn, finding nothing but the dried skeletons of small mammals littering the floor. Here and there the earth was disturbed, as if objects had been stored, and later moved. At last, having almost given up hope, as they infiltrated the last of the five corridors, they turned a corner and found what they were seeking.

Only two lidless coffins from the original twenty. But each contained one of the dreadful sleepers. Each one as if asleep, lying prone on a sprinkling of sour earth. The air was foul with the smells of blood and decay. All three men snatched a peep over the first coffin's edge. One glimpse was enough. They had found their prey. The hunter had become the hunted.

"Go ahead," whispered Forman to Saywell, who was clearly unnerved by what he had seen. With trembling hands the minister opened his book, and in a quavering voice, began to read aloud the office for Evening Prayer. He began with the Lord's Prayer. At the end, the other two mumbled a half-hearted Amen.

"O Lord, open thou our lips," intoned the priest. He paused, and looked meaningfully at the other two.

"Oh sorry," said William. "I was miles away. And our mouth

shall show forth thy praise."

"O Lord, make speed to save us." And so it went on, the priest reading the office, and the other two responding with more or less accuracy, and even less enthusiasm. Saywell went through the prayers, the *Magnificat* and *Nunc Dimittis*, the Collects:

"Lighten our darkness we beseech thee O Lord, and by thy great mercy defend us from all perils and dangers of this night ..."

Then came the Creed, which seemed both interminable and obscure. "The Holy Ghost is of the father and of the son neither made, nor created, nor begotten, but proceeding. So there is one father, not three fathers, one son not three sons; one holy ghost, not three holy ghosts ..."

There was no room for misunderstanding. During this recital, Forman leaned against the wall with his head bowed. William was unsure whether he was praying, or sleeping. After the Creed came the Litany, which was even longer.

"Spare us, good Lord, from all evil and mischief, from sin, from the crafts and assaults of the devil, from thy wrath, and from everlasting damnation ..."

It went on. And on. Each time the priest seemed to reach a peroration that signalled a conclusion, it was no more than a pause, and he was off again.

"What's he doing?" whispered Forman in William's ear.

"Don't ask me," was the reply. "You brought him here."

"Father," said William timidly. "Do you think you could maybe proceed to the casting out bit? We still have to find the rest of them."

The minister turned a severe white face towards William. "Understand this, brother," he replied precisely. "The Ministry of the Word is a necessary preface to the operation of the sacraments. These poor possessed creatures are not to be denied the light of God's eternal word, just because you're in a hurry. However lost they may be, the Lord will seek them out and offer them salvation. It is not a matter of performing certain dumb ceremonies, as if we were mountebanks or players. They must hear the voice of reason, in order to find the path to redemption." And he continued with his prayers.

"It'll be getting dark soon," hissed Forman.

"I know," said William. "But he's unstoppable."

"It's all very well, but I don't think they're listening."

Just as the priest was preparing at last to round off the office, something else stopped him in his tracks. A yellow, glistening face suddenly rose above the edge of the first coffin, and stared at them with empty eyes. Saywell was dumbstruck. The Vampyr rose to a sitting position, and ran a black tongue over cracked lips and yellow fangs. Then his companion rose from the coffin in the same way, looked around, and grinned, horrible, a ghastly smile.

"*Cine este el?*" asked the first Vampyr of the second.

"*Nu stiu,*" said the other.

"*E un preot? El arata ca un preot.*"

"*El nu poate fi un adeverat preot. El nu are o cruce!*"

Both laughed their horrible, mirthless laugh. "*El nici măcar nu vorbeşte limba latină!*"

"*Sa-l ducem.*"

And with a speed and agility beyond human power, the two obscene apparitions leapt from their coffins and fell upon the priest, striking at him with the rash and rush of a wild boar's fangs. The Reverend Saywell screamed in terror, and then in pain, as the monsters tore at his flesh and lapped his blood. His tall black form collapsed in on itself like a falling tower, and the Vampyrs fell on him, snarling and biting like fighting dogs. William and Forman again turned on their heels and ran, leaving the Vampyrs to feast on the fallen. There was nothing they could do. Back to the shaft-bottom, up the ladder, out of the house, door slammed behind them, through the dark streets of Westminster they ran for their lives.

22 February 1606. Silver Street

"There is one thing we can be sure of, William," said Forman, once he had caught his breath. "Protestant Christianity has no power over these Vampyrs."

"You think?" exclaimed William, still gasping for air.

"Yes," Forman continued, taking out his notebook and writing. "We have learned much from this encounter. We know now that these Vampyrs, which we thought dumb brutes, have the power of speech. They can communicate with one another. They can reason, and act upon their knowledge."

"But what on earth were they saying? Do you know?"

"Oh yes. I took the trouble, on my voyage back from the Netherlands, to learn a little of the Romani language spoken in Transylvania. They asked whether the Reverend was a priest, since he looked like one. But they did not think him to be a real priest. He doesn't have a cross, they said. He doesn't even speak Latin. They displayed towards him neither respect nor fear. Their final words were 'Let's get him.' So we know that the ministers of the reformed Church of England are of no use to us. And things being as they are, we can hardly call for assistance upon the Catholic Church."

"Then what can we do?"

"We must go it alone. We will arm ourselves, and return to the house at first light. We will find these creatures asleep in their coffins. Then we will drive, through their hearts, stakes made from the wood of Our Saviour's cross. Many such relics have been confiscated from the church during these past years."

"Have they not been destroyed?"

"No." Forman smiled enigmatically. "They are safely stored, in a place where very few can enter. There is a large storehouse beneath Lambeth Palace where such articles are kept under lock and key."

"And who has the keys?"

"I do," said Forman simply. "We will pierce these Vampyrs with the sacred wood. And with sharp blades of the purest silver, we will sever their heads from their bodies. It will be dreadful work. They will seem like living beings, helpless in their coffins. They will cry in fear, and plead for their lives, and scream in pain. It will be a massacre. But we are destroying monsters, slaughtering vicious beasts, not murdering men. We must be bloody, bold and resolute to accomplish this great task. I can rely on you, can I not, William?"

"Well, to be honest, you know, it's not really my line of work."

Forman looked at him steadily. "You are my indentured assistant. You are a trained and experienced butcher. You have knowledge that has helped to track down these creatures. You possess that knowledge because all this is partly your fault. I can't really imagine anyone better qualified. Can you?"

William shrugged. It was all true. Forman had him on the hook. And all the time a dark shadow lay across his mind. The Countess. He had seen her disappearing into the Westminster house. Perhaps he had been wrong about her? Perhaps he could save her. Things must be as they may. He was beginning to talk like one of his own characters.

"That's it then," said Forman with an air of satisfaction. "Tomorrow we must collect our tools, and make our assault. Meet me at Lambeth Palace at daybreak. We will make a great team, William, you and I. Forman and Shakespeare."

"Shakespeare and Forman," said William automatically.

"Let's not quarrel about the billing. Look what happened to poor Marlowe."

"That was a quarrel about the *bill*. In a tavern. Not the *billing*."

"It wasn't a tavern, William," Forman said with an air of superior knowledge. "So there was no bill. It was a private house, owned by Eleanor Bull. Our late lamented Queen Elizabeth's beloved Nanny."

"Really?"

"Oh yes. I was involved in Marlowe's inquest. This is not my first foray into intelligence work. The place was a nothing less than a safe house for government spies. The other men there were all agents of Sir Francis Walsingham."

"I'm not altogether surprised. Kit was a spy. But he *was* murdered, was he not? Come to think of it, he didn't mention it."

Forman paused with his notebook half way into his bag. "What did you say?"

"Oh, nothing. I had a dream. Marlowe was there."

"I see," said Forman mysteriously. "But let me tell you this, William. Should you ever chance to cross the Channel, and find yourself walking the streets of Flushing, and you bump into a man who looks exactly like Christopher Marlowe, don't be at all surprised. His death was … doubtful. Unless …" he said thoughtfully, almost to himself, as he closed his bag, "he became a Vampyr …"

"No, I'm sure he's in Hell," said William, trying to be helpful. "Making the best of it."

"Whatever you say. Well, he's not our problem at the moment. Though if you'd like me to try and raise his spirit for you, I'll have a go."

"Oh, no thanks. If it's all the same to you. We've got enough on our plate, without bringing him back again."

As soon as the Doctor had left, William slumped on his bed, and plummeted into the first real sleep he had experienced in weeks. As blackness crept across his mind, he saw an image of a butchery, his father's old shop, hung outside with carcasses of naked men and women, dangling from hooks and swaying slightly in the breeze, and with a sign above the door that read: "Forman and Shakespeare. Vampire Hunters."

21 February 1606. Lambeth Palace

Shortly after sunrise, refreshed by an unaccustomed night's rest,

William was loitering before the gatehouse of Lambeth Palace. While he waited for Forman, he gazed up at the rosy red-brick magnificence of the gateway, with its massive five-storey towers jutting forward at either side of the entrance. The first rays of the sun caught and highlighted the ornate diaperwork of black header bricks. Window dressings and tracery, copings and battlements, quoins and bands, all of stone. He admired the mullioned window on the south front. What craftsmanship! An artistry of brick and stone. Above the entrance a stone vaulting with moulded ridge, attached angle shafts, moulded caps and bases, carved bosses. The Palace was a portal to an older, finer world, where Cardinals were great princes of the church, and no expense was spared. But today, in this lovely building, power and beauty still went hand-in-hand. Why had he sought to destroy them? He sat down on the black wooden settle beside the entrance. Though the air was cold, the wood of the bench was warm against his back. He closed his eyes, and was glad to be alive.

Forman came walking briskly along the river from his Lambeth house, carrying his ubiquitous bag. He too seemed cheered by the thin February sunshine.

"Morning, William, morning." They could have been meeting for a fishing expedition, or a walk in the country.

Forman knocked on the smaller of the two gates, exchanged a few words with the turnkey, and beckoned William inside. They crossed a quadrangle between the honey-coloured ragstone buildings, threaded the cloisters, and entered a low archway. Before them was a stout old oak door, fastened with iron bands, which Forman proceeded to unlock with a huge iron key. As William entered, he closed the door behind them.

The room was dimly illuminated by light filtering through dusty stained glass. Down the centre ran a long oak table. Each wall was piled high with numbered and labelled boxes.

"What we have here, William," said Forman, "is a repository

of religious artefacts, captured and confiscated from churches and from recusant Catholics. For us it will prove, I trust, to be a kind of armoury. Most of those 'Popish trinkets' were destroyed in the persecutions, of course: rosaries, crosses, bells, books and candles. But artefacts of any value were spirited away and locked up here. In these boxes you will find some items of extraordinary antiquity and beauty: jewelled crucifixes, golden patens, silver chalices, costly ecclesiastical vestments, adorned with amethyst and orient pearl. Here also you will find relics, taken by the reformers from the churches they vandalised. Objects that were once thought to possess extraordinary powers. Here you will find the bones of St Cuthbert, and the skull of the Venerable Bede. Below this room there is a crypt, a secret chamber even I am not allowed to enter. There are stored relics of immense sacramental power. It is rumoured that it contains the shroud in which Our Lord was buried, and the skin of St Bartholomew. Who knows what really lies down there? The Ark of the Covenant, perhaps? The Holy Grail? The Spear of Longinus?"

"I don't understand," said William. "The church has decreed such objects to be of no value, mere popish impostures, the trickery of mountebanks who practised on popular superstition. Why on earth would they want to keep them?"

"In one word, William: power. They were once believed by the population at large to contain some kind of influence. Though the church decrees they are nothing more than paltry baubles and worthless trinkets, the stock-in-trade of mendicant priests and fraudulent friars, our government does not wish to discard anything that might conceivably be useful as an instrument of force – whether or not, officially, they believe in its efficacy. They keep these things so no-one else can access even the potentiality of power. One day, the nation might face some threat that would require such potency, a black day when men will use anything that lies to hand to defend themselves. And who knows? Maybe one day the church will want these things back in place again. Such revolutions have happened, as recently as the last generation. But now, to work. We must arm ourselves with the breastplate of faith, and the helmet of salvation."

Forman picked up a large box, set it on the table, and proceeded to unpack its contents. Two large silver crosses on chains, designed to be worn on the breast. Two rosaries, each made from fine cut-glass crystal beads, with a pendant silver cross. A collection of smaller crucifixes, also of silver. A small engraved silver box, which he opened to reveal a pile of round and thin white wafers. The consecrated host. Some glass flasks of transparent liquid: Holy Water.

Then a number of larger objects. A bag of ancient and rusting square iron nails, each about a foot long. Some lengths of wood, also of great antiquity, sharpened at one end. Two wooden mallets, with heavy rounded heads. And lastly two very old swords, fashioned in the manner of the Roman *gladius,* with a broad three-foot blade, simple hand-guard, and leather-bound grip. The mountings bore the patina of age, but the blades were bright and undefiled.

"Pure silver," said Forman. "Not strong enough for battle-blades, of course, but perfect for our purposes. Here, feel the edge."

William put the heel of his thumb to the edge of one of the swords. It was keen as a razor. Looking more closely he could see that the edge had been heat-tempered to an intimidating sharpness, with etched along the blade a wavy line like the *hamon* on a Japanese sword.

"I spent last night studying the book van Helsing gave us. It details all the methods of killing a Vampyr. First we subdue it with Holy Water, and bind it by laying a silver crucifix on its chest. Then we drive through its brain one of these nails, reputed to be taken from Our Saviour's Crucifixion. We pierce the heart with one of these stakes, also taken from the wood of the True Cross. We cut off its head, and in its mouth place a piece of the consecrated host. And all the while we are protected by these crosses on our breasts, these rosaries wound about our arms."

William pored over the objects with some scepticism. There seemed to be a surprising number of nails for one crucifixion, and the stakes looked like ordinary wood to him. He wanted to believe. "Will they work?" he asked.

"Who knows?" Forman replied simply. "Everything is an experiment. This is a new kind of medical practice, its objective being to take, rather than preserve, life. It is not unprecedented in my profession. I once met a physician from Liverpool, who confided that in that town, the death of a patient who seems beyond recovery is often hastened, by the simple expedient of enforced starvation. Doctors kill their patients. It is a strange method of healing, but he insisted it was prompted by a kind of care for the patient's welfare. His suffering is shortened. His family's medical bills reduced. The 'Liverpool Care Pathway,' he called it.

"These Vampyrs are our patients. But we must treat them by administering to them the sharp cure of a sudden and violent death. The best prognosis for them, is immediate destruction. If the patient lives, the doctor dies. Have faith, William. You are a Catholic. You may in the end prove that your own religion truly possesses all the powers it claims."

"And if we fail?"

"We fail? But screw your courage to the sticking place, and we'll not fail. Come. Arm yourself, Sir William of Stratford. Take your shield, your favour, your lance." Around William's neck he draped a pectoral cross, about his arm he twined a rosary, and in his hand he placed a silver sword. "Fight valiantly, under the banner of Christ, against the world, the flesh and the devil."

Together they crossed the river and made their way towards Westminster. Forman concealed all their tools in the apparently infinite capacity of his bag. They reached the house, and Forman again picked the lock. This time they entered as quietly as they could, and in the darkened entrance room, removed from the bag their arsenal of holy weapons. The pectoral crosses were slung around their necks, the rosaries wound about their forearms. Each man filled his pockets with little silver crucifixes. Forman had brought along two broad leather bandoliers, worn across the body like those of a musquetier. But in place of powder and bullets, they held the small flasks of Holy Water, and the blessed crucifixion nails. Lastly they each took up a sword in the right hand, a mallet in the other, and a sharpened stake thrust into the belt.

Forman led the way down the shaft, and into the corridor where the priest had been killed. His exsanguinated corpse lay twisted across the passageway, his white face turning yellow, his wide open eyes staring in horror. The upper lip was already receding from the teeth, showing the enlargement of the canines. He was turning. The boxes were still there, their occupants lying inert like huge overfed leeches, bloated with blood.

Killing the first two Vampyrs was not as bad as William had feared. Forman lost no time in sloshing both with Holy Water. As soon as the liquid touched their skin, it seemed to burn, scalding and hissing, jetting a pungent smoke. The Vampyrs both screamed in agony, and began to shake violently within their coffins. Quickly William laid, on the chest of each, one of the small silver crucifixes. The effect was immediate: the screaming stopped, and as if paralysed, the Vampyrs merely opened their mouths wide in a silent rictus of pain and fear. Ruthlessly Forman placed an iron nail against one of the creature's staring eyes, and with his mallet smashed the point through his skull. Again the monster yelled out and writhed violently. William thought of Marlowe, stabbed through the eye, screaming his blasphemies against the vaults of heaven.

But there was no time for thought: the deed was upon them. Seizing his sharp stake, he held it over the Vampyr's ribs, and with an enormous blow struck the sacred point home. Then he tore it out, breaking bone and ripping soft tissue. A jet of blood erupted from the wound, and splashed and soiled his face. But the writhing thing was still. Forman's blade flashed for a moment in the air, then fell like the vengeful scythe of Death himself, to sever the hideous face from its ruined body. They repeated the operation on the other Vampyr, and finished by placing pieces of the Blessed Sacrament in each monster's mouth. It was done.

As they turned from the scene of their butchery to retrace their steps, they observed that the corpse of the priest had changed. The face was no longer yellow and distorted, but candid with an expression of ineffable peace.

"Ah," said Forman. "I read something about this. The Vampyr's bite turns its victim into another Vampyr. But kill the first creature, and the curse is lifted. The victim assumes a natural death. This poor soul will not rise again to trouble the waste night watches. He is truly dead. And, let us hope, he dwells with his God. But come, William. We have more dreadful work to perform."

Knowing the Vampyrs had forsaken the territory of their initial rest, where Fawkes had first installed them, they sought through the excavation for the remainder. Since they were not to be found in the passageways off the main shaft, they must needs be down the tunnel. Holding their lanterns aloft, William and Forman crept quietly along the length of the tunnel. Half way through, they came across what looked like a cave-in, a pile of loose earth blocking the aperture. It took them a while to clear the debris away, and continue their progress. At last they entered the foot of the shaft at the Westminster Palace end. Still no sign. The ladder remained in place, and looking up, they could see that the top of the shaft was roughly covered with boards. Gingerly they ascended, shifted the planks aside, and poked their heads up into the cellar beneath the Parliament House, the vault of the Gunpowder Plot.

There were the other lidless coffins, all eighteen of them,

neatly lodged around the walls of the vault. Once the Plot had been discovered, the powder found and removed, the Vampyrs must have moved into this deserted space. In any event there they all lay, supine and helpless, eyes closed in their unnatural daylight sleep.

Steeling themselves to their bloody work, the Vampyr hunters began. A sprinkling of Holy Water over the first creature's ravaged face. At his sudden cry of pain, every monster in the vault awoke, and began to scream in his turn. Terrified bodies noisily knocked against coffin wood, with a sound like stabled horses driven mad by the scent of a wolf.

But the hunters kept their nerve. A silver cross on the breast. A nail driven through the soft tissue of an eye. The sharpened wood of the Holy Cross, battered through fragile ribs, piercing the dried and evil heart. Then with a flash of the healing blade, the hideous head lopped from the undead, unliving, dying body.

The vault was like a slaughterhouse. For hours they worked, methodically slaying each monster in turn, deafening their ears to the screams of horror, wiping the curtains of blood from their eyes.

Nineteen boxes purged and sanctified. Nineteen Vampyrs slain. At the nineteenth violent stroke, Forman cut his own hand with the sharp sword-blade. Dropping the weapon, he inspected the wound.

"William," he said, "I must anoint and bind this laceration. For fear of infection. The ointment is in my bag. Can you handle this last one on your own?"

William looked down at his reeking hands, subdued to what they worked in. "Yes, of course. Take care of it."

Clumsily Forman descended the ladder, holding his injured hand to his chest. William approached the last coffin. Strange! This one was closed, its lid resting across it at a slight diagonal, as if pulled into place from inside. William remembered that the twentieth Vampyr had escaped from the ship. And Fawkes had told him of the escapee's return. Twenty was the right number. This one must be the last. But why was it closed? He bent down, and rotated the coffin lid to expose its occupant to his view. Stood back and looked into the coffin. And felt his heart, literally, stop beating.

It was the Countess. There she lay, in all her unnatural beauty, red lips redder than the stained stones of the Vampyr's vault. The long fringes of her eyelashes swept down onto her cheeks, and her dark hair framed her lovely face. Her breasts moved gently, as if in sleep.

Lines from *Romeo and Juliet* came back to him. He had played the part himself, and could recall every word:

Death, that hath suck'd the honey of thy breath,
Hath had no power yet upon thy beauty:
Thou art not conquer'd; beauty's ensign yet
Is crimson in thy lips and in thy cheeks ...

So it was all true. The Countess was one of the Undead. Yet she seemed so alive, so beautiful! She stirred in her sleep, and softly sighed, as if at some innocent dream of loneliness and loss. But as she moved, the upper lip drew back a little from the protuberant teeth. They were flecked with dried blood. She was a monster. She lay on her unconsecrated bed, foul with her crimes. With trembling hands William took out a flask of Holy Water, and removed the stopper. He must destroy her. Yet her beauty arrested him, stayed his hand.

Why art thou yet so fair? shall I believe
That unsubstantial death is amorous,
And that the lean abhorred monster keeps
Thee here in dark to be his paramour?

In the play Juliet was not dead, merely drugged, death-like only in her sleep. The Countess was a true bride of darkness, Death's own paramour. But still, he had loved her. Could he not spare her? Could he not join her, marry himself to corruption, share in the monstrous desecration that kept her undead body young and beautiful? He could not bear the thought of her destruction. He could not hand her over to insubstantial death. The thought of it robbed him of all decision, and the sharp sword dangled from his nerveless hand. She was indeed his Dark Lady. Yet he would not sacrifice her to the Dark Lord.

For fear of that, I still will stay with thee;
And never from this palace of dim night
Depart again:

He could hear Forman running back along the tunnel, shouting something unintelligible. Heard his body crash into the ladder. Heard his boots knocking and slipping against the creaking wood as he climbed. "William! William!" His head appeared above the parapet. "*Sunset!*"

William glanced back, and gripped his sword. But as he turned again to stare into the coffin, it was empty. Above him there was a movement in the air, like a windswept shadow. A fluttering. A faint squeaking. A bat, circling and zig-zagging around the vault, seeking some means of escape. "She's gone!" he cried.

"*She?*" was Forman's uncomprehending reply.

"The Countess. It was her, in the last coffin. She's one of them. But she – disappeared."

"With the last rays of the sun." Forman nodded. "Come, we must go. Bring your tools. We have not yet finished our task." And he slipped over the edge onto the rungs of the ladder.

As William followed him, he noticed the bat flitting around the pile of firewood that had concealed the barrels of powder. His feet on the ladder, his head over the rim of the shaft, he paused to watch. Something was moving among the faggots. There was a faint stirring of dry wood. Someone was there. Someone, or something. A hand emerged from the brushwood, clearing it away. Another hand. A face. A form. The body of a very tall man, dressed in a long black cloak and hood. He stood upright among the broken branches, opened his swirling garment, and enfolded within it the fluttering form of the bat.

Forman was calling him. Tearing his eyes away from the unnatural scene, William slid down the ladder and ran after the doctor. He could not believe what he had seen with his own eyes. The face of the man in the cloak and hood, was the mask of Guido Fawkes.

21 February 1606. Silver Street

"It is time, William," said Forman meaningfully, "for you to enter the confessional." So William told him the whole story of how he had followed the Countess, and watched her at her deadly work. "You should have told me," Forman reprimanded him. "We could have been prepared. Now we know there is at least one Vampyr still on the loose."

"Maybe more than one." And he told him about the tall, black-cloaked figure with the visored face of Guido Fawkes. "And what about all the others? The one we saw in Spitalfields? The victims of the 'plague'?"

"Unless I am much mistaken, they will all have died the natural death that was denied them by the intervention of these foul creatures. Remember our priest was turned back, and released, his soul restored, before he had the chance to rise. We will see. Our immediate concern must be to find and destroy the Countess."

"I'm sorry," said William. "Really sorry."

"I daresay you couldn't help it. The lunatic, the lover and the poet. You've managed to be all three at once."

"How did she disappear?"

"I'll have to do some more research. The book van Helsing gave me must have the answers. I have also written to him, and expect an answer any day. I'll study the book again tonight, and re-read Fawkes's letters. Good-night, William. Come to my house tomorrow. I think we will be taking a trip down the river."

22 February 1606. The River Thames, Lambeth

The boat moved noiselessly through thick river-fog. Just a light splash, as the oars were skilfully dipped and feathered, a faint creak of wood from the rowlocks, and the soft sound of the hull being urged smoothly along the silent waterway. One man took the oars, another was sitting aft, and handling the rudder. Wreaths of fog curled and parted before them. Occasionally the steersman would change direction slightly, in response to the ruddy glow of a light looming near, or when the low cry of another boatman echoed like a bird-call across the water.

William had called on Forman at his Lambeth house, and found the doctor busily collating his papers. He had had a letter from van Helsing, which he added to *The Natural History of the Vampyr* and Fawkes's letters, stuffing the whole collection untidily into his bag.

"There is a boat waiting for us down at the Lambeth landing-stage," he said. "We are going to the Tower."

William, accustomed by now to Forman's penchant for mystery and deferred explanation, didn't bother to ask why. Perhaps he was going to be re-arrested. What a relief that would be.

"Now William," Forman began as they settled into the boat for the long, slow journey down the Thames, "I have managed to unravel the tangled skein of our mystery. Most of it, anyway. The clues are all in Fawkes's epistles. The solution is to be found here, in this book, and in the letter I have just received from van

Helsing. Your Countess is the last link in the chain of explanation.

"Fawkes was drawn into this business, like a moth to a flame. His inquiries in Eastern Europe led him inexorably to Transylvania, and to the Castle of Count Dracula. You remember how that name struck fear into the hearts of the local people? How when his name was mentioned, they muttered amongst themselves of devils and hell, in their language of 'ordog' and 'pokol'? How the Slovaks who guided Fawkes to the castle fled for their lives before the setting of the sun?

"The reason? This Count Dracula is nothing less than the oldest and most powerful of all the Vampyrs. He has lived for over a century. In life he was a great man. His name was Vlad III, Prince of Wallachia. His father founded the Order of the Dragon, to protect Christendom against the Turks, and thence comes the family name of 'Dracula.' Vlad signed himself *Wladislaus Dragwlya, vaivoda partium Transalpinarum*. Wladislav Dracula, Lord of Transylvania. He was a great warlord, and ruthless in battle. From his custom of impaling his enemies on spikes, he derived the nickname 'Vlad the Impaler.' On his death in 1476, nobody knows how, he became a Vampyr.

"Now you recall the portraits Fawkes observed in the south wing of the castle? One was the portrait of this long-dead Vlad, the very image of Dracula himself. But alongside that picture was another: the portrait of a beautiful dark-haired woman. She was the wife of Vlad. No-one knows her name. She died after her husband. Fawkes thought he saw her, just after sunset, in the south wing of the castle. How could that be possible? But van Helsing sent me a picture of her. Her name was Ilona." And he handed William a small miniature portrait of a dark-haired woman in the dress of the 15th century.

She had a name! There could be no doubt. It was her. It was the Countess. She was no novice Vampyr, newly turned in some dark alleyway in Clerkenwell. Like her husband, she was one of the old ones, a long-surviving member of the Undead.

"She said her husband was old," said William thoughtfully.

"Aha," returned Forman. "And *you* thought he was just another senile cuckold from one of your city comedies, eh? An old husband you could gull, and fleece, while you fucked his pretty young wife right under his bespectacled nose? Not a one-hundred-and-thirty year old Vampyr!"

"But how did she get here?"

"The evidence is all here in these writings," said Forman, "for those who know how to decipher it. You remember Fawkes's story of the man who stole the silver cross from one of the coffins? Poor wretch, his petty theft released one of the Undead from its confinement in the hold of the ship. They left him tied to the mast, and in the night the Vampyr took him. Think, William. That night Fawkes dreamed that the dark-haired woman from the castle was near him in the darkness. It was her. The Countess. She was on the ship."

"But how …?" Suddenly it dawned on William. "The empty coffin!"

"Exactly," said Forman. "The Countess smuggled herself into one of the boxes, and left the castle without her husband's knowledge. She escaped from the ship when it landed at Foulness, and made her way to London. And there you met her: beautiful, cold, cruel. Always at night. She was your Dark Lady."

"Why did she not kill me?"

"I don't know. Did she ever offer any signs of violence?"

"Yes. Yes, she did." And William told Forman about those moments where the Countess seemed possessed of some rage or hunger; of how his poetry calmed her; and of how she required him to write poems for her by way of propitiation.

"That's why you brought your sonnets to her. I see. Like the girl in the old Arabian tale? Scheherazade. You had to tell a new story every night, to save yourself from death. You were very fortunate. But tell me again about your sex life with her."

William told him. Forman listened avidly. "So she would not let you inside her. Fascinating. She told you it would be your death. Perhaps you would, by entering her body, have encountered, and been destroyed by, the Undeath within. But she masturbated for you? I wish I'd been there. For clinical observation, of course, I mean. Strictly scientific. And she performed fellatio on you? Did you come in her mouth?"

"Yes," said William reluctantly, sensing that Forman had a more than professional interest in his descriptions. "If you must know, yes."

"Did she spit, or swallow?"

"Why? For God's sake. She swallowed."

"Did she seem to like it?"

"As a matter of fact she did. She liked it a lot. She lapped it up as if it was mother's milk."

"To her perhaps it was. You didn't think that in any way odd? You know a lot of women, do you, who really like the taste of semen? William, tell me. Have you at any time, in the last six months, had treatment for the *gonorrhoea passio*? I am not your doctor, I know, but you can tell me in confidence."

"Yes, of course I have. I'm a celebrated actor. An occasional dose of the clap is a professional obligation."

"That's it then," said Forman with a smile of satisfaction. "Men who have had gonorrhoea often secrete, in their semen, tiny droplets of blood. She could taste blood in your seed, and drank it to quench her dreadful thirst. You see, William, your whore-mongering may have saved your life."

"But what happened to the Countess last night? She just seemed to vanish into thin air."

"I want you to recall one more detail in Fawkes's letters. When the ship lay beached on the shoal at Foulness, did not Fawkes see a beautiful black horse on the deck, which leapt ashore and made off into the darkness?"

"He said it was a trick of the light. It was never really there."

"Be assured it was. This book tells how the Vampyr can change its shape at will, though only between sunset and sunrise. A Vampyr may transform itself into a wolf, a horse – or a bat. Thus transformed, they enjoy through the hours of darkness the powers and abilities of these creatures: the wolf's savagery, the horse's speed, the bat's mastery of the air. That horse was none other than the Countess. In that form she escaped from the ship, made the shore and reached London. There she would have turned herself back into a woman again, and found her resting place before sunrise."

"At the Westminster house!"

"The very same. By some magical power she found her way home, back to that box of earth from her native land. And now we have no alternative but to destroy her."

"And her companion. The one who wears the mask of Guy Fawkes. He too must be a Vampyr."

"Yes," replied Forman thoughtfully. "The man in the mask. Bitten and turned by the Countess. It must be so. For you saw Fawkes put to death, did you not, with your own eyes?"

William was silent for a space. Water lapped and gurgled along the prow, as the boat inched its way through the fog.

"Whoever he is," Forman went on, "that tall stranger, it is the Countess we must destroy. She is the source of the evil."

"Yes. I'm just not sure I'm up to it."

"You are right to be afraid. That is exactly why we are now on our way to the Tower. The *Natural History of the Vampyr* explains that there is a huge difference, in strength and power and cunning, between a newly-made Vampyr, and one like your Countess, or indeed her husband the Count, who has endured and survived for centuries. It seems that with the years, they increase in strength, augment their powers, sharpen their wits and expand their intellectual capacities. They are not like human beings, who grow feeble and incapacitated and demented with age. They improve, they mature, they evolve. This explains, you see, how one Vampyr can exert such authority over others, as the Count dominated and compelled his minions of newly-made Vampyrs. It is not an aristocracy of birth, where natural authority can be inherited by an infant. It is the survival of the fittest: an aristocracy of death, or rather Undeath. Those who manage to sustain their horrid career of murder, and bloodlust, and prolong it for years, decades, centuries, are able to exert their rule over their own creatures. Indeed, in their dark perverse world, they are like gods, who create beings in their own image, and then compel their obedience. These creatures are truly the ones to be feared. We are lucky to have escaped with our lives yesterday, since the Countess is one of the very old ones, one of the most powerful Vampyrs on earth. And so today we seek help from an authority capable of matching hers, strength for strength. In the Tower lies one who, I trust, will guide us safely through the perils of the vault, so that we may perform our bloody work."

"Who?"

"You will see."

The thick fog still obstructed all visibility, so it was only by a slight shock of the boat's prow, softly bumping and grazing against a mooring, that they knew they had arrived. The landing-stage of the Tower. Home from home, thought William as he stepped off the little craft's dipping edge and found his feet on the firm planks of a jetty. Silent men were there to meet and guide them to a postern gate. Once inside, they were led through the usual maze of corridors and stairways, to the door of a chamber on the upper floors. Here the guards left them, and Forman knocked for admission. The voice that bid them enter was firm but melodic. Forman opened the door, and they found themselves in a large, fair chamber, unusually spacious and well-appointed for housing a prisoner. A fire crackled in the grate, and around the room were scattered books, pens and paper, sheets of writing, musical instruments. The man they had come to meet sat at a desk beneath the window, with his back to them, his eyes on a book. With a scholar's reluctance, he closed the volume, and turned to meet them.

William had never met this man, but knew instantly who he was. He was of middling height, with a strong, well-muscled body and an erect carriage. His hair was cut very short, in an ascetic or military style, and like his close-cropped forked beard, was streaked with grey. He wore beautifully-tailored clothes of black silk, with a collar of purest white.

This was none other than Father Henry Garnett, superior of the Jesuits in England. Father Garnett held out his ringed right hand for them to kiss. Both did so, Forman in courtesy, William with a kind of avidity that surprised him. Looking up into the Jesuit's large, luminous eyes, he felt suddenly and unexpectedly the stab of contrition. He wanted to confess: to pour out his soul to this soldier-priest; to give assurance to God that he was sorry for his sins; to receive, upon his heart, like sweet spring rain, the infinite and inexplicable gift of God's own mercy. Garnett was a gentleman in whom he felt he could repose an absolute trust.

Forman introduced them by name, and as doctor and poet conscripted into government service. The priest revealed no particular curiosity about them, or any anxiety to give account of himself. He seemed a man without vanity. He beckoned them to be seated, Forman on an upright chair, William on the edge of the prisoner's bed.

"Monsignor," Forman began, "do you know why we are here?"

Garnett replied with a polite smile. "I believe so. I have been informed that there is a service His Majesty wishes to undertake on his behalf. And that an earnest and successful performance of this service will go some way towards mitigating my punishment."

"Punishment?" William interrupted in surprise. "What are you in for?"

Again the Jesuit smiled, this time not without some sign of

strain. "Between ourselves – and any spies who may be listening, though they know it all already – I am incarcerated here for my faith. As are other Jesuits. The specific charge against *me* is that I had foreknowledge of the Powder Plot, and failed to reveal it to the proper authorities."

"And did you?" asked Forman bluntly.

"To answer that question," the Jesuit said softly, "would violate my priestly oath, by breaking the seal of the confessional. This is my only defence. It has the advantage of truth; the disadvantage, that in the eyes of my accusers, it constitutes no defence at all, since it has no place in common law."

"So you are charged with treason?" William asked.

"Indeed. And am likely to die a traitor's death. Unless you gentlemen have brought some good news pertaining to my deliverance."

Forman explained, guardedly, that the Jesuit's help was needed on a grave spiritual mission; that he would be granted temporary release from confinement, on condition that he swear to surrender himself back to the Tower on its completion; and that he would remain, at all times, in the company of the two men who were to take charge of him, and would stand security for his restoration.

"And in return for this service," said Father Garnett, "I am assured of some remission to my penalty, whatever that might be?"

"So are we assured," Forman replied, "though the details are, as you will appreciate, beyond our remit. But I can tell you this. The realm is facing an attack from a dreadful foe, capable of wreaking a terrible catastrophe. If we can vanquish this enemy, you will deserve more at His Majesty's hands than mere gratitude."

"Well," said Garnett, apparently satisfied by the assurance. "My trust is in you. The rest is in God's hands."

"And ours," said Forman, whose atheism was growing a little

restless in this atmosphere of devout belief. "You may leave with us immediately, Father, and we will take you to the place where the great work awaits us. On the way we will explain to you the nature of the task."

"There is no need," said the Jesuit mildly. "Surely you do not think the enemy of God and man can send his emissaries amongst us, without our Order having some prior knowledge? I know they are here. I have felt their presence everywhere. I have seen it, in despairing faces in the street; heard it, in hopeless voices in the confessional; read it, in the swirling black dust of the Powder conspiracy. He is near. 'The Devil is come amongst us, having great wrath, for he knoweth he hath but a short time.'"

"The devil he is!" said Forman sceptically. "But these creatures are like nothing we have encountered before. I have taken great pains to understand their natural history, and to know the sources of their power. They are of a very specific kind ...''

"No," replied the Jesuit mildly. "There is only one kind. It travels in many forms, and under many titles, for its name is Legion. But I know only too well what it is. I have encountered it before, in Rome. And on behalf of my God and my order, I will face it, and send it back whence it came. Or die in the attempt."

"Spoken like a true soldier of Christ," said Forman, impressed by the priest's courage, and trying to rise to the rhetorical occasion.

"We all owe God a death," said William, ransacking his own work for some sentiment matching the Jesuit's easy command of oracular speech.

"Indeed, Master Shakespeare," Father Garnett replied. "And He will decide when repayment is due."

"Are you ready to leave, Monsignor?"

"May I have half an hour to walk in the garden below my window?"

Forman called the guards and relayed Garnett's request. They took him down, while Forman and William remained in the chamber. Presently, though the window, they were able to see the Jesuit walking in the garden.

"Why on earth is he in here?" William asked of Forman.

Speaking very low to avoid being overheard, Forman brought William up to date. "The government has long wanted to implicate the Jesuits in some major act of treason. The Powder Plot gave them the opportunity. To kill two birds with one stone. Once they had caught and executed the plotters themselves, they set out to prove that the Jesuits were behind it all. They even coined a new name for it, the 'Jesuit Treason.' It took them a long time to find Garnett, who was kept hidden, in various houses, by members of the faithful. Eventually they ran him to ground. You will know of him as a man of honourable and upright character, who preached a gospel of peace and submission, rather than one of violent resistance. But there was just one detail that exposed him to accusation."

"And that was ..."

"He was Catesby's confessor. And that one detail will hang him, or worse. Unless we can save him. By affording him the opportunity of saving us."

At the end of half an hour, they went down to find him in the garden. His black-clad figure could be seen strolling between the flower-beds, hands clasped behind his back. He was like one long deprived of the open air, relishing the light and space. He paused to examine a brightly-coloured butterfly, that hovered weightlessly against the leaves of a flowering currant. The bright fragile thing seemed to fascinate him: its elusive beauty, its brief intense life. Transient, yet eternal. Changed in a moment, in the twinkling of an eye. To William the priest looked like someone who was saying his goodbyes.

23 February 1606. Westminster

They stood on the rim of the crater, and prepared to enter Hell.

The three men were armed and equipped as soldiers readying themselves for some last battle. Father Garnett wore cassock and surplice, a purple stole, and on his head a simple biretta. Looking like two overgrown altar boys, Forman carried a vial of Holy Water, and William a censer with a pastille of smouldering incense, that he swung gently to and fro on a long chain. Under their coats, however, they also wore the leather bandoliers that carried their grim tools of execution. For this was to be an exorcism, followed swiftly by a sentence of death.

The priest bowed his head to pray. The others followed suit. *"Gràtia Dòmini nostri Jesu Christi, et càritas Dei, et communicàtio Sancti Spìritus, sit cum òmnibus vobis."* (3)

"Et cum spirito tuo," (4) William responded fervently. It was all coming back to him.

One by one they descended into the darkness of the shaft. With Forman leading the way, bearing a lantern, and William bringing up the rear with another, they walked through the newly-enlarged tunnel. Pacing between them, the Jesuit carried with him a kind of regal majesty strangely combined with humility. And no trace of fear. He could just as easily have been processing down the nave of a church at Sunday Mass.

Soon they were at the bottom of the second shaft, and mounting the ladder to emerge into the vault. William was not sure if the coffin of the Countess would still occupy the same place. But there it was, exactly as he had last seen it, this time with the lid lying beside it on the cellar floor.

And there was she, lying in the extraordinary dark radiance of her unforgettable beauty. For some reason she had assumed a white dress, of almost bridal candour, that illuminated by contrast the darkness of her skin. Her fine brown hands lay across her partially-exposed breasts. Her dark hair spread out on the pillow like an aureole. But her face! Such loveliness of living colour in the cheeks, such soft redness of lips, such exquisite veined beauty in the closed blue eyelids. It was the face of an angel, though fallen, an angel ruined, but still bearing the traces of a heavenly beauty.

The Jesuit looked long on her, and his look was one of pity. Through the forgiving lens of his sacerdotal eyes, William could see her quite differently. For the first time he saw her, not as a dark lady, or a sexually-charged woman, but as the lovely, soulful creature she once had been, though now possessed by the enemy of mankind. He realised that he himself had never been able to separate the woman from the demon, so surely had her sexual charisma held him in thrall. He had adored the evil in her, along with the good. He had worshipped, in the darkness of his secret heart, her unspeakable obscenity of violence. He had knelt, in craven deference, before her blood-stained altar. Suddenly, in the presence of the priest, he became aware of her as a victim, a tender and loving creature, mercilessly ravished by the fierce and ruthless powers of the air. And he could feel nothing but loathing for the foul thing that had taken her shape, without her soul. If the Jesuit really could expel the demon from her, might she not regain her soul, and die peacefully in his arms, in love, if not in faith? Was it, after all, his destiny to save her?

William suddenly became aware that Garnett's hand was extended, to take the thurible from him. Carefully and gracefully, the priest censed the four corners of the coffin, and the two men who stood on either side. William bowed as the familiar sweet smoke drifted around his head, and reverently crossed himself. Forman followed suit, clumsily copying the unfamiliar gestures.

Then the Jesuit began, in his strong mellifluous voice, to pray over the sleeping body of the woman the ancient ritual of exorcism: "*Exorcisámos te, ómnis immúnde spíritus, ómnis satánic potéstas, ómnis infernális adversárii, ómnis légio, ómnis congregátio et sécta diabólica, in nómine et virtúte Dómini nóstri Jésu Chrísti, eradicáre et effugáre a Dei Ecclésia, ab animábus ad imáginem Dei cónditis ac pretióso divíni Ágni sánguine redémptis."* (5)

He paused. The potent words seemed to have had no effect. But in the silence that followed, the Countess awoke. Her long-lashed eyes glanced at each of them in turn. Her upper lip drew back in a feral grin, exposing the gleaming white canines, and her face contorted with cruel amusement. Then her baleful eyes fixed on the face of the priest, as if she recognised him as the true enemy. She snarled, and growled, and made little snapping dog-like gestures with her teeth. As Garnett continued the prayer, she grew increasingly restive, her head writhing from side to side, her hands clenching and unclenching, her lips champing violently against her teeth.

"Non últra áudeas, sérpens callidíssime, decípere humánum génus, Dei Ecclésiam pérsequi, ac Dei eléctos excútere et cribráre sicut tríticum. Ímperat tíbi Deus altíssimus, cui in mágna tua supérbia te símile habéri ádhuc praesúmis." (6)

Her throat stretched back, the Countess howled like a wolf. Then raising her head from the pillow, she spat full in the Jesuit's face a dark gob of blood-stained mucus. Undeterred, Father Garnett wiped the filthy sputum from his cheek, and continued with the ritual, his voice growing stronger, though not louder, at the great exhortations of compulsion:

"Ímperat tíbi Déus Pater; ímperat tíbi Deus Fílius; ímperat tíbi Déus Spíritus Sánctus." (7)

Again the Countess spat blood at him from pursed, snarling lips. Impassively the priest traced over her the sign of the cross.

"Ímperat tíbi majéstas Chrísti, aetérnum Dei Vérbum cáro factum, qui pro salúte géneris nóstri tua invídia pérditi, humiliávit semetípsum fáctus obédiens úsque ad mortem ..." (8)

She was silent now, watching him warily. Thin streams of blood bubbled and dribbled from the corners of her mouth.

"Ímperat tíbi sacraméntum Crúcis, omniúmque christiánae fídei Mysteriórum virtus." (9)

With a terrible retching sound, the Countess vomited and projected from her mouth a solid stream of blood, that fountained from the coffin and splashed and soiled the Jesuit's face, filling his eyes and blinding him. As she jeered and cackled and howled, he signalled to Forman and William to assist him. William censed the hideous, grinning face with the sweet smoke of sacrifice. The doctor uncorked his vial of Holy Water, and splashed it over the writhing thing in the coffin. Clapping her hands to her burning face, the Vampyr began to vent snorting sounds, like one choking on her own blood. Then the priest stood back, and unleashed upon her all the majesty and power of Christ's own words.

"*Váde Sátana, invéntor et magíster ómnis falláciae, hóstis humánae salútis ...*"

Again the perfumed smoke, again the lashing stream of Holy Water, again the charm of execration: "*Vade Sátana ...*" The Countess was weakening now, her body crumpled into snorting sobs and retching hiccups, her hands still covering her face. "*Vade Sátana ...*"

Then the Jesuit leaned over the coffin, and with an act of the utmost tenderness, laid his hand on her brow, and intoned, in English, the beautiful old prayer for the sick: "They shall lay their hands upon the sick, and all will be well with them." Gently with his fingers he wiped the filth of blood and mucus from her cheeks. As his hand brushed her mouth, her lips parted, and it seemed to William as he watched her through the swirling clouds of incense, that she kissed the hand that caressed her. Was she saved? The priest instinctively drew back his hand for a moment, and then resumed his caring ministrations. "May Jesus, Son of Mary, Lord and Saviour of the world, show to his suffering servant Ilona, favour and mercy." At last she was still. Her eyes were closed. Was that an expression of peace on her face?

"Now," said the priest, stepping back from the coffin.

Quickly Forman drew a stake from his belt, and held it in position over the Vampyr's heart. "William," he said, "it is for you to strike the blow." William hefted his mallet, and held it in place above the stake. "No hesitation, man," urged Forman. "You have seen what she can do. Let us end this. Give her peace."

And with all the strength he could muster, William brought the mallet down, with irresistible force, to drive the mercy-bearing stake deep into the heart of the woman he loved, deep into the heart of the monster who possessed her. The be-all and the end-all. At the first blow, Ilona's eyes widened, and her hands seized the stake where its point had entered her body. William paused, helpless, unable to proceed. But the expression in her eyes was no longer a look of hate and anger, but one of love, and longing. They pleaded with him to give her the rest she had been denied, the peace she craved. She slid her hands higher up the stake, as if begging him to thrust it deeper. Her lips formed a word, though they could make no sound. Goodbye.

With one tremendous blow William battered the stake right through the Vampyr's body, and into the wooden floor of the coffin below her. Her eyes closed for the last time. Over her face there stole that look of peace he had seen on the corpses of those who died in faith. She was truly dead.

"Rest eternal grant her, O Lord," said the priest, in English, "and let light perpetual shine upon her."

"*Requiescat in pace,*" added William, feeling the Latin was more fitting. "*Et lux eterna luceat eam.*" Then he turned aside and left Forman and Father Garnett to complete their gruesome work of redemption.

24 February 1606. The Tower of London

The next day, in the evening, William and Forman met, by arrangement, under the walls of the Tower, and were admitted again to Garnett's chamber. Forman had spent the day reporting

back to Robert Cecil, and bore in his hand the papers empow-
ering Garnett's release. They found the Jesuit on his knees beside
the bed, in an attitude of prayer, and waited respectfully for him
to complete his devotions. When he rose to greet them, William
noticed he was nursing his right hand, which was loosely
bandaged in the stole he had worn the day before. He seemed
tired, his face drawn, his hair perhaps a touch greyer.

Forman explained to Garnett the results of his negotiations
with Cecil. He had told the Secretary the whole story, and given
him assurance that it was only Garnett's spiritual power that had
enabled them to destroy the Vampyr. Cecil was deeply
impressed, and moved to extend the utmost clemency. Not only
would the charges against Garnett be dropped: the Jesuit would
be released from confinement immediately, and permitted to
leave England. It was strongly suggested that his future lay
abroad, rather than at home. But the Secretary had wished him
well. Garnett was a free man.

There was a silence. The Jesuit looked out of the window at
the darkening sky, and heaved a deep sigh. "No," he said.

Forman looked at William. "*No*, Monsignor? You are saying
'no' to Secretary Cecil's offer of mercy? Are you not satisfied with
this outcome?"

Father Garnett turned back towards them, and shook his
head. "Do not imagine I am anything less than grateful for your
efforts to help me. I thank both of you, and Secretary Cecil for his
offer of clemency. But for me, I'm afraid, it is too late."

"Too late?" said William. "Whatever do you mean?"

Slowly and painfully, Garnett began to unwrap the stole that
bandaged his hand. Beneath it they could see a wound in the
flesh on the back of his hand, the skin around it crinkled and
puckered, the centre festering with inflammation. A rough red
rash had begun to trace a line up the Jesuit's arm. Amidst the
bubbling green pus, the two tell-tale puncture marks could
clearly be seen. Forman gave a gasp of surprise and concern, and

leaned over to examine the wound more closely.

"Yes, you see," said the Jesuit in a tired voice, re-bandaging the infected hand, "before that poor creature died, while she was still under the sway of the demon, she bit me, as I wiped her face. Just a little nick, a mere scratch. It was enough. 'Twill serve.'"

"But surely," said William excitedly, glancing to Forman for confirmation, "now she is truly dead, the bite will no longer affect you. We ourselves have seen a man turned by the Vampyr's bite, and then turned back again, once the monster is destroyed. Have we not, Simon? Is it not so?"

"Yes," said Forman heavily, "of this we have seen examples. But this is different, William, and the Father here knows it. Like a dying man's curse, the Vampyr's death-bite is of extraordinary power. It can bind the living, even after the monster's own destruction. From the mouth of one so ancient and powerful as the Countess Ilona, the death-bite cannot be anything less than fatal."

"I am glad to have done the state some service," Garnett went on, "to have rid the realm of so foul a creature, to have released a poor soul from a terrible bondage. To have saved many from death, and a fate worse than death, eternal damnation. But the creature's bite has infected me with the same terrible curse. Within a few days my body will change, my soul will vanish quietly in the night, and the foul fiend will take up his residence *here*," and he beat his breast. "But it is not to be. I will cheat Satan of his prize. The charges against me will not be withdrawn. I will go on trial, and be condemned, and suffer the utmost rigours of a traitor's death. For only thus can I be redeemed from this terrible affliction. You, my friends, must remain near me during my trial and my execution. You must ensure that everything is done to me as the law prescribes: let them take out my heart, and burn it; let them sever my head from my body; let them wholeheartedly ruin this anointed temple which the monster has broken into, this fair vineyard ravaged by the roaring beast from Hell. Only then will my soul be freed. Only then may I return to my God. For *that*, my dear companions: *that* is my only hope, my only desire."

28 March 1606. The Guildhall

And so it came to pass. Despite his innocence, and his work of salvation, Father Henry Garnett was, at his own insistence, tried for treason in the Guildhall. By sheer strength of mind and spiritual discipline, he was able temporarily to resist the incursions of the demon that hovered at the threshold of his being, ready to possess him. But the Vampyr nature was beginning to leave its indelible traces on his body.

Knowledge of his true condition was clearly restricted to a very small coterie. His guards simply received orders and obeyed them, however arbitrary and idiosyncratic they might seem to be. Forman and William were allowed, without explanation given or requested, to remain near him, and to assist him when required.

It was the normal practice for accused traitors to be led through the streets, as the objects of public derision and recrimination, but Garnett was conveyed to the Guildhall in a closed carriage, to avoid his exposure to sunlight. Before entering the Guildhall, he was permitted to pray for a space at the lovely old church of St Mary the Virgin, an unprecedented liberty. Though his sight had always been sharp and true, at his trial he made use of spectacles specially constructed from a kind of smoked glass.

During the trial, which of course took place during the day, he seemed to his observers so heavy with sleep that he could scarcely hold up his head, or keep his eyes open. Watching him, William realised that his overpowering instinct now was to sleep in his coffin, and to wake only at sunset, to prowl forth in search of blood. As the questions were put to him, his eyelids dropped and closed. He rested his chin on his hand, but the hand would slip away, and let fall his heavy head. He could barely manage to formulate replies to his accusers. He kept his hand across his mouth, to hide the accelerating protrusion of his canine teeth. His voice was thick and roughened, his throat seemed dry and sore. They offered him water to drink, but he refused, with an expression of aversion. William knew that he could drink no water. His thirst now was purely for the thrilling taste of living blood.

Throughout the trial Garnett stood in a kind of pulpit, giving the spectators a clear view. They came to satisfy curiosity, or verify reports, or simply to feast their eyes on the man who was caricatured, in this parody of justice, as the architect of the Powder Plot, now represented by the prosecutor Sir Edward Coke as "the Jesuit Treason." Only a few observers knew the truth of his innocence and the value of his service to the realm: William and Forman, Robert Cecil who participated in the prosecution, and perhaps King James himself, who was watching the proceedings, so it was rumoured, from behind a curtain. All but these few stared at the traitor, the equivocator, the author of the most horrible conspiracy, as a terrorist who had sought to murder their king. Forman saw only his weakness, as he struggled against his condition: the drawn face, the thinning grey hair, the trembling fingers. To William, Father Garnett stood in the dock as innocently as Christ had stood before Pilate in the Praesidium. A lesser man would have succumbed to the demonic assault, and embraced the curse of the Vampyr. Garnett held out, endured, clung to his soul, as a drowning man clings to a spar of wreckage. William thought of St Paul:

> For I am persuaded, that neither death, nor life, nor angels, nor principalities, nor powers, nor things present, nor things to come, nor height, nor depth, nor any other creature, shall be able to separate us from the love of God.

3 May 1606. St Paul's Churchyard

Garnett was borne to his execution on the day of the Feast of the Invention of the Holy Cross. The choice of day had been Garnett's own. The festival commemorates the discovery in Jerusalem by St Helena, mother of the Emperor Constantine, of the buried rood. No better day for such a man to mount the cross of self-immolation.

Forman and William helped him dress in the Tower, ensuring that his body was completely covered in a black cloak, his head and face by a big black hat to protect him from the light. As they left the chamber, the cook who had served him tried to grasp Garnett's hand to say a tearful farewell.

"Farewell, good friend Tom," said Garnett courteously, "this day I will save thee a labour to provide my dinner."

In the courtyard the Jesuit was strapped to a hurdle, to be drawn by three horses to the place of execution. Forman and William walked on either side, whispering words of comfort, adjusting his hood to keep the light from touching him.

On the scaffold Garnett stood in silence, like a man in deep contemplation. Attempts were made to engage him in debate, but he cut them off quickly. "I came here prepared," he said, "and am resolved." The Recorder Sir Henry Montague tried to make Garnett confess to his crimes. "I have committed against the king no offence," was the Jesuit's reply, "nor treason."

"Upon this day," he said, "is recorded the Invention of the Cross of Christ. Upon this day I thank God I have found my cross." And then he spoke Christ's own words from the cross: "Father, into thy hand I commend my spirit." Contrary to common practice, and on Cecil's direct orders, they dispensed with the stripping of the prisoner's garments, else the daylight would have destroyed him without the hangman's help.

Then, at last, Father Garnett crossed himself, and went to his death. His heart was torn from his chest, and held aloft for the crowd to see. "Behold the heart of a traitor!" But there was nothing there, only the executioner staring at his empty hand. Then Garnett's head was severed from his body. Immediately the crowd gasped at its extraordinary pallor. The face emitted a kind of radiant candour, a pure and irreproachable whiteness. Strangely, the head did not incinerate at the touch of sunlight. Perhaps the Jesuit's soul, that God-given spark of divinity he had so resolutely clung to, had there at last taken up its dwelling place, tabernacled in the pious skull.

Certain it is that later, when the head was exposed on London Bridge, that unearthly whiteness drew crowds of spectators, who found it nothing less than miraculous. At Forman's request, Garnett's head was then turned upwards. Ostensibly this was so that his pale features would not reproach the state and disturb the peace. But in reality it was so that his dead eyes could gaze towards the heavens, where his martyred soul now peacefully reposed.

Drama

15 May 1606. The Globe Theatre

"Welcome, Horatio: welcome, good Marcellus."

"What, has this thing appear'd again to-night?"

William sat in the back of a box at the Globe, shielded by a curtain from the eyes of the audience, and for the umpteenth time watched the re-opening, by popular request, of his own tragedy *Hamlet*. The sentries met on stage, exchanged their greetings, and once again the play was away, intriguing in its mystery, reassuring in its familiarity.

After Garnett's death, William had thrown himself into his work, hoping to forget the Countess, and Vampyrs, and all the thrilling and terrifying events he had lived through in the course of that action-packed year. He and Forman went their separate ways. He felt he'd had quite enough drama in his life, and couldn't wait to get back into the theatre, where the extraordinary was a mere effect, and danger his servant rather than his master. At night, when sleeplessness still oppressed him, he pushed on with writing the Powder Play commissioned by Cecil, an unfulfilled promise he felt obligated to keep. During the day, he immersed himself in the endless pettiness and triviality that characterises the everyday life of an acting company. Vanity, hysterics, stage fright, drunken absenteeism – all these were nothing compared to what he in the recent past had had to endure. So he relaxed into the routine, the quotidian, the normal, and began to feel like himself again.

After the execution of the Jesuits, a historical line had been drawn beneath the Powder Plot. There were no further signs of insurrection from that quarter. The English Catholics once again fell to their knees, and took their punishment. The exorcism and destruction of the Countess had likewise set a *terminus ad quem* on the Plague of the Vampyrs. He and Forman had returned to the vault, and made a thorough search for the mysterious tall man. They could find no trace. Nor was there anything left alive, or undead, in the workings of the mine under the Westminster house. They could only assume that Forman's surmise was correct: the figure William had seen belonged to a Vampyr who had been made by the Countess's fatal kiss, and destroyed in the repercussions of her destruction. He must have crawled off somewhere to hide, and found his true death when the wood of the true cross had pierced her heart. Forman and William had thrown all the wreckage of their massacre into the pit, which was then filled in by a group of silent soldiers from Cecil's secret service, who handled their trenching shovels without question or curiosity. By the time they had finished, there was no trace of the excavation that had linked the conspirator's house to the Palace of Westminster. In the future, William said to himself, this is a mysterious tunnel that will be spoken of, but never found.

Though the company knew *Hamlet* well, staging it this time was proving unusually difficult. William had found the theatre, on his return, mysteriously changed. He knew that actors were a superstitious bunch at the best of times. None of them would dream of wishing another good luck, preferring phrases like "may your ship sink," or "hope your head falls off." None of them would be caught whistling in the theatre. Some of them refused to wear green, some yellow, others blue, which created endless problems for the costume department. They would refuse to speak the final line of a play in rehearsal, since no play should end without an audience present. And the sight of a single peacock feather was capable of creating mass hysteria.

But this time the company seemed to be in the grip of a nameless nervousness that surpassed all conventional theatrical superstition. William had to assume their mood to be some kind of fall-out from the Powder Plot, a form of collective anxiety. Some of them might have been pulled in for questioning after his arrest: he was not the only theatrical professional who knew more than he should have known about the Plot. He hoped it would all wear off in time. For the moment the dark shadow of superstition lay across the white boards of the Globe like a curse, and nothing seemed to be able to dispel it.

Once they had started to rehearse *Hamlet*, the company's corporate trepidation started to focus on the play itself, which of course with its ghosts, and gravediggers, and final scene in which virtually everybody died, easily lent itself to superstitious imaginings. William was forced to leave the theatre dark for one day a week, so that the thespian ghosts could stage their own production. The actors even developed a superstition about the play's title, refusing to hear it spoken, and insisting on everyone employing the euphemism "The Danish Play." If a player inadvertently pronounced the unlucky name, he had to go outside, spin round three times, cough, sneeze, curse and knock on the door to be re-admitted. Naturally this wasted quite a lot of time.

He remembered how it had started. Beneath the wooden stage of the Globe there was an under-space, connecting by a trap-door to the stage, and giving access to the tiring-room at the rear. Actors playing ghosts and devils could crawl from the green room to the trap door, and enter from below. Beneath the under-space there was an old cellar, reached by a spiral stone stairway, in which the company stored props and costumes. William had asked a stage-hand to fetch something from below, but he had refused. He claimed that when down there alone, he had heard some kind of noise, that struck him with terror.

"What sort of noise?"

"A kind of sigh – long, sad, heart-breaking. I'm not going down there again."

"But we need those spears!"

"Don't make me, Master Will. Please. It's more than my job's worth."

William had gone down under the stage with a lantern, and looked around. Of course there was nothing there. He gathered the props himself, and carried them back up again. But the company's anxiety did not go away. Every time a group of players gathered, for example to march across the stage as the Norwegian army, someone would insist that he could sense one supernumerary member of the troupe. They would stop to count, and the total was invariably correct. But there was always that feeling of one extra walking beside them, one who could not be accounted for. One who should not have been there.

And the plague of superstition was catching. Public complaints from the adjoining community increased. At night local people heard noises, glimpsed strange lights in the theatre, saw ghostly figures flitting to and fro. Someone had heard the sounds of sawing and hammering, and peering through a crack in the wall, had seen a man in a broken mask that only partially concealed a hideously deformed face. People started wandering in, looking for their lost pets. My dog's missing. Have you seen my cat?

On the day in question Burbage, who was playing the Prince, called in sick. Whether his malaise was connected with the pervasive climate of irrational fear, or was just a coincidence, William didn't have time to consider. Short-handed in any case, re-casting was a nightmare. He himself would have to take the part of Hamlet, leaving no-one to play the Ghost. He had two actors to spare. One was a big tall fellow, Robin, who would carry the old king's spectral figure excellent well. But he spoke in a clotted cream West Country accent that would have provoked howls of derision if let loose in the Globe.

"'Amlet, oi am thy father's spirit …"

The only other supernumerary, Peter, was a tiny short-legged man with a big head and a barrel chest, who would look ridiculous in costume, but who happened to have a tremendous bass voice. William hit upon the idea of combining their talents into one. The tall man would personate the Ghost, but remain silent. The dwarf would supply the lines, when required, from offstage. It could work, he tried to convince himself. It could work really well.

They got Robin into the Ghost's chain mail and long black cloak, and pulled the hood over his head and face. He was to enter from below the stage through the trap-door, and exit the same way.

"Don't forget, Robin," William urged him. "You don't say anything. Just walk around. Make some ghostly noises, if you like. Some sort of long slow exhale, say? Peter will give your lines for you."

Robin drew in, and slowly but noisily released, a breath, that echoed around a little inside his makeshift visor. The effect was good. Chilling, even. William directed Peter to deliver the lines on-book, from a hiding-place in the gallery. He himself got into Burbage's Hamlet costume, which hung a little loosely on his smaller frame. It was time. Places.

The opening scene started well. Now it was time for the apparition of the Ghost.

"Last night of all,
When yond same star that's westward from the pole
Had made his course to illume that part of heaven
Where now it burns, Marcellus and myself,
The bell then beating one …"

The trap-door silently opened, and the tall black-cloaked figure of Robin rose from beneath the stage, to an audible gasp from the spectators.

"Peace, break thee off; look, where it comes again!"

"In the same figure, like the king that's dead."

"Thou art a scholar; speak to it, Horatio."

Robin paced around the stage a little, in a slow and dignified silence, while Horatio and the sentries tried to address him. He returned on cue to the trap-door, paused only to vent one of his long rasping sighs, and disappeared the way he had come.

Thank God for that, thought William. It worked. The scene continued, with the three actors huddling closer together, and lowering their voices, to discuss the portent of the Ghost, and the rottenness of Denmark.

"In what particular thought to work I know not," said Horatio,
"But in the gross and scope of my opinion,
This bodes some strange eruption to our state."

Then without warning, to the astonishment of the entire company as well as the audience, the trap-door opened again. From the aperture rose the tall apparition of the Ghost, enfolded in black cloak, head scarfed inside the big black hood. What the hell's he doing? thought William. Why's he coming on again? There was a terrible hiatus of collective paralysis.

Then Horatio tried to ad-lib a way out of the impasse.

"But soft, behold! lo, where it comes. *Again?*"

From the back of the box William attempted a loud and strangled imitation of a cock crowing, to give Robin the cue to get off again. *Cock crows.* Cock-a-doodle-doo!

"Shall I strike at it with my partisan?" cried Marcellus, looking helplessly at the others. It was a genuine question. Nobody had a clue what to do.

"Do, if it will not stand," ad-libbed Horatio. It seemed the obvious thing to say. All three actors made a clumsy lunge at the tall figure that traversed the stage, but it seemed to slip past them like so much smoke, and disappeared in the direction of the tiring-house.

"'Tis here!"

"'Tis here!"

"'Tis gone!"

"It was about to speak," said Bernardo, looking meaningfully across at William, "when the cock crew." Robin was out of control. If, in addition to entering at the wrong time, he started to talk in that mackerel-and-pasty accent, all was lost.

The actor playing Horatio took over. He had been a poet before becoming an actor, and could improvise lines at the drop of a hat.

"And then it started like a guilty thing
Upon a fearful summons. I have heard,
The cock, that is the trumpet to the morn,
Doth with his lofty and shrill-sounding throat
Awake the god of day; and, at his warning,
Whether in sea or fire, in earth or air,
The extravagant and erring spirit hies
To his confine."

Why that's a nice speech, thought William, watching, with a kind of morbid fascination, the long slow wrecking of the scene. I might keep that in.

Horatio looked to Marcellus for the next line, but without a script, the young actor was stumped. "To his confine," Horatio repeated, pointing at the trap-door. Cue. Say something, for God's sake. Marcellus gulped, and in his desperation grasped at the obvious.

"It faded on the crowing of the cock."

"Aye," replied Horatio meaningfully. "For this we have both seen, and spoken of. Already." His closing lines were addressed to William, in the manner of a direct accusation.

"Let us impart what we have seen to-night
Unto young *Hamlet*; for, upon my life,
This spirit – dumb to *us* – will speak to *him*."

William went in search of Robin to have a word with him, but he was nowhere to be seen. There was no time: he had to be on for the Court Scene. Hopefully Robin had just gone out for a puff of Nicotan, and would be back for his big scene with William.

Which was coming up fast. It was night again on the battlements of Elsinore. With William on stage, the other actors recovered their confidence, and the dialogue went back and forth with expert timing. Horatio virtually shouted the Ghost's cue, so it could be heard below the stage: "Look, my lord, it comes!"

And once again a tall black figure rose from the grave and confronted William. But it was not Robin, and it was not the ghost of Hamlet's father. It was now William's turn to be struck dumb. For the Ghost had partly shaken back his hood, revealing, to William alone, a familiar countenance, that yet was not a face. Peering white and sinister from the folds of black cloth, eyebrows strangely tilted above hollow, empty eyes, the incongruous apple cheeks, the inscrutable smiling mouth. It was the mask of Guido Fawkes.

In the script William had only to follow the Ghost's beckoning, and exit with him. But struck to the soul by the apparition of Fawkes, risen from the grave and standing before him, he improvised as he had never improvised before.

"Angels and ministers of grace defend us!" he cried, automatically making the sign of the cross. "Be thou," he said to the apparition he now believed to be Fawkes himself, inexplicably back from the dead:

"Be thou a spirit of health or goblin damn'd,
Bring with thee airs from heaven or blasts from hell,
Be thy intents wicked or charitable,
Thou comest in such a questionable shape
That I will speak to thee, and bid thee tell
Why thy canonized bones, hearsed in death,
Have burst their cerements? why the sepulchre,

Wherein we saw thee quietly inurn'd,
Hath oped his ponderous and marble jaws,
To cast thee up again? What may this mean,
That thou, dead corpse, again in complete steel
Revisit'st thus the glimpses of the moon,
Making night hideous; and we fools of nature
So horridly to shake our disposition
With thoughts beyond the reaches of our souls?
Say, why is this? wherefore? what should we do?"

Slowly and deliberately, the apparition stretched out a black-gloved hand, and crooked a finger to beckon William away. The other actors sensed his fear. Something was wrong.

"It beckons you to go away with it," cried Horatio, in a voice of genuine alarm.

"But do not go with it," cried Marcellus. "No, by no means."

The figure turned, slipped into the trap-door and disappeared. William made to follow him. Horatio tried to stop him, but William shook him off. "It will not speak," said William decisively. He must get to the bottom of this. "Then I will follow it." He stepped into the trap-door, and down he went.

The Ghost preceded him through the under-stage, and took the stone stairs down into the cellar. Here a lamp was burning, and they could stand upright. The apparition turned, and in a voice readily recognisable as that of Guido Fawkes, said to him: "William: I owe you an explanation."

"Well, I've heard some understatements in my time," William replied. "But that one takes the biscuit."

"I'm sorry. It could not have been otherwise. I regret the deception."

"Where would you like to start?"

"At the beginning. Sit down," said Fawkes, gesturing towards an upturned pail. "When are you needed back on stage?"

"Oh, not for a while. The next scene is mostly Polonius. He

goes on for ever. They can manage without me."

Above them a murmur of voices testified to the progress of the play. "Very well." Fawkes sat opposite him, on a pile of costumes, and shook back his hood. The mask had been broken somehow around the left cheek, so part of his face was exposed. William recognised beneath it the ulcerous yellow skin of the Vampyr. Fawkes seemed embarrassed, perhaps by his appearance, or his unwillingness to embark on confidences. He turned the unbroken side of his mask to William, and the soft glow of the lamplight rendered his white features even more sinister and indecipherable.

"If it helps," William began, anxious to cut through the awkwardness, "I know you're a Vampyr. But I don't know how; or why; or what you're doing here; or what your future plans are; or how I can help you."

Fawkes turned that unnerving fixed smile towards William. "Yes, I am a Vampyr. I am one of those monsters I brought here from Transylvania to dig the tunnel, the creatures you and your friend Dr Forman destroyed. But I was glad to see them dispatched. Believe this, William: Though I cannot bear the sunlight on my naked skin, I do not drink human blood."

"So you live on what – small mammals?"

"Yes. It is disgusting. But necessary."

"That certainly explains all those missing pets. But how did it happen?"

"I was bitten. I was turned. That's when I began to wear the mask."

"I see. What about your 'execution'?"

"You were there, I know. I saw you, at the window. Fortunate for me that our slaughter was planned for the hour before dawn. You saw the gang of men wearing this same kind of mask? They were my company of Vampyrs. I made the leap from the gallows, and broke my own neck: painful, but not fatal for one such as I. My comrades concealed my body, and offered up to the executioner one of their own. The body you saw being disembowelled and beheaded was that of one of the miners, not mine. It was not my head that was shown to the baying mob as the head of a traitor."

"Yes," said William thoughtfully. "I didn't think it looked like you. Though of course I haven't seen your face for a while. And the head seemed to burn, when struck by the first rays of the sun. I should have guessed."

"Yes, of course. Sunlight destroys my kind. And so I had to live underground, in the darkness: brooding on my injuries, plotting my revenge. My only consolation was that the Lord sent me a comforter. A companion to ease my solitude."

"A companion?" asked William, beginning to piece the jigsaw together, and not liking the picture that emerged.

"Yes. But let me tell the story. I lay in hiding under the Westminster house, guessing at what was going on above: the arrests, the torture, the brutal executions. I lived on rats, and moles, and the occasional bird that fell down a chimney. I had to endure the company of my miners. There I hid, day after day, night after night, planning how I could secure my revenge. The miners were the only force I commanded now, so they formed the cornerstone of my schemes. But you and your friend the doctor put paid to that, William, when you massacred the entire troop."

"I'm – sorry," said William. "Sort of."

"No, no. They were vile creatures, whose very existence blasphemed God's creation. Death was a gift to them. In any case, I have another plan." Fawkes fell silent for a time, again turning to William the intact cheek of his mask.

"It was you, wasn't it," said William after a pause, "I saw that evening. When we tried to destroy the Countess?"

"Yes, it was me. She was able to escape from you when the sun set. But not for long …"

"You seem a little reticent in telling me *her* story," said

William. "Where exactly does she fit it?"

"Yes. You will understand. I know you loved her, William. She told me everything. She killed many men such as you. You she spared. But she became – everything to me. She was my companion, my comfort, my consolation. I loved her more than I have loved any mortal being. At times, I feared that I loved her more than my God."

"You knew *I* loved her?" said William with no little asperity. "And you just stole her from me?"

Fawkes turned his fixed smile towards William. "Not exactly. After all, I saw her first."

"Ah. She was the woman you saw in the castle. And again on the boat."

"Yes. She was the wife of Count Dracula. Ilona. A woman deeply unhappy, desperate to escape centuries of loveless marriage to an immortal monster. I saw her apparition in the castle, and she begged me to help her. At the time, of course, I did not understand. So she smuggled herself into one of the coffins, and we carried her unawares to England. That night in the ship she was there, in my cabin, and could easily have killed me. She needed sustenance. But she saw me as her liberator, and her finer nature prompted her to spare me. When we landed at Foulness, she turned herself into the black mare I saw on the deck, and disappeared into the darkness. Then one night, there she was, at my door, seeking the shelter of her coffin. I took her in, and we remained together until the end."

Two loves have I, William thought to himself, of comfort and despair. "Did you sleep with her?"

"We shared a coffin."

"That's not quite what I meant." Perhaps after all Fawkes had been a more suitable mate for the Countess. William could not imagine for himself such a degree of necrophiliac intimacy. "Were you – lovers?"

"No. Not in your sense. My love for her was chaste, impersonal. A kind of adoration. And her body was not made for sexual love. Her passion was – otherwise."

"Were you there when we destroyed her?"

"No. I was out seeking a new home for us. I returned to find her ..."

Quickly William told Fawkes the story of the Countess's exorcism, hoping it would comfort him in his bereavement. "We expelled the demon, and released her soul."

Fawkes nodded slowly. "Then it is possible. Redemption. I had given up hope. Father Garnett, you say? Perhaps he could do the same for me?"

"I'm afraid that won't be possible."

And William recounted the narrative of Garnett's trial and execution.

"God rest his soul. No matter. I have work to do before I shuffle off this Vampyr nature. Perhaps I will be damned, on account of the demon within me. But I will ask God's forgiveness. He may choose to pardon me at the last."

"His mercy is for ever sure," said William fervently. "But listen, Guido. Forman and I have gathered an unrivalled knowledge of the Vampyr. But there are many things here I just don't understand. You don't seem to – well, fit the bill. Those miners you brought home from Transylvania were hideous abominations, cannibals. The Countess, though I loved the woman in her, was a blood-sucking monster who fed on human flesh. They were demons. The signs and sacraments of our faith were anathema to them. We destroyed them with Holy Water, blessed metal, sacramental wood. You still talk of God as if you were innocent of demonic possession. You can control your thirst for human blood. You are not afraid of the Cross. What makes you so different?"

Fawkes gazed upwards for a space, as if trying to see, beyond the ceiling of the dingy cellar, the light of the sunlit sky. "I do not know. Something to do with the manner in which I was bitten, perhaps."

"What do you mean?"

"Ilona told me there is a great difference between the bite of newly-made Vampyr, and a bite from one of the old ones."

"So *she* turned you?"

"The young ones are clumsy, half-formed creatures, with little strength and no intelligence. A Vampyr who has survived for centuries harbours enormous powers: physical strength, cunning, acute sensitivity, the ability to read thoughts, even a kind of prescience."

"Yes!" said William, remembering. "Forman told me something of this."

"She could hear what was being said and done half a mile away. She could tell what was going on in someone's mind. She could easily anticipate human action and behaviour. She could turn herself into any shape she wished. I wanted those powers, William, to pursue my work. I needed to acquire them. She said she could give them to me."

"And she obliged?"

"Yes. At my request. Had I not begged her, she would have left me unscathed, unbitten, as she left you. But I pleaded with her to bestow on me the dark gift of her Vampyr nature. Eventually she did. My surrender was voluntary, and for the sake of an ideal. Now I have the monstrous strength, the intelligence, the force of character you will find only in one of the oldest of these demons. I can read minds, a little. But there are other things I cannot do: change shape at will, for example; or see the future. I cannot fly. That may come in time. If there is time. But I am a strange, hybrid creature. A Vampyr with a soul. A Vampyr who does not murder. Does not drink human blood. Keeps the demon within himself perpetually at bay. And is still resolved, despite everything, to serve his God."

"Serve?" said William cautiously. "And how might you do that?"

"The Powder Plot was my life's work. Its collapse caused me, for a time, to despair, almost to give up the ghost. But I rallied. Of late I have realised that this Vampyr curse may have been inflicted on me for a reason. That I might again attempt a catastrophic assault against the powers of the infidel. That I might launch a surprise attack, against the citadels of ungodly authority. That I might succeed, where I failed before. To kill the king."

"The king? How?"

"You have heard of Leonardo da Vinci?"

"Of course. A wonderful painter."

"That, and much more. Da Vinci was an inventor, an engineer, a scientist. He designed and constructed many ingenious machines: modes of transport, weapons of war. Among them was a machine able to render a man capable of flight."

"Flight?"

"Flight. He drew a set of wooden wings, hinged to a frame that will carry the weight of a man. The wings to be covered with silk, so they would carry the machine aloft. A cranking mechanism to move and flap the wings. A tail-flap to act as rudder, and give the craft direction. The machine was based on the wings and tail of a bird. Or perhaps a bat. Wonderfully simple. Truly ingenious."

"And you have built such a flying machine?"

"I have. I got Little John working on it before his arrest. He prepared the wood. After he was gone, I put it together."

"And it works?"

"That remains to be seen." The fixed smile of Fawkes's mask seemed to bend a little in the lamplight.

"And your plan?"

"I intend to load it with a barrel of gunpowder, and pilot it into the tower of St Paul's. The king will be attending a service in the church, at that precise moment."

"Good God. When? Where is this machine?"

"Enough, William. I trust you as a true Catholic, but it is best that you know no more of my scheme. The less, the better. Though I know it was not you who betrayed the Powder Plot. I can see it in your mind."

I'm not so sure, thought William to himself. Only because someone else got there first.

"There is no way you, or anyone else," said Fawkes decisively, "can stop me now."

"You will fly through the sky … but – the daylight?"

"Cloaked and hooded, masked, booted and gloved, I can endure sunlight for a brief space. Long enough to fly across the river."

"How will you ignite the powder?"

"As I approach the tower, I will simply remove my cloak. My body will burst into flames, and touch the powder. By the time I hit the building, I will have become a raging whirlwind of flame. The impact will bring the tower crashing to the ground. All below will perish."

"So it's a suicide mission? But how can you possibly know the king will be …" Before his curiosity could be satisfied, William's attention was caught by a silence above them. The murmur of voices and the shuffling feet had stopped. Oh God, he thought. My cue. His ear picked up a line, spoken loudly and insistently, as if the speaker had had to repeat himself.

"But look where sadly the poor wretch *comes reading*."

"I've got to go, Guido. I'd wish you good luck, but we don't do that in the theatre."

"Why ever not?"

"It's bad luck. To wish someone – good luck. Let me just say farewell. Old friend."

"Remember me," Fawkes called after him, as he bolted up the stairs to regain the stage. "Remember me."

16 May 1606. Lambeth

Once again William stood in Dr Forman's study in his house by the river. Through the open window came the sound of the fast-running tidal Thames, and the smell of flowers and herbs from his garden. On the bookshelves were books of medicine, books of astrology, books of alchemy. Everywhere bottles, phials, pillboxes, jars. Astrological charts on the walls, and on the floor, a large five-pointed star.

Though out of breath, William managed to blurt out to Forman everything Fawkes had told him.

"He's going to do it, Simon. He said nothing could stop him."

"We'll see about that. We need to know when, where and how. First of all, when. That should be easy enough. The where-abouts of the king. What did I do with the *Gazette*?" Forman scrabbled among the untidy papers on his desk, found a printed sheet, and began to pore over it. "Let me see … St Paul's … ah. You're right. It is a matter of the utmost urgency. The king is to attend a memorial service, in St Paul's, for Tsar Dimitri II of Russia."

"Who?"

"The king of Russia. He was killed by a mob in the Kremlin, a few days ago. Apparently James feels sorry for him. As he does for all royal martyrs. Fellow-feeling, you see. There but for the grace of God."

"When is the service?"

Forman put down the newspaper, and looked him squarely in the eye. "Today."

"God in heaven. Can we stop the ceremony?"

Forman shook his head. "Not enough time. To persuade them of something so – incredible. Cecil might believe us. But he will never convince the king. Who now believes himself to be invul-nerable, and under God's particular protection. No, we must stop Fawkes. There is no other way. Now, did he say where he keeps this machine?"

"No."

"Think, William. He said Little John had worked on it? And he finished it himself."

"Yes."

"That would require woodworking tools. A carpenter's workshop."

"London is full of carpenter's shops."

"Indeed. But this one managed to house Little John, working on a secret project. And the machine must have been kept hidden. So we need to look for some space of concealment. Set that aside. Let us consider: motive, means, opportunity. I know something of Leonardo's flying machine. The 'ornithopter.' Some say he tested it, even flew in it himself. Once launched, the craft would glide through the air for a certain distance. But there was no way of persuading it to leave the ground. I read somewhere that they managed to launch it from the top of a hill outside Florence. And that it glided, like a kite, for several miles, and landed safely in a field."

"A hill? So where's he going to launch it from? Surrey? The Cotswolds? Ben Nevis?"

"No, William. Try to keep up. He doesn't need a hill *per se*. Just an elevated point, to get the machine off the ground, and into the air."

"A building, then!"

"Quite. So we are looking for: a place containing a space of concealment; the equipment and tools of a carpenter; and a tower of some kind, from which a flying machine could be launched. A building, then, with a clear line of sight, and a short flying distance to St Paul's."

Suddenly William saw where Forman's logic was pointing. "The Globe!"

"Which is where Fawkes happens to reside. Hm. Coincidence? Obviously the Globe," said Forman impatiently. "It's not rocket science, William."

"What's rocket science?"

"Oh, it's just a saying among scientists. Meaning, 'it's not complicated.' Unlike the complex calculations needed to determine the force, speed and trajectory of a rocket. Though come to think of it ... if you did attach rockets to a flying machine, would that be a way of lifting it into the air? Jet propulsion ..." He shook away the inventive thoughts that began to crowd his teeming brain. "There's no time to lose. The memorial service begins at three o'clock this afternoon. Fawkes must plan to launch his craft shortly thereafter. He will need to manhandle it to the roof of the Globe. How will he do that?"

"He said he has prodigious strength. But also of course in the theatre we have ropes, pulleys, block and tackle, weights and counterweights."

"Yes, yes. That's how it will be done. No doubt. And there we must stop him. How would Leonardo have done it? How would he have stopped one of his own machines? Suppose someone stole it, and used it against Florence as a weapon of war ... let me think ... let me think ... What else did Leonardo create?"

"The *Mona Lisa*?"

"Apart from that. He designed guns, for the Medici. Breech-loading cannons. Artillery with multiple barrels, that could be fired and re-loaded rapidly. Machine-guns. William, do you have any cannons in the theatre?"

"Yes. Small pieces, that we fire off for sound effects."

"Would they fire a round?"

"Yes, of course. We could charge, load them with shot and prime them."

"Would you have need of such a device in tomorrow's play?"

"We're still doing *Hamlet*. I mean the Danish Play. Shit, I'll have to go outside for a bit ..."

"Never mind that now," snapped Forman.

"Sorry. Yes, there are directions for ordnance to fire. About half an hour in. To celebrate the king's rouse."

"Then we will shoot him down. Over the Thames. Blow him out of the sky, before he has chance to execute his deadly plan."

"That's a tricky bit of marksmanship."

"I can do it. It's only mathematics. Anyway, it's our one chance. What time does the play begin?"

"Two o'clock."

"Start half an hour later. And have some buckets of water standing by, in case of accidents. And stewards to evacuate the theatre in a hurry. Set and prime the cannon. I'll bring the shot. Get back to the theatre now, William. Make everything ready."

17 May 1606. The Globe Theatre, Southwark

From across the river, a battering of kettle drums, and a braying of brass horns, told William that the royal procession was approaching St Paul's. He could see bright breastplates of the mounted guard gleaming in the sun, pennants fluttering gaily from the lances of pike men. At that distance it resembled some chivalric panoply from the *Tres Riches Heures du Duc de Berri*, rather than a rout of drunken Scotsmen weaving its way unsteadily up Ludgate Hill. The royal carriage followed, coal black, drawn by six black horses. A couple of white ostrich feathers, he thought, and it could be a hearse. Crowds lined the streets, and cheered for their sovereign, little suspecting the invisible terror that hovered above them, ready to attack from the air.

William drew away from the window, and traversed the circular corridor that circumvented the theatre, making for the tiring-house. The audience was thin on the ground. The company had deliberately omitted to patrol the streets beforehand, banging drums and bullying people into buying tickets. And many of their potential punters were in any case across the river, watching the royal show. Pails of water stood round the pit, ready, as Forman had put it, "in case of accidents." A larger than usual number of stewards in purple baldrics lined the yard, prepared to evacuate quickly in an emergency.

William was playing Hamlet again. Under the tiring-house roof for most of the time, he was relying on Forman to spot Fawkes's emergence. They had set up a small cannon by the gallery rail at the front of the stage, its barrel pointing skywards. From there the doctor could command a clear view of the thatched roof, with its flagpole and company banner that danced in the stiff breeze. Ideal weather for a manned flight. Trying the patience of the actors, and provoking loud complaints from the scattering of spectators, William directed the play to start half an hour late. At last the time arrived, and the play could begin.

Half an hour in, and once again they were atop the cold battlements of Elsinore.

"The air bites shrewdly; it is very cold."

"It is a nipping and an eager air."

"What hour now?"

William could see Forman, sitting behind his cannon, a thin stream of smoke rising from the lighted match in his hand. His eyes were fixed on the roof.

A flourish of trumpets.

It was the cue. From backstage came a shrill blast of music. Forgetting the play, William ran over to the front of the apron, and craned his neck upwards. There he was, Fawkes himself, standing tall and dark beside the flagpole. He wore his customary concealing uniform of black cloak and hood, and his broken white mask gleamed uncannily in the sunlight. He had strapped the flying machine to his body. He held his arms outstretched to horizontally extend his wooden, batsilk wings. He seemed like some heavenly messenger, poised to post with speed on some God-given errand, an angel of the north. To William he looked rather like some great hawk, preparing to stoop and hurtle earthwards like a thunderbolt upon his unsuspecting prey. I saw Lucifer fall like lightning from heaven. Around his waist, William could see he had strapped a series of small barrels, like brandy casks, filled no doubt with gunpowder. A suicide vestment.

Again the flourish of trumpets. Fawkes raised his wings to catch the wind, and bent forward for flight.

Ordnance shot off within.

At exactly the same moment, William was deafened by a colossal explosion behind him, and the whistling whine of a projectile whizzed past his ear. Forman was taking no chances, and had decided to take his shot. Fawkes glanced downwards at the smoke of the report, only to see a missile land at his feet, and lodge harmlessly in the thatch of the theatre's roof. Oh my God, thought William. It's a dud.

But it was not. A secondary explosion rocked the theatre as the missile Forman had fired detonated at Fawkes's feet. An incendiary shell, William realised. Forman was fighting fire with fire. The flames that spurted and spiralled upwards from the explosion snatched at the billowing hem of Fawkes's cloak. Flapping his hand downwards, hampered by the wooden wings, he tried to beat back the flames, but they lapped about him greedily for all that. Soon his lower body was engulfed in a whirlwind of fire. His clothes, devoured by flame, fluttered and floated away in a tatter of burning shreds and patches. Exposed to the sun, his naked skin began to crinkle and burn.

Tearing his gaze away from the rooftop conflagration, William realised that the theatre was burning. The stewards had already ushered the few spectators out of the doors. Pails of water were passed from hand to hand and dashed, with little effect, over the rapidly-spreading flames. A man in the yard screamed as his trousers caught fire from a drifting spark, but his neighbour had the presence of mind to douse it with the contents of his beer-bottle.

There was no reason for William to stay longer. Leaping from the stage, he grabbed Forman, who was staring upwards open-mouthed.

"Nice shooting," yelled William, "but we've got to get out of here."

Reaching the door, William thrust Forman through in front of him. Turning back for one final glance, he saw Fawkes's barrels of powder explode with a devastating thud. Fragments of wood and metal rocketed skywards, tracing bright arcs of flame across the sky. The wooden wings disintegrated, and crumbled into smouldering ash. His last glimpse of Fawkes was of a body torn in two by the explosion, his legs gone, nothing left of him but a severed torso that lay at an ungainly angle above a bonfire of blazing thatch, more like a stuffed dummy than a human form. The rigid smile of his mask gurned eerily through the smoke. Works of fire, fire-works, banged and crackled, whizzed and popped.

Truly it was Guy Fawkes's day.

Play

1 July 1606. Hampton Court Palace

Everyone was waiting. What was Robert Cecil going to say about *The Tragedy of Macbeth*?

To William's horror, Cecil shook his head. Wagged a finger in a gesture of reprimand. And uttered one final and decisive word.

"No."

"No?" repeated William, baffled. "I'm sorry, Your Excellency, I don't understand."

"Oh, it's very good, of course," said Cecil smoothly. "Good story, great characters, terrific poetry. Quality work. But it really – won't do, you know."

"In what way won't it do?"

"We prefer not to dwell too much on this late unfortunate – business. Best to let it be forgotten. But here you are, dragging it all up again. And I did tell you to include only things that are of interest to His Majesty."

"But I have," William protested. "It's all about what happens to the regicide when a king is killed. It's an awful warning to rebels and traitors. And it's a compliment to the king. All about Scotland. About the king's own ancestor, Malcolm. In fact it's exactly the story you requested."

"Yes," said Cecil. "But His Majesty won't want to be reminded about …" – silently he mouthed the word, like an adult swearing in front of children – "*Vampyrs*. Just take them out. Replace them with – I don't know – something else."

"Does Your Grace have any suggestions?" William's tone was growing insolent.

"Something the king will like. Something that interests *him*. Surely there are plenty of other supernatural creatures, in folk-tale and myth, capable of tempting a man into wickedness?

Fairies, maybe. Yes. Or nymphs. No. Wait a minute. I've got it. *Witches.* His Majesty is fascinated by them. He's written a whole book on the subject. Witches. Yes, That'll do. Just take out your" – again he lip-synched the word – "*Vampyrs,* and replace them with Witches. That's all."

William was torn between arguing the point, and just giving up. He hated having to change his writing, but this was a fight he couldn't win. In any case, Cecil was already getting up to leave. As far as he was concerned, it was all settled.

Forman rose and came over to sit by him. "Simon?" William said, as if hoping the doctor might be able to intervene. Instead Forman held before William's eyes the notebook in which he had been writing his eyewitness account of the play. There it was, *The Tragedy of Macbeth.*

To Hampton Court on 1 July 1606 to see the *Tragedy of Macbeth,* by William Shakespeare. There was to be observed first the 3 Vampyr sisters, terrifying but comely with their sharp teeth and bright red lips.

Where he had originally written "Vampyrs," Forman had crossed the word out, and replaced it with "Fairies."

Then he had crossed out that word too, and substituted "Nymphs."

Finally "Nymphs" had been scored through, and replaced by "Witches."

"But ..." William began.

"Leave it," said Forman decisively. "You're a writer, aren't you? And he's the boss. He's in charge. Go back to the drawing-board. Re-draft. Revise. Produce a new textual version. Relegate this one to the status of a Bad Quarto."

"But I don't know anything about witches."

"That's all right," replied Forman, with a hint of self-satis-faction in his voice. "*I* do. How do you feel about collaboration?"

Notes

1. "By the sacred mysteries of man's redemption, may almighty God remit to you all penalties of the present life and of the life to come: may He open to you the gates of paradise, and lead you to joys everlasting."
2. "By this holy unction, and his own most gracious mercy, may the Lord pardon you whatever sin you have committed by sight, hearing, smell, taste and speech, touch."
3. "The grace of the Lord Jesus Christ, the love of God, and the fellowship of the Holy Spirit be with all of you."
4. "And with thy spirit."
5. "We cast you out, every unclean spirit, every satanic power, every onslaught of the infernal adversary, every legion, every diabolical group and sect, in the name and by the power of our Lord Jesus Christ. We command you, begone and fly far from the Church of God, from the souls made by God in His Image and redeemed by the Precious Blood of the Divine Lamb."
6. "No longer dare, cunning serpent, to deceive the human race, to persecute God's Church, to strike God's elect and to sift them as wheat. For the Most High God commands you, He to Whom you once proudly presumed yourself equal."
7. "God the Father commands you. The Son of God commands you. God the Holy Ghost commands you."
8. "Christ, the Eternal Word of God made flesh, commands you, Who humbled Himself, becoming obedient even unto death."
9. "The sacred mystery of the Cross commands you, along with the power of all mysteries of Christian Faith."
10. "Depart, Satan, father and lord of all lies, enemy of man's salvation."

Historical Note

Some of this actually happened

I have described this book as "historical fantasy" because it is a work of imagination solidly grounded in historical fact and documentary record.

Details of the Gunpowder Plot of 1604-5 are taken from the main primary sources. The leading protagonists of the conspiracy, Robin Catesby, Thomas Percy, Guy Fawkes, the brothers Wright and Wintour, all dedicated their lives to the Catholic cause, and all met with violent deaths. I have frequently cited their actual recorded words. The plot was hatched on 20 May 1604, in an inn called the Duck and the Drake in the Strand, traces of which historians have been unable to find. The plotters swore their oath on a prayer-book called *The Little Office of the Blessed Virgin,* a favourite text of Christian warriors (I own a copy printed in the 17th century for the Knights of Malta).

Nicholas Owen, also known as Little John, was also a real historical character, who built priest-holes in Catholic houses throughout the kingdom, and was arrested for complicity in the Gunpowder Plot. He died violently in captivity. The conspirators had special swords of Spanish steel, engraved with scenes from the Passion of Christ, forged for them. The tunnel dug beneath the conspirator's rented Westminster house to the Palace of Westminster is authentically on record in the conspirators' confessions, though its existence has been doubted by historians, and no trace of it has ever been found. The Jacobean Parliament was prorogued several times in 1604-5, eventually scheduled to meet on 5 November 1605. Guy Fawkes travelled abroad in April 1605, ostensibly to Flanders. When the Plot was discovered, thirty-six barrels of gunpowder were found in the vault beneath Parliament.

Sir Edward Hoby was involved in the Powder Plot interrogations. His wife was daughter to Lord Hunsden, patron to Shakespeare's company the Lord Chamberlain's Men, until his death in 1596. On 26 October 1605 the Catholic peer William Parker, Baron Monteagle, received an anonymous letter, possibly from his brother-in-law Francis Tresham, warning him to stay away from Parliament. He immediately took it to Robert Cecil, and triggered the discovery of the plot. At this time Burghly House, built by William Cecil, stood on the Strand, inside the space now bounded by Exeter Street. The arrests, trails and executions of the conspirators took place more or less exactly as described.

Dr Simon Forman was a physician and astrologer who had extensive contacts across 17th century London society. He attended Shakespeare's plays at the Globe, and wrote eyewitness accounts of performances in his *Boke of Plaies*. Many of the details I have used to construct his character, including many of his recorded records and observations, are taken from history, and the various treatments he prescribes are taken from his casebooks. He had a long-standing affair with a married Catholic, Avisa Allen. His case-book notes when he first had intercourse with her, on Saturday 15th December, 1593, at 5pm. He was suspected, in Plymouth in 1602, of being a Jesuit priest and conducting illegal masses. He did study in the Netherlands, he did survive the plague and wrote a poem about it, he did treat Shakespeare's landlady, he was asked to divine the whereabouts of Thomas Percy after the discovery of the Gunpowder Plot, and he did write up an account of a performance of *Macbeth* at the Globe. The Swan with Two Necks and the Talbot were inns close to Shakespeare's lodgings in Silver Street.

Father Henry Garnett, Superior of the Jesuits in England, was arrested in the wake of the Powder Plot (specifically on the grounds that he was Robin Catesby's confessor), confined in the Tower of London, and executed in 1606. At his trial he was unable to stay awake, suffered from terrible thirst, and wore spectacles. He was taken to his execution in a closed carriage, though the normal practice was for the condemned man to walk or be dragged through the streets. His severed head, when exposed on London Bridge, appeared to be of a miraculous whiteness.

Throughout the book I have drawn extensively on Shakespeare's own work, quoting his poems and plays exactly, while speculating freely about the sources of his inspiration. There are some inconclusive verbal parallels between *Measure for Measure* and Dante's *Inferno*. The data detailing Shakespeare's Catholic connections, especially his father's 'Spiritual Testament', is well-documented, though disputed by scholars. The 'Spiritual Testament' was found by builders in the rafters of the Shakespeare family's Henley Street house in Stratford. The Globe Theatre was burnt down by an accident with a cannon, though this was in 1613, not 1606. *Macbeth* is thought to have been performed before King James at Hampton Court in August 1606. Simon Forman's account of a performance at the Globe dates to 1611.

The series of tapestries by Pieter Coecke van Aelst, commissioned by Henry VIII, depicting scenes from the life of Abraham, still hang in the Great Hall of Hampton Court Palace. The encyclopaedic *Glory of the Duchy of Carniola* (Nuremberg, 1689) by Johann Weichard von Valvasor cites as fact the existence of a vampire, Jure Grando, who rose from the dead, haunted cemeteries, and prowled in search of human blood. He was destroyed by exorcism and decapitation. The historical accuracy of this account cannot be verified.

**TOP HAT
BOOKS**

Historical fiction that lives.

We publish fiction that captures the contrasts, the achievements, the optimism and the radicalism of ordinary and extraordinary times across the world.

We're open to all time periods and we strive to go beyond the narrow, foggy slums of Victorian London. Where are the tales of the people of fifteenth century Australasia? The stories of eighth century India? The voices from Africa, Arabia, cities and forests, deserts and towns? Our books thrill, excite, delight and inspire.

The genres will be broad but clear. Whether we're publishing romance, thrillers, crime, or something else entirely, the unifying themes are timescale and enthusiasm. These books will be a celebration of the chaotic power of the human spirit in difficult times. The reader, when they finish, will snap the book closed with a satisfied smile.